"What did the rest of read past the first paragr̶ ____ wanted his engagement details when she couldn't score a decent date.

"Have a look." Marco scanned the room as though expecting the letter to be casually sitting on the coffee table.

"I threw it in the trash." She lifted her chin in defiance.

"I see."

"What? You expected me to frame it and hang it on the wall?" She bit out, embarrassed of her jealousy.

"No." His lips twisted with humor. "I thought you might have read the letter to the end."

Jenna's mind searched for excuses. "Yeah, well, I…I was busy. My phone rang and distracted me."

He threw her a "yeah right" look, inflaming her more.

"Who the hell writes letters, anyway?" She glared.

Stepping Stone

Invested In You Book Two

by

Liv Arnold

Stepping Stone

Contact Information: info@thewildrosepress.com

Cover Art by *Diana Carlile*

The Wild Rose Press, Inc.
PO Box 708
Adams Basin, NY 14410-0708

Visit us at www.thewildrosepress.com

Publishing History
First Edition, 2022
Print ISBN 978-1-5092-4136-1
Digital ISBN 978-1-5092-4137-8

Published in the United States of America

Dedication

To my brother Bon Oh for brainstorming
the novel's game of cat and mouse.

Author Acknowledgments

I loved writing an edgier romance with relevant topics like mental health and PTSD. I am pleased to donate some of my profits to Anxiety and Depression Association of America.

Massive thanks to my wonderful husband Tim, mum, dad, two brothers Bon and James, and only fur-child, Groot.

A note of appreciation to my mother and father-in-law Susan and Martin.

Thank you to my friends Matt Ross, Melissa Haslam, Jenna and John Mladenis, Jenny Zeng, and Jeffrey Bennett. Especially to Matt and John who explained coding for my plot.

I was blown away to have women I admire— Meredith Wild, J. Kenner, and Cherry Adair—provide a cover endorsement.

Special thanks to the talented Desiree Holt, Samantha Vérant, and Sara Bond.

To my critique partners—Hollee Mands, Sadira Stone, and Georgia Tingley—you are amazing.

Shout out to Stuart Lo and Kate Callaghan for the army life and PTSD insight.

I adored working with my editor Judi Mobley and cover artist Diana Carlile.

Finally, thank you for reading. I'm always flattered when someone picks up my book.

Chapter One

Good news filled the letter.

For Jenna Kravitz's ex.

He was getting married and requested custody of their dog. The word "engagement" dropped inside her stomach like a ton of bricks. Sinking back onto her living room couch, she gritted her teeth.

"He can have the bitch." His new fiancée, not the dog.

"I'm not letting anyone take you," she cooed to the little pooch. "No, I'm not. No, I'm not." She scratched Scruffy behind her ears. Her dog's ears reminded her of her deceased grandfather—gray and hairy. Scruffy rolled onto her back for a belly rub.

She tore the offensive letter into pieces, scrunching it in her fist for good measure. No one wrote letters these days. Marco could have easily texted. But she supposed the news was a little more formal, more important, warranting more than a message. She threw the torn paper into the can.

Her chest heaved. She clutched the edge of the windowsill. "Screw you, Marco Kravitz."

He had been with this woman for…a month? Maybe he knocked her up. What was the young twit's name again? She had never met the girl before. One of her daughters mentioned he was seeing someone. Her precious child then told Marco's fiancée that Jenna said her name was "airhead" and exclaimed it was a funny word. The girl hated Jenna since. Some women were strange like that.

Jenna and Marco had been separated for over a year. He turned up every day at home for six months to reconcile. Although the decision to end the relationship was hers, she couldn't picture Marco spending life with someone else. But this letter...her stomach vanished, leaving a hollow space under her ribs. Tears stung her eyes.

To distract herself, she leaned out of the living room window. The view of the steep San Francisco street would be fantastic, as long as she overlooked the trash heap in the neighbor's backyard. She and Marco moved in fifteen years ago because they couldn't afford a nicer area. They had every intention to upgrade when they secured better jobs, but life got in the way—first her pregnancies, then the separation with Marco.

After the army discharged him, he was not the same person. They spent time apart for him to sort out his head. The last thing she'd thought he'd indulge in was a boy's trip to a brothel in Thailand. He claimed he'd left once he realized his location. Still, no excuse.

Their relationship had turned into a sitcom. Except...a separation in her thirties wasn't funny. Unfair he moved on. She must be strong. No more pining.

She left the neat living room. One foot stomped on a small plastic piece. She hopped up and down. "Crap, shit, fuck."

People did not know real pain until one of those pointy blocks studded into the soles of their feet. Unless they had undergone childbirth. Noting to remind her girls to clean up after themselves, she picked up the pieces and dropped them on the bookshelf.

Inside the bedroom closet, she plucked out a yellow tank top and sweat shorts folded in the drawer. Marco had collected their daughters for their weekend sleepover, passing the note at the same time.

She wiggled into gym gear, slipped on running shoes, and grabbed the classy tall gold bottle of perfume Marco gifted her. No way she'd throw the expensive violet fragrance out. Her absolute favorite. After two sprays, she sprinted out of the house. The door banged behind her. At a steady pace, she jogged up the hill. Oxygen gushed into her lungs.

Her legs burned a little, but she loved the adrenaline each time her sneakers hit the pavement. Packed-together houses whizzed by. The homes were almost identical—multiple windows, pastel colors, and small entryways. A teenager on a pink bicycle with a basket at the front raced past.

Jenna's clothes and hair, damp and slick, stuck to her body. The air cleared her mind. She gave zero shits about Marco. Stupid, stupid Marco. Her one-time soulmate, now the person she must get over.

She sped down another hill and veered off one street until she slipped into a trail. Trees lined up on both sides, trunks somber brown, sable cracks gnarling the bark. The small path widened. A creek came into view. Rocks of every size scattered the ground—from boulders big enough to climb on, to grains sticking between the tread on her shoes. The creek expanded into a lake. On this warmish Saturday in late September, the water remained still. The lake calmed her, although this one had the occasional candy wrapper and chip bag. She needed a "reset" button—one where her life had never revolved around Marco.

"Good riddance." Slowing down, she peeked to the left, then right and twirled again to confirm no one roamed nearby. Lifting her top, she flung off her shorts. Now stripped down to underwear, she jumped into the water. The liquid slithered through her panties. She stifled a yelp. A rude shock to the system but refreshing. Skin prickling, she rubbed her arms.

She waded to keep warm and dove underneath the surface. Swimming in the lake was her life's metaphor—she must paddle through the rubbish.

****

The crowd erupted, stamping their feet. Men screamed profanities. Marco Kravitz's body was electrified. Awake. In the ring's center, he held up fisted hands, the red gloves gleaming under the dim lights. His opponent, Joaquin "Dippy Dog" Barker, famous for mutilating someone's lips by biting the bottom off, circled Marco in jerky steps.

The organizers had disqualified Dippy Dog for a week. The audience desired more blood. More pain. Typical for an illegal boxing match. Only two rules— no weapons or blows to the face.

Joaquin raised his hands to his broad chest, cracking his neck side to side. His white, peroxide, blond hair with skull and crossbones shaved into the sides of his crew cut screamed douchebag.

"Get on with it," a tall, burly man yelled from the herd. "Past one in the afternoon already."

Perfect. Marco had enough time to let off steam. He had collected his daughters from Jenna's, dropped them off at ballet, and afterward, they were attending a friend's birthday.

"I aim to please." Teeth bared, Joaquin charged.

Marco dodged to the side in one smooth motion. His enemy swiveled in his direction. Marco hit Joaquin's chest. Joaquin stumbled and rested his hands on his knees.

"Is that all you've got?" Marco's knuckles stung. He needed this. Needed a distraction to bleed the power of his painful Afghanistan memories. The extra money was a bonus.

A pop banged in his ears. He jumped and pivoted. Only a young man from the front row bursting a chip bag. Nausea lined his stomach, one layer at a time.

His mind jerked back to the place *the moment* happened. He had crawled on the ground, reaching for the team. *Is anyone still alive?* His lungs squeezed until the air released at the smoke and fire's sharp odor. Dead bodies, splattered gore, and missing limbs surrounded his feet in a sea of red dirt.

Joaquin threw an uppercut to Marco's jaw.

Marco collapsed to the floor, head first. His tongue soaked in the metallic taste of blood.

The referee blew a whistle. "Foul."

People shouted, voices blurring into one.

Dark, curly hair flashed in his peripheral vision. *Jenna?* He tilted his head. The woman had pale skin. Jenna's was a creamy coffee color. He had to stop thinking about her. His inability to pull himself together caused their marriage breakdown.

Dippy Dog advanced toward Marco before he could stand. His eyes red, he punched Marco in the stomach. Another blow landed on the same spot. Then three, four, five.

Bruised and winded, Marco groaned. He flung his arms to block the attacks but stopped midway. *No energy.*

Two men seized Joaquin from behind.

Joaquin kicked and thrashed, veins bulging out of his neck. *"Me cago en todo lo que se menea."*

The crowd roared. Piercing whistles, stomping feet, and clanging chairs rang through the room.

"Don't stop," Marco croaked as the men dragged off Dippy Dog. He longed to surrender to death and end his pain.

"We'll fix you up, buddy." The dreadlocks guy hauling Joaquin away shot Marco a sympathetic look.

Marco clutched his abdomen and squeezed his eyes shut. Jenna didn't need someone broken. Someone who made wrong decisions, leaving a destructive trail wherever he ventured. Jenna must've read his letter by now. The words had to be right. Despite what almost happened, she was still his world.

He deserved the beating. Every last bit. For the part he played in his comrades' deaths. For what he did to Jenna. For failing his entire family.

Chapter Two

Jenna might have enjoyed visiting Aunt Louise, if not for the hundred and ninety-nine questions on Jenna's split with Marco or snagging a new boyfriend.

She sat in the dining room at her parents' house. Pictures of Jenna and her brother Josh lined the light peach walls. Some from her dance performances. Others of Josh becoming School Captain—the last and only achievement her parents bragged about their son.

"Surely, you can give Marco another chance. Pride comes before a fall." Aunt Louise spooned cream onto a scone. Jenna's great, great grandmother's, from England, recipe. "He had a lapse in judgment."

"If you call a naked bath with a prostitute a lapse in judgment…" Jenna stuffed a piece of scone into her mouth to keep the edge from her voice.

Mom waved her hands. "He was unwell. When your grandfather experienced war, he was never the same. Taking someone's life provokes horrors in a man. You and the girls stayed here while he stationed overseas. Marco didn't have support. You should've followed him."

"His friends were sketchy when they dragged him to the brothel. I can't believe Ken was my buddy." Josh's words shot out razor-sharp. "Marco thought the place was a bar."

"Phew…Marco won't contact another prostitute?

We should be best pals. You're cruisin' for a bruisin', Josh." Jenna held her breath and counted to three. They rehashed the same conversation over and over. She forced a calm expression on her face—tranquil, layered over a cyclone.

Aunt Louise licked jam off her index finger. "His friends are thorns in the flesh."

Josh fisted his hands on the table. "Marco trusted them because they had gone through war together. Glad Marco decked Ken."

"Hail Mary. Marriage is for life." Not a single strand of dark hair on Mom's head swayed as she spoke. She reminded Jenna of a talk show host—immaculate and the voice of reason.

Her family were devout Catholics, and she used to attend church every Sunday. They didn't believe in sex before marriage, and she grew up wearing buttoned-up-to-the-top cardigans and headbands. Imagine her parents' horror, when over a year ago, she announced she and Marco had separated.

Jenna wanted to say, "He's met someone else." The words lingered on the tip of her tongue, but voicing them turned her tragic life real. They were meant to grow old together. Now he desired another woman. She'd never imagined a household where her children stayed with their father every weekend. Those were for other people. Not her.

A teapot collection, several wearing knitted sweaters, lined the shelf to the right. A cozy, homey setting felt like a police interrogation. But she didn't retort to her family whining on and on—she refused to engage in a battle of wits with unarmed people.

She shot her brother a pleading look. *Help me.*

The left side of Josh's lips tilted up. He faced their dad. "I have an acting audition next week."

Adoration swelled her chest. She always had Josh by her side. With enthusiastic yet strict parents, she and Josh often took turns to take one for the team.

"When will you find a real job?" Dad loosened his tie. Whenever he visited friends or extended family, her father suited up.

Dad picked up another scone from the plate centered on the table. "You can't live with us forever."

Josh brushed a dark curly lock away from his face. The same hair that matched Jenna's. Everyone always exclaimed he resembled the male version of her. "I don't want to spend my life thinking, 'what if?' I'm still young. There's a short lifespan in show business."

"Can't you buy a house and give us grandchildren?" Mom leaned forward and tsked.

Josh rolled his eyes.

Jenna and her brother loved their parents. Really. They were supportive with the children, but their most essential values were a stable job, climbing the corporate ladder, and having kids. No room for goals outside the box.

Dad's bushy eyebrows pinched together. "You only spend time in your room, memorizing lines. You need friends too."

Josh's dark eyes narrowed. "I have friends."

Josh had aspired to be an actor for as long as Jenna remembered. Since he watched his first musical with the flying car and performed plays for the whole family.

"I don't recall the last time you went out with anyone. For the grace of God, you will never find a girlfriend." Mom stood and walked to the fridge.

Opening the door, she grabbed another jug of homemade lemonade.

Dad pointed a fork. "Name one friend."

"Jenna." Josh wiped his mouth with a napkin.

Jenna clapped and laughed.

"You can't name your sister as your friend." Aunt Louise snorted, her round face contorting.

"Sure, I can." Josh gave a tight smile, but his voice rose. "Anyway, let's return to the subject of why Jenna isn't forgiving Marco."

Jenna's mouth flattened. Her gaze shot poison darts.

"Sorry," Josh whispered. "Either you or me."

"Yes. He's such a good man." Mom's mouth crinkled around the corners.

"You're old now," Dad added.

"Don't want you to end up alone like me." Aunt Louise waved a finger as thick as a sausage.

Sharp pains shot from the base of Jenna's skull and settled in her temples, pounding a staccato beat—so close to escaping the conversation. Even if she wanted Marco back, and that was a big if, he had a new partner. Nausea wormed through her body at them kissing and cuddling. Cursing under her breath, she sank into the chair. She might as well settle in for an inescapable, stomach-curdling grilling.

****

When Jenna walked through the front door, the place felt empty. Usually, one girl yelled, "Mommm," every few seconds. Eve's small sweater hung over the sofa. Tugging at the material, she folded the sleeves into perfect lines. A sigh escaped her lips. She picked up the remote and turned on the television. The conversation of a daily soap opera resounded through the room, and the pinch in her shoulders relaxed.

Her cell pinged in her jeans pocket. She whipped out the phone.

A guy from the dating app *Finding You* had swiped right and commented:

—*I showed u mine. Show me urs. xxx*—

A dick picture revealing ginger pubic hair accompanied the text. Acid filled her mouth. *Oh, no.* He was one of *those* men. One with a level of moron beyond belief. His profile picture displayed lips curled into a "you're welcome" smile and too much gel in his red hair. Yes, he was the same guy who, months ago, had messaged her a cringeworthy, face-scrunching sentence.

—*Hai pretty. What u up2 2nite?*—

He obviously contacted many girls on this app and didn't keep track. Some people hit on everyone in the online dating scene. His juvenile English offended her, coming a close second to the graphic picture.

She let her thumb hover over the trash icon. Bursting with laughter, she typed.

—*I'm concerned. The lump on your left testicle looks funny. Please visit a doctor for a consultation. I popped your photo and details on Finding You's forum for another opinion. You can thank me later!*—

Within a second, faint words formed at the bottom of the screen. "Macca is typing…"

Giggles bubbled at her throat. Tears leaked at the corners of her eyes. How she wished she could see his face. Although she was bluffing, her retort might scare him to stop sending explicit pictures to innocent women.

11

She blocked and reported him to *Finding You*.

The dating world was harsh, but she might as well have fun. Singledom sure as hell was better than staying with Marco, who shattered her heart. No matter how much she missed him.

****

Keisha, Jenna's nine-year-old daughter, burst through the front door, holding two silver balloons. "Mommy. We had the best weekend with Dad."

Eve followed behind her.

One decent trait about Marco was his devotion to their girls. They adored every moment together.

"Can we talk?" Marco leaned against the door. The tattoos of their two daughters on his left arm peeked underneath his T-shirt. His sleeves cut into his biceps.

She jammed her heart back into her chest. Those arms used to wrap around her, reminding her of better times.

Scruffy stayed close to Jenna's heel and let out a soft growl. *Good girl*. Two months ago, she adopted the Schnauzer when she wanted a positive to focus on. An adorable walking teddy to take her two daughters' minds off their dad no longer living with them. Zero sense why Marco claimed Scruffy. He had moved out before they rescued her.

She ruffled Keisha's curly hair and kissed Eve's plump cheek. "Did you two have an amazing time?" If she kept snubbing Marco, maybe he'd go away.

"Yes, yes, yes. The dance studio had pretty balloons. They let us take them home." Eve pranced around Jenna and pirouetted, balloons bobbing.

"How nice, sweetie." Grabbing Eve's hand, Jenna twirled her. Both her daughters' techniques were

12

coming along well. She missed her dancing days, tutu, and performing in front of a crowd.

"Eve, find a nice spot to tie the balloons." Marco stepped inside their home, not taking his gaze away from Jenna. His deep chocolate brown eyes sparkled like jewels. When they met at church as teenagers, his eyes were the first feature she adored. How unfair he grew better looking with age.

Her lips dipped into a scowl. He hovered around her like a ghost figuring out how to haunt her. She set her gaze on the painting behind him—a cliché fruit basket. Walking over, she adjusted the frame's position.

"Can we tie the balloons to our beds?" Eve sucked her thumb. Even though she'd turned six recently, she still hadn't grown out of this habit.

"Sure." Marco lifted the two girls, spinning them. They squealed before he let them go.

Keisha and Eve raced to their rooms. Scruffy trotted behind, always the faithful protector.

Jenna snapped her teeth shut, her insides twisting.

Marco marched toward the living room and sat on the plush navy-blue leather sofa.

Sighing, she plonked on the other end. Silence stretched between them. She might as well get this over and done with. "How may I help you?"

They remained civil in front of the kids. The last outcome either wanted was their children being insecure or disruption in their lives. But when left alone, the insults preloaded on her tongue and itched to fly. They didn't have comfortable silences anymore, nor their natural back-and-forth banter. Out of every aspect she missed about their relationship, the friendship loss stabbed right through her chest. Marco had been half her life, and they'd continue to drift further away with his upcoming wedding.

"Did you read my letter?" He stretched his long legs out.

"Yes." She shifted in the seat. "Congratulations."

He rubbed the back of his shaved head. "For what?"

"On your engagement. I suppose we can't stay separated. You require a divorce." Jenna's voice stiffened. To stop her hands shaking, she secured them under her knees. The idea still hadn't sunk in that he'd be spending the rest of his days with someone else.

His eyebrows shot up. "No one's getting married. Did you read until the end? I wrote Bluebell's parents were traditional and misunderstood our friendship. They asked for a proposal. I didn't agree to a wedding."

Her heart perked up. They were only friends. "Oh, Bluebell. Who names their child after an ice cream flavor? Not even a real name." The knot in her stomach loosened. He still had a powerful effect on her. She should be relieved he was moving on with his life.

"Some people find the name…quaint." He shuffled closer.

Her body sizzled like cold water dripping into a hot pan. She tamped down the temperature in her chest. "Yeah, for a bird. Keisha tells me she irons her socks. She's evil."

"Are you jealous, Jenna?" His musky scent flooded her senses. The steam hissed from the scorching pan again.

"Jealous? Sounds like you're speaking English, but I don't understand a word you're saying." She threw each word like a punch.

His lips quivered. "If you insist."

"What about intending to take Scruffy?" Jenna crossed her arms. Marco barely knew the dog.

An excited squeal burst from Keisha's room, followed by Eve's giggles. They both turned their heads for a second.

Marco sighed. "I should've said my thoughts in person, but I didn't want my words to come out wrong. I clearly did a great job. I meant for Scruffy to visit sometimes with the girls. They love her and don't like leaving her at home."

He definitely was a caring father and considered their kids' needs.

"What did the rest of your note say?" She hadn't read past the first paragraph. No way she wanted his engagement details when she couldn't score a decent date.

"Have a look." Marco scanned the room as though expecting the letter to be casually sitting on the coffee table.

"I threw it in the trash." She lifted her chin in defiance.

"I see."

"What? You expected me to frame it and hang it on the wall?" She bit out, embarrassed of her jealousy.

"No." His lips twisted with humor. "I thought you might have read the letter to the end."

Jenna's mind searched for excuses. "Yeah, well, I...I was busy. My phone rang and distracted me."

He threw her a "yeah right" look, inflaming her more.

"Who the hell writes letters, anyway?" She glared.

He brushed the back of his fingers across her arm,

leaving goose bumps. "I miss you. I miss us. I miss talking to you."

"You surely considered the consequences before…the incident." A ball of fury spun in her stomach. Whenever her mind wandered to his admission, the nearest object often ended up as collateral damage.

"Not a single day goes by when my heart doesn't fill with regret." His eyes shone.

Deep down, she believed he was sorry. They had known each other for too long to pretend otherwise. Yes, not many men ventured into a brothel and did nothing sexual. But Marco had a twitch in his right eye when he lied. He'd confessed straight away—much easier not to utter a word. Still no justification. Although he never slept with the prostitute, he still betrayed her by entering the brothel.

"Can't change the past." No sarcasm infiltrated her tone. Her rage was destroying her. Holding on to anger wasn't healthy to find someone special. He was in a bad place back then. Mentally. After his army discharge, he woke up in a sweat most nights. One occasion, she arrived home from work early, and Marco was in bed curled into a ball, their room trashed. She still didn't understand the full horrors he faced overseas. No PTSD brochure clearly painted the picture.

Now when she thoroughly studied him, a blue and purple tinge lingered under his jaw. "How did you get the bruise?"

"Accident at the construction site." His right eye twitched. The telltale sign.

Jenna sighed. "You don't have to tell me. Anyway…what is going on with…Bluebell?" She bit her lip to stifle a laugh. No way she'd ever take the name seriously.

He chuckled, a deep rumble warming her like a cup of tea in front of a fireplace. "No romantic relationship. Bluebell is a friend who served. I cut off ties with Ken and the others."

Her head shot up. His buddies were his brothers, his lifeblood. And Bluebell…Jenna jumped to the wrong conclusion when Keisha relayed she spotted him with someone. The mention of another woman clouded her vision red. Avoiding the temptation to hop up and down with glee, she dug her feet to the floor.

"You're smiling." Marco tucked a stray lock of hair behind her ear.

She didn't lean into his touch, but for the first time in over a year, her body didn't squirm away. "No, I'm not. You are."

"You haven't smiled for a long time. Is there a chance we can be friends?"

She pondered his words. Maybe they could. They had been through so much together—a shame to throw their history away. They created the two most perfect angels, deserving parents who got along.

Keisha and Eve ran out of a room, giggling.

"Dad's birthday is coming up." Keisha sprinted past, toward the backyard. "Let's have dinner."

Eve trailed after her sister. "Please, Dad."

Marco's gaze drifted to Jenna, an unspoken question on his face.

Jenna's legs jittered at the idea of spending an entire evening together, but the gesture would mean a lot to the girls. "Yes, come over."

Marco's eyes widened. His face broke out into a

slightly crooked earth-shattering grin. The type to thaw her soul.

"I'll bring dessert." He wrapped his strong arms around her.

Her back stiffened before she melted into his solid body. Shivering, she shut her eyes. The familiarity sprinted her heart up a tower. A closeness she sometimes denied she missed.

Chapter Three

Sunlight seeped through the gaps in the curtains. Marco had finished work early today, and he had closed every single blind to hide from the light. Darkness greeted him like an old friend.

He adjusted his sleeping position on the couch. A crippling spasm hit his stomach and doubled him over. His muscles ached like they had been flash-burned with acid from the inside out. Although his body was sated from fists pounding into his flesh for now, he still needed a new fight date in sight. Usually, he won.

Throughout the weekend with his daughters, he acted like he wasn't in a world of agony. His pretense was worth the stress, though. Jenna and the kids were the only ones to give him happiness. He would not waste the precious moments.

A half-drunk bourbon bottle gleamed on the coffee table, beckoning him. His mouth watered. The drink lowered the noises in his head. An image of Jenna flashed through his mind. Holding her in his arms again elevated his spirits. Her sweet violet scent still lingered on his shirt and soothed him. Maybe her wearing his present hinted at prospects around the corner.

He dozed off to the sound of her voice, dreaming she was stroking his back and whispering everything would be okay. And who knew, maybe things would be.

****

Stone Corp's building, one of the largest investment companies in the US, appeared in Jenna's view. A modern workplace in the financial district—slanted light gray walls, angling inward and outward. A canyon of tall buildings surrounded her. Office workers in suits buzzed this way and that.

She walked inside. The two security guards stationed in the lobby nodded as she swiped an access pass. After waving to Andy, a business development manager, she headed toward the stairs. The staircase wrapped the atrium, connecting each office floor. Her strides complemented the continuous hum of conversations, phones ringing every ten seconds, and people typing furiously to meet deadlines.

On level three, she strolled to her desk through the open office space and plonked her stuff down. A photo sat on the counter of Keisha tickling Eve's feet when they were little. Her daughters had grown so big. This picture always tipped up her lips.

She had been with her employer since it was a start-up ten years ago, but she wouldn't work elsewhere. Her heart still beat with excitement of a new puzzle every day. She loved her job, especially since she'd received a promotion a few months ago for a data analytics role.

"Good morning to you too." Vanessa Lang, her work best friend, arrived at the pod minutes later. Her sundress showed off her slender arms and delicate fingers.

Jenna twisted her dark curly hair into a bun above her head. "What do you mean?"

"You're rather chipper." Her colleague's cherry

lips quirked up.

"I'm always a ray of sunshine." Jenna opened a PowerPoint presentation on the company's current targets. Luckily, their initiatives mostly rated in the green.

"Yes, but now's way too early in the morning to be this happy. Even for you." Vanessa pointed a finger at Jenna.

Jenna had always been a morning person. She loved the sunrise, crisp air on her skin, and birds chirping their cheerful song. The day full of possibilities ahead.

"Marco and I had a good chat last night and sorted out our misunderstanding. He has dated no one. We're celebrating his thirty-fifth birthday as a family in two weeks." Her stomach backflipped three times in a row—how she craved him.

Vanessa's dark eyes enlarged as she switched on the computer. "A huge deal. Are you sure you're ready?"

"Yeah. I'm kinda nervous. We haven't spent time together in a year and might not gel anymore. We're different people now."

Vanessa wheeled her chair closer. "The first time is the hardest. The icebreaker. You'll be fine."

"Fingers crossed. My life will be easier if I stop competing with him on, 'who'll die miserable.' "

"Does this mean there's a chance of reconnecting?" Her friend lowered her voice even though few people sat around them right now.

Jenna straightened. She hoped Marco didn't have the wrong idea. "No way. He was my light at the end of the tunnel but turned into a train instead."

Too much had happened to reconcile. He ripped her heart out. For months, she churned through the motions. She must be strong and capable for her kids. Motherhood and Stone Corp were her saviors to take her mind off him.

Desiree West from the policy and advocacy team sauntered over, nose held a little high. "Hello, ladies."

More people had filled the office, holding coffee cups and bagels.

Jenna nudged Vanessa, already picturing duct-tape over Desiree's mouth. Desiree talked everyone's ear off, usually about herself. When she strutted closer, Jenna flinched. Desiree looked a lot like the Bluebell girl, based on photos Jenna had stalked on social media. *Bluebell is Marco's friend*, she reminded herself.

Desiree waved a phone in front of them. "I bought a house over the weekend."

"Congratulations." Jenna admired the patio. Vines twisted around the wooden railing. "With your boyfriend?"

"Love the backyard," Vanessa added.

"No, Nathan isn't on the loan. I wanted a place for me. I can't wait to host dinner parties and invite people over. You live in a tiny house, don't you, Jenna? Not much space." Desiree flipped her long amber hair. Her big, duck lips spread into a huge grin.

Jenna recoiled. Maybe Bluebell smiled in the same demeaning manner when chatting to Marco. They must have a special relationship sharing the army experience. Perhaps he told Bluebell secrets he had never confided in Jenna. Her heart fisted. She shook her body to snap out of her absurd thoughts. The possibility of Marco's friendship affected her more than expected.

Desiree puffed her chest. "Don't worry. You'll own a bigger place once you're as high up as me."

Jenna didn't know what her colleague's problem was but betted Desiree couldn't pronounce it. Desiree had a gigantic head, figuratively and literally. But right now, she hated the woman more than her boastful comments merited.

A shriek rent through the air, jolting Jenna in her seat. The siren grew in volume, then fell again, before peaking like a crying baby. A monotone voice followed the alarm. "Warning. This is a fire drill. Please listen to the fire wardens and proceed to your nearest emergency exit."

Groans and sighs echoed the room. The procedure took up to an hour of their already busy day.

"I'm a fire warden. I better find my team." Desiree spun on designer heels and strode away.

Jenna sighed in relief when the woman disappeared. For a possible friendship with Marco, she should get used to him dating other people. No jealousy.

"Shall we ditch the drill and grab a coffee?" Vanessa stood from her seat.

Jenna raised her hands in mock outrage. "Vanessa Lang, as the CEO's girlfriend, I am shocked you do not set a better example."

"Yeah, yeah, yeah." Vanessa grabbed a handbag. "Like you're not tempted."

"Okay, you've twisted my arm." Jenna followed Vanessa out of the building. Even though the day had barely started, maybe she needed a break. Not normal to rage over a lookalike woman her ex had befriended.

****

After the excitement of the morning's fire drill, Jenna settled into a busy day. At a little past two in the afternoon, the light on her cell flashed. She swiped to open a text from Marco.

—*Thanks again for the birthday dinner invite. Looking forward to seeing you Thursday.*—

Her brows knitted together. He only mentioned "you" and not their girls. She typed on the phone.

—*You're welcome. Xx*—

She stared at the unsent message. A habit to put kisses at the end no matter the recipient. She backspaced the two x's and hit "send." Placing the cell down, she clicked into AnaStone, the software she had created years ago to predict stock trends. Out of her work accomplishments, the program outranked everything because she saved the company from layoffs. An error message flashed across the screen. The occasional bug popped up in the system. She recreated the bug to find the problem source.

Her cell buzzed again. Another message from Marco.

—*xoxo*—

Oh, hell no. Exes turned potential friends did not respond with hugs and kisses. She'd have to set boundaries, no matter the anticipation flowing through her veins like a sugar rush. Maybe because she hadn't had sex since him, her mind drifted to the time they made love in their garden. The warmth of the rays kissed her face and the freshly mowed lawn scent enticed her. She didn't mind the occasional ant crawling over her.

She rubbed her temples. Her stomach grumbled. She cursed for forgetting lunch. Grabbing her handbag, she left the office in search of food. Her shoulders loosened since her gossip session with Vanessa. Usually, guilt overcame her about taking another break, but she often arrived at work before most people and finished projects at home.

The afternoon's sun warmed her as she stepped out of the building. People bustled. Rows of shops crammed close to its neighbor. Historic and contemporary buildings shot to the cloudless sky.

Passing cafés, takeaway joints, and restaurants, she strolled down the crowded street. A hard decision to choose lunch. Since she worked central to the action, she had exhausted every food option until nothing pleased her. Mentally, she ran through the contents in her fridge at home and the meal to cook for Marco's birthday. She shook her head. Her thoughts kept reverting to him.

A breeze drifted past. Her hold on the handbag loosened. She stumbled. A guy with a gray hood covering his face sprinted off with her belongings.

"Stop, thief," a husky female voice yelled from behind her.

He scurried faster. The man had the same frame as the person who snatched her bag last year. But at five-foot-eleven, many men fit his description.

A woman with long, glossy locks chased him.

Jenna hurried to catch up. Adrenaline zipped up and down her body. Her breaths grew hot. No way she'd let this guy steal from her again. Not on her watch.

The man peeked over his shoulder, wide lips curled into a smirk.

The wind kicked Jenna's hair, and gravel bit into

her sandals. He turned the corner. She followed, slowed, and spun in every direction. He had disappeared. Guitarists played in front of the brick walls, displaying graffiti artwork.

The woman clutched her hands on her hips.

Jenna's jaw tensed. He escaped again and would keep terrorizing unsuspecting citizens. For a second time, he targeted her. A black handbag lay on the ground. Her heart galloped with relief.

"Thank you for scaring him off," Jenna called.

The woman turned. A waft of vanilla hit Jenna. Her mouth hung open at the most beautiful creature. She blinked three times to take in the vision.

The lady had a knowing smile and confident stance. Almost a living doll—small waist, full bust, slender legs, and startling blue eyes like Baker Beach's rippling ocean on a summer's day. Too perfect to be real.

The woman picked up the handbag. Her sky-high heels clicked as she walked toward Jenna. "My powers can sometimes be used for good. He escaped, though."

"You still saved me from losing money. I appreciate you coming to my rescue."

"You're welcome. I'm Claudine De la Harp by the way."

What an exotic name. Rolled off the tongue. Jenna's mouth dried. She stared at Claudine's lips for several long seconds. That generous mouth would be cushions across Jenna's neck, inner thighs, and…higher. Her attention snapped back to Claudine. The other woman had her hand out. Heat climbed her neck. Something was wrong with her today.

She offered a hand. "Jenna Kravitz."

Their fingers clasped. A bolt of static electricity shot up her arm.

Claudine's lush pink lips twitched. "Lovely to meet you."

Jenna gave a full inner body shakedown. She wasn't attracted to the same sex. Then again, many months ago, a random woman at a food stand had flirted with her. Or so Vanessa claimed. The server left her flustered. Still, the past situation was nothing. Just like this. The shock of coming face-to-face with the man who robbed her mixed with a new friendship with Marco confused her—nothing else.

Jenna mustered up a small smile. "I'm afraid I might know the man."

The guy had robbed more than money and credit cards. He left her unsettled. For weeks, she glanced over her shoulder, paranoid everyone had sinister motives. Maybe Marco's experience day-to-day. The knot in her throat rose. Perhaps she was an utter bitch for not being more understanding. Every soldier's partner received PTSD information and the signs to notice. Not one brochure mentioned a bath with a prostitute, though. She shoved her ex into the far recesses of her mind.

Claudine raised an eyebrow, her gaze flittering up and down Jenna. "Do you keep company with those types of people? You look too classy."

Surely, Claudine was not flirting.

"Yes, me and petty criminals are like 'this.' " Jenna lifted two fingers and twisted them together. "He snatched my bag ages ago. The police never caught him. No idea why he tried me again. Are you okay?"

"I'm fine. Glad you were here so I wasn't alone."

Claudine's breathy voice allured Jenna.

"I'll report him to the police. The more they're informed, the more likely he'll be arrested."

"I can't believe he's done this before. Some people have no shame." Claudine's button nose scrunched up, appearing chipmunk-like.

"For a long time, the incident had me quaking in my stylish yet affordable boots." Jenna's gaze trailed the woman's soft and milky neck. She longed to trace the tip of her index finger down Claudine's collarbone and over her slight cleavage.

Seriously, her mind was playing up today.

Claudine's mouth twisted in sympathy. "Of course."

"He's still getting away with stealing. I'd love to end him." Jenna forced her gaze to Claudine's face. Unable to form a full sentence, she had transformed into a schoolgirl. For God's sake, she was a corporate professional. People sought her advice and opinion. But still…the woman fascinated her. From the impeccable way she dressed to the glint in her eyes—comfortable in the world and her place.

Claudine tossed her dark chocolate hair over a shoulder. Her eyes twinkled like she knew Jenna's most inner-secret thoughts. "I'll help you. Let's catch the bastard."

Chapter Four

"What do you do for work, Claudine?" Jenna stirred a protein shake in the antique-style café, Le Morning Sunshine. The interior had multitoned shades of brown and red. Marble, dark timber, and lipstick-red leather upholstery at the entrance. Black and white photos of flowers hung on the walls. Jenna invited Claudine for coffee to thank her for saving her handbag. Claudine shrugged the gesture off. After Jenna insisted three more times, Claudine chose the venue. Even though she met Claudine today, Le Morning Sunshine suited her new friend.

Chatty customers crammed the room. Light classical music played in the background. A group of suits sat at a nearby wooden, rustic table. The perfect people-watching spot. Tall windows, warm ambient lighting, and central location overlooking a busy intersection. Cozy. Through the glass, a couple frowned and waved their hands in an argument.

Claudine sat against an exposed brick wall. Lush cleavage gaped through her blouse to reveal a red lacy bra. "I'm in computer science and data analytics. Or at least I was before my layoff."

"Oh, I'm sorry. I'm in a similar field." Jenna clutched her hands on her lap to resist the urge to lift Claudine's top and caress her breasts.

"Don't be. The situation has allowed me to

29

contemplate my future." Claudine raised the small coffee flute to her full lips, tilted her head back a little, and sipped.

Jenna's breath hitched. Caffeine was never sexy. Groaning, she gulped the protein shake to cool the temperature beneath her skin. "What are you hoping to do?"

Claudine's eyes flickered. She set the glass onto the counter. "I'm still figuring out my life."

"There must be something you always fantasized about." Why did she utter the word "fantasized?" A heatwave rose from her core to hair roots.

"Well…can you keep a secret?" Claudine opened her deep blue eyes wide, almost child-like.

"Not really."

"Ha ha. I've enjoyed baking since I was a child. Petit fours, croissants, eclairs, you name it. I have my recipes written on a notepad I carry around in case inspiration strikes." Claudine slid her legs to the side of the table, crossing them. She adjusted the straps on her heels. The split down the side of her knee-length skirt revealed the V of soft thigh flesh and the promises of upward.

Jenna swallowed, rubbing her hands up and down her arms.

A car roared past the café. The music's base thumped at full volume. They glanced up. Some people were idiots. The car skidded.

Jenna turned to Claudine. "Perfect. Why don't you open a bakery or café?"

A waitress grazed a tray against Jenna's arm. The server smiled in apology.

Claudine shook her head fast. "A faraway dream to

own a place like this. I used to visit here as a little girl and watch the baker prepare bread." She gestured a hand to the elderly woman at the counter featuring rows and rows of tiny desserts. Strawberries, pears, and peaches on pastries—fruits ripe enough to burst in your mouth. "Isn't the owner amazing?"

"Her creations look delicious. They remind me of my family's scone recipe passed down from my British ancestors. Mom bakes the scones at least once a month."

"Ooh. Sounds delicious. Will you share the method with me?" Claudine shuffled her seat forward. So close, the heat radiated off her.

"My parents might kill me if I divulged the secret to anyone outside family."

Claudine's tongue peeked out at the corner of her mouth. "Now I'm even more eager to know the ingredients."

"No chance. Anyway, what's stopping you from buying a place like this?"

"Money for one. I have no job. And..." Claudine snapped her lips shut.

"You can tell me." Jenna reached for Claudine's hand but yanked back when she realized. Her blood hummed at the stranger's nearness.

"My parents. They always likened running any sort of food place as second-class jobs. My mother's particularly snobby. They didn't send me to private school to bake muffins. It may not be worth the argument."

Jenna's heart sank. She also had a strict family. They gave her the universe, but a tiny box confined her growing up. Sometimes she yearned to break free or

31

shock people. For people to raise their hands and yell, "Oh, my God," at a random impulsion.

"Worry about your parents later. I can help with the first part. There are vacancies at the company I work for, Stone Corp." Jenna flexed her stiff fingers. She met this woman thirty minutes ago, although Claudine showed great integrity when Jenna was in trouble. Either way, it didn't sit right to leave a person in the lurch when she could help.

Maybe the mother in her wanted to cheer Claudine up. Or the pull Claudine had over her. She had never experienced such a strong, sensual magnetism from anyone besides Marco.

Claudine's perfectly arched eyebrows raised high. "Are you sure? Isn't Stone Corp huge? The jobs are out of my league."

"I can't guarantee an outcome, but send me your resume." Jenna rifled through her huge handbag.

Claudine exuded confidence in every area besides her career. Her parents must've had other plans. Jenna could relate. Removing a notebook and multiple pens, she found her wallet.

Claudine giggled, laughter tinkling like a music box. "Have you stashed enough in there?"

"Not quite." Jenna slipped out a business card from her wallet's front compartment and slid it across the table. "Please contact me."

Claudine picked up the card, gaze lingering on the details. She peered up at Jenna and licked her lips. "The perfect excuse to see more of you. However can I thank you?"

Every sentence Claudine purred implied a double meaning. She had a raw, compelling aura no one could ever ignore.

"Buckets full of money will do." Jenna released a pent-up breath, completely out of her depth.

****

Twenty feet away from Marco, the forklift reversed. A colleague sat in the machine, lowering the ten slabs of concrete and dropped them to the ground. Four piercing beeps rendered the site.

Marco tilted the opening of the concrete machine upward, stopping the flow pouring into the formwork. A knot worked into his gut. The noise reminded him of the time…

Shaking his head, he banished the negative images.

Think about another topic. His lips tugged up at having dinner with Jenna and the girls. Happiness floated through his body—the first time in ages. *His* Jenna, the sweet and incredible woman. He missed her like he had a limb amputated.

When he blindly followed his friends inside the brothel, the setting appeared to be a bar. Liquor bottles covered the shelf, seating scattered the room, and people played pool in the middle. His mood stabilizer medication mixed with alcohol and insomnia fogged his mind.

He should have told Jenna about the drugs for his mental health. They already had other relationship struggles. Too embarrassed to confess his weakness, he shoved the admission to the bottom of the list. He had stared unblinkingly upstairs in the bar for a short minute…or perhaps hours. Either way, the moment lasted until the unbroken part of him remembered his love for Jenna, realized his location, and rushed out of the room.

"You a'ight, Marco?" Douglas, the concrete laborer next to Marco, called out.

Marco inclined his head. His breath trickled from his lungs before the air gusted out. He continued emptying the bucket's contents for the small pathway. After the pummeling from the other night's fight, his stomach gnawed at every movement. But the wounds were worth the pain. When he smashed his fist into someone's face, and they thrashed him in return, he came alive—unlike his current husk state.

Brad, the construction manager, marched to his section, a clipboard in hand. "We're half a day behind schedule because of multiple lazy asses calling in sick."

Douglas saluted their boss. "We're wrecked, though. My arms are fucked." He rested his hands on his knees and panted.

Yeah, yeah, yeah. Marco scowled. Who cared if a job ran behind or someone had sore muscles? The only consequence was this private school wouldn't have a fancy new pool in time for their next round of swimming lessons. Every task appeared trivial, but he'd worked on rebuilding projects in Afghanistan during his army years. The construction role was the only area he qualified. He straightened his hard hat.

"Let's double our speed to get back on track. Drinks and pizza are on me tonight," Brad said.

Cheers rang through the air. Douglas whistled.

Marco flinched. The last activity he wanted to do was socialize.

"I already have plans after work." Not a blatant lie. His mouth watered at the scotch bottle awaiting him.

Douglas removed his gloves and wiped the sweat off his forehead with a sleeve. He bent over the long, straight, stiff tubing and rolled it to smooth the wet concrete.

Marco gritted his teeth. "Put your gloves back on."

"My bad." Douglas slid the gloves through his fingers.

"Not good enough." Marco's stomach rocked like he sailed out at sea. He dropped the bucket to the ground.

"Chill. Only a second."

"Only a second? There are motherfucking chemicals. Guys have had hands amputated after working cement without gloves." Marco's words shot out like fireballs. Rage slithered around his body, wrapping tighter and tighter.

The other workers glanced up from their stations.

Brad narrowed his eyes and secured a hand on Marco's tensed shoulder. "No harm done."

Marco jumped back, his chest labored. "There's a reason we follow shitty rules. Someone might get hurt or die."

"Marco. Calm down. Skin damage occurs over a long period of time." Brad lowered his voice into a gentle tone.

Fury clawed Marco's throat like a crab tearing apart its prey. People strode toward their group in slow, even steps. They held their hands up as if approaching a wild and unpredictable animal, speaking at the same time.

"Totally fine, Marco."

"You're okay."

"We're good."

Their voices became a radio tuning in and out of his head. His chest heaved, and a chalky, bitter taste filled his mouth.

Brad shifted on his feet. "Marco, take the rest of the day off."

A moment ago, Brad requested everyone to operate at twice their speed.

Heat rushed to his face. Marco couldn't get any part of life right. Everywhere he turned, a set of eyes accused him. Or worse, pitied him. A pressure built in his throat. Invisible walls enclosed him. His legs shook like he walked through an earthquake. These fuckwits had no idea. Safety breaches converted any site into a shitstorm.

"Yes, boss." Marco forced the words out. He stalked out of the site, ripping off his gloves and helmet.

****

A cinnamon and cherry scent perfumed the lingerie shop. Jenna browsed the racks for new underwear on her way to the BART before heading home. Every one of her undergarments was old, had holes, or appeared too *mommy*. Not one item screamed, "Take me now." But she had no one to impress. Not Marco.

She had skipped work a little early. Reporting the almost theft to the police left her rattled. One awful experience affected her. Marco coped with years of army memories. A part of her delved deeper into this line of thought, but she nudged the unpleasantness away. These feelings led to confusion and sometimes guilt. Anyone could tell Marco had issues. Maybe she should've tried harder to break through his tough exterior.

She studied Claudine's resume on her cell. Throughout the day, she had second thoughts on recommending Claudine but didn't know why. She was as smart as she was beautiful, working at big banks, government, and investment firms, including Stone Corp's rival company. TMC Investments was crazy to let her go. No one was indispensable from a company saving a few bucks. If Jenna lost her job, she hoped someone might help. She forwarded Claudine's files to Hayley Snow. Her boss decided on new recruits.

The sales assistant hung corsets on the rack nearby. "Can I help you?"

"I'm fine browsing." Awkward to ask for underwear advice. Did anyone actually reply, "Yes, I want something to make him immediately come in his pants?"

A red transparent teddy caught her eye. On the price tag, a luscious model had her entire body on display underneath the sheer lace. Damn, her boobs looked fantastic. A sexy number wasn't practical in Jenna's day-to-day life. Maybe a racy getup Claudine wore. Meeting the woman was a sign telling her to be more out there. She had been on multiple bad dates. No reward without risk.

She grabbed the teddy—must act and dress like someone with a spicy love life to translate into reality. From the hooks, she picked six practical underwear in black, beige, and blue, on sale for "buy two, get one free." She checked the time on her phone. Five o'clock. If she left soon, she could collect the girls from after-school care in time.

The cell rang. She answered. "Hi, Hayley. You're quick."

"Where did you find this girl?" Hayley's voice rose in excitement. "Claudine's resume is impressive."

"I met her on my lunch break." Jenna's gaze snagged on the sex toys at the back corner—a kink she had never experimented with Marco.

"She's almost too qualified. I stalked her online. Quite a stunner too."

Jenna's mind drifted to Claudine's luscious lips. "Yeah, she's attractive."

"I'll contact her for an interview. I need someone ASAP. Is she prettier than me, though?"

"Not a chance." She pictured Hayley fluffing up her hair at a computer screen's reflection. Her heart skipped a beat at Claudine sitting on the edge of her desk, leaning over Jenna's shoulder to study the computer.

Hayley laughed. "Right answer. I'll call her now. Thanks for the referral. See you tomorrow."

"Bye, Hayley." Jenna ended the call and stared at the screen.

Claudine confronted her with thoughts she never had. She would have to deal with the uneasiness every day if Claudine secured the job. A knot settled deep inside her stomach. Hayley had always been casual about her pansexuality even with a long-term boyfriend. Freaking out was uncalled for.

Her reactions had no merit…only her mind overplaying from stress. Curiosity got the better of her about the sex toys. She headed toward the back and lifted a pack featuring leather handcuffs, rope to tie against bedposts, and a whip. A long, deep-down desire fluttered in her belly. Her legs trembled. When she was alone in bed, sex toys and rough sex popped into her mind, although she never voiced the fantasy out loud— not to Marco or anyone. She had longed for the fetish, but he might've thought she was a freak.

The same salesgirl appeared beside her. "The rope gives the right pleasure amount. Leather is surprisingly soft." Her tone was casual like she discussed the weather. Her lips shone a bright pink gloss. Doubtful she was even old enough to discuss adult toys.

"I see. Thank you." No way she'd have this conversation. Some people had zero boundaries.

"Sing out with any questions." The assistant returned to the counter.

Jenna's thumb grazed across the elegant ropes. The leather would chafe Claudine's creamy skin, leaving a red mark. Trembling, she chose a plastic box containing metal balls from the bargain discount bin. A red "80% off" sticker was stuck at the top. She twirled the pack in her fingers. The description read, "Small, round weights to strengthen your pelvic and vagina muscles for one explosive orgasm."

Her core tightened. Claudine wouldn't hesitate to try something new and glowed from her head to her toes. Jenna needed some of that. Forcing her knees together, she glanced around the room. No one loitered nearby.

The clerk winked.

She'd hide her purchases somewhere deep inside a closet when she reached home. Her skin prickled with this naughty secret. A little wicked self-indulgence hurt no one.

Chapter Five

The week flew by. Work kept Jenna busy. Too hectic. Desperate for a qualified professional to fill the data analytics position, Hayley interviewed Claudine the day after they spoke on the phone and offered the job an hour later. The process happened quicker than Jenna anticipated. Her heart thumped fast and erratic at Claudine starting today.

"Howdy, stranger." A familiar husky voice sounded from behind Jenna.

Jenna swiveled in her chair, absorbing Claudine's black dress accentuating every curve. Her blood simmered. She pictured Claudine underneath her clothes.

Beside her, Hayley gestured a hand. "I believe you two have met."

Jenna beamed at Claudine—an automatic reflex. "I'm glad you got the job."

"Thank you. I couldn't have won this role without you." Claudine brushed a hand over Jenna's shoulder.

Jenna's nerve endings zapped. "You sure didn't muck around hiring, Hayley."

"No point wasting time after finding the perfect person." Hayley laughed. "I'm doing the rounds, introducing her to everyone. Let's do a team welcome lunch today to bribe Claudine not to leave."

Claudine placed her hands on her hips. "I'm not

going anywhere, but I'll still take the food."

"Sounds good. Have fun." Jenna waved.

"I'd love to catch up." Claudine's gaze lingered on Jenna's with a sensual urgency. "You smell delicious by the way." She leaned closer. "Violets?"

Jenna's core squeezed tighter and tighter. She agreed to be friends with Marco. A new team member she had an unexplainable attraction to should be a piece of cake.

****

"I'm too full from lunch." Jenna groaned as she dawdled down the strip of shops, patting her aching stomach from eating dozens of dumplings.

A street performer played an eighties rock song on the guitar at the supermarket's front. The music took her back to Marco serenading her when they started dating. Although only kids, even then, they really loved each other. A longing inside her morphed into a rope, tightening itself around her chest, strong and constricting.

"Yummy, though." Vanessa tied her dark straight hair into a ponytail.

"Don't take offense when I say this…" A twinkle shone in Hayley's hazel eyes as she hip-bumped Claudine.

"People always say that when they're about to say an inappropriate comment." Claudine's voice floated in the air, light and playful. "Like when someone says, 'I don't mean to be racist but…' "

Jenna chuckled. Claudine was a firecracker.

They plodded past a man in his late thirties clutching a sign stating, "Jesus Saves Lives."

Jenna believed in God, but why oh why did people

hound others in public?

Hayley entered Stone Corp's building, and the others followed. "I mean...you don't look like a computer geek working in analytics. What attracted you to this field?"

Hayley had a point. Claudine wouldn't appear out of place in a swimsuit magazine with her round ass and lush breasts.

Jenna tapped the elevator's "up" button and shoved her clammy hands into her pants pockets.

"Oh, God." Claudine chuckled. "I was an ugly duckling. You should have seen me. My friends were other online nerds who introduced me to the tech world."

Jenna's eyebrows shot up. Claudine attracted her like a bee to honey. Not a chance she was a loner when Jenna wanted to eat her up. She'd taste as sweet as honey.

The elevator doors sprang open.

Hayley stepped in and held the door until everyone hopped inside. "Get outta here. You were never plain-Jane. Pics or it didn't happen."

Claudine grabbed a phone from her handbag and tapped the screen. Grinning, she turned the mobile to face Hayley. "See."

Jenna and Vanessa hovered for a better peek. Claudine was in her early teens. Bleached blonde hair, dark roots growing out at the top, and heavy bangs drooping past her brows. Her eyes squinted as she played the clarinet. A natural beauty with a small button nose and sumptuous lips. Claudine was attractive even back then when you looked at her features individually.

"How adorable," Vanessa gushed. "I played the

flute at school for a few months."

Hayley examined the image. "Wow. What a dork. You weren't being modest."

"Heyyy." Claudine punched Hayley's arm.

The elevator opened, and they exited while other people waited.

"You were always stunning." Jenna averted her gaze, heat singeing her cheeks.

"I meant a cute dork." Hayley nudged Claudine.

A nineties girl band tune tinkled from Claudine's phone. Jenna turned her head to hide a grin. Someone potentially jeering at Claudine's music taste or old nerdy school photo had zero effect on her. Lust flittered through her chest.

Claudine twisted her mouth in apology and lifted the cell to her ear. "Hello, Claudine speaking."

A loud crackling ejected from Claudine's phone as they ambled down the hallway.

Jenna shot Claudine a sympathetic look. Anyone recognized the annoying sound.

"Ms. Claudine. Please let me reassure you, this is not a sales call." The male voice from the other end boomed from Claudine's device.

Damn, telemarketers were loud even when not on speaker phone. Jenna rolled her eyes. "That's what they all say."

Claudine scrunched her face and sighed. "Good to know."

"You have won free tickets to a seminar to lead a better life. Just spend a twenty-dollar minimum on our wellness products."

Jenna waved to Tina Ly from accounting who strode into a meeting room.

Claudine's lips twitched. "I'm sorry, I can't talk right now. What's your number? I'll call you back."

A few beats passed before the man answered. "Sorry, I can't give you my details."

"Do you not want someone calling your personal number?"

"Umm…no." The telemarketer's voice came out hesitant.

"Now you know how I feel." Claudine hung up the phone and giggled.

Jenna, Vanessa, and Hayley exploded into laughter. Claudine's humor was a turn on. Wait…what…?

Hayley clutched her knees, gasping for air. "You're going to fit in with the team fine."

****

After work, Jenna strolled through the shopping mall with her daughters for Marco's birthday gift at Keisha's insistence. The domed ceiling rose higher than any cathedral. Walkways spiraled skyward, flowing like salmon fighting their way up a river. Soothing music played in the background, gentle rolling notes to take customers' cares away.

There were no rules in gifts for an ex. The underwear shop beside her displayed posters of a muscular man and an athletic woman. No way. Too intimate. Still, she loved going out on an excursion, the three of them.

Eve slipped her fingers into Jenna's. "Why don't we hold hands much anymore?"

Jenna's heart burst with love. She grabbed onto Keisha with her other hand.

Together, they skipped along and pointed out the flower stand and the cupcakes with delicate frosting at another stall. Maybe the type of treats Claudine baked. A jewelry store lit up in front of them. The window's bold sign boasted, "Gift your loved ones an engraved watch."

Ugh. Too romantic. And couple-y. Which they weren't. She needed a gesture appropriate for the father of her kids. One not giving Marco false hope.

Keisha tugged Jenna's hand at a shop. Picture frames and photos hung on the walls. "My friend Monica gave her dad a giant canvas of the family."

Jenna cringed at the joyful family snaps. They once used to be happy—hypocritical to gift Marco one of these cheesy shots.

"Ooh. They can turn a picture into a jigsaw." Eve towed Jenna inside.

The counter listed photo options. Jenna examined the puzzle. She had read ages ago that jigsaws provided peace and tranquility. Marco stressed more since returning from the army although he'd never admit his problems. The activity might help take his mind off his trauma.

She whipped out a phone from her handbag. "Okay, help me pick a photo."

****

The week working with Claudine hadn't been awkward in the slightest. Jenna looked forward to Claudine's smiling face every day, and she waited for the subtle vanilla scent to enter the space.

Today was Marco's birthday. She grabbed her phone from the desk and tapped the device against her chin.

In the end, she typed a quick message.

—Wishing you many happy returns on your special

day. See you tonight.—

Minutes later, the phone beeped.

—Thank you.—

She smiled. Marco respected her boundaries. Exes could be friends. Her recent reminiscences of him were a computer glitch in her brain.

She clicked her email tab open. Angie, Sebastian's assistant, sent a meeting invitation on his behalf. The subject line read, "Jenna, Sandeep, and Sebastian catch–up." The location was at Sebastian's office. Angie didn't include details, but the time was ten minutes away.

Sebastian Stone, founder and Stone Corp's CEO, had the face to turn every single head. Not that she blamed anyone. He was delicious and also an amazing boyfriend to Vanessa. Jenna was the first person at work to discover their relationship.

Sandeep was Hayley's boss and the Executive of Strategy and Business Insights. A man in his mid-fifties, his communication style was curt and to the point.

They gave little notice and did not invite Hayley. Jenna's section for the financial year report wasn't due until the end of month. She grabbed a notebook and her favorite floral-patterned pen. Keisha gifted her the stationery for Mother's Day two years ago. Standing, she left her desk and arrived at Sebastian's office with one minute to spare. Even a second late caused anxiety to swirl within her.

Sebastian and Sandeep already sat at the table in his office space. Knocking once, she lingered at the entryway.

"Come in." Sebastian's smile didn't reach his

brilliant emerald eyes.

She gulped. Usually, Sebastian checked in on people no matter his busy schedule. Vanessa hadn't mentioned the meeting either.

"Take a seat." Sandeep adjusted his tie—always in a full suit, even on casual Fridays. He had an air saying he was much smarter, better looking, and cooler than everyone else. Even his voicemail was obnoxious. "Yep, leave me a message."

Strolling over, she slid out of the nearest chair. Whatever the issue, she'd fix it.

Sandeep pivoted his laptop. A chart displayed on the screen. "There're discrepancies with the software, AnaStone, you created last year."

"What? How?" The system predicted market trends to inform Stone Corp when to buy and sell. A revolutionary piece of genius if she said so herself.

Sandeep double-clicked on a red line and pointed. "Right here, AnaStone recommended selling stock for the University of San Francisco. A week later, the institution received a major donation from a known philanthropist. The university's programs had been in the news for their latest science technology advancements. Can you explain why the software predicted the organization would go under?"

Her eyes narrowed. "This doesn't sound like AnaStone."

"There's other unreliable instances." Sandeep connected to another tab. "For the broker services company, Homelander, the software told us to buy stock when at a high. Bankruptcy rumors have been following them because of their brokers' unethical tactics."

Jenna wished she'd brought toilet paper because Sandeep was an ass. His beady eyes and sharp little turns resembled a cruel-eyed, clawed vulture, attacking her repeatedly.

"I'm sure there's an explanation. What does Hayley say?" Her voice remained steady and strong. She had worked on AnaStone for many years with immaculate testing before the product launched—no way her baby created errors now.

"Hayley thinks there must be a mistake because she trusts your abilities." Sebastian ran a hand over his thick, raven hair. He reminded her of the dreamy princes people swooned over in movies. "We still wanted to chat to understand your views. The IT department will study the problems too."

"I can't give an opinion until I investigate the miscalculations." Thank God her manager backed her. Gratitude wrapped her body, almost lifting her.

"There's a lot at stake with the software. We're losing money, and jobs are on the line. Must cut somewhere. You don't wish your colleagues' livelihoods on your conscience." Sandeep stuck out his jaw.

If Jenna murdered him, she'd probably get off with justifiable homicide.

Sebastian patted her shoulder. "Angie will email our findings. Hopefully, the software only has a glitch."

She didn't want company layoffs based on her failures. Staff had financial obligations. Determination washed over her like a tidal wave. "I won't let you down."

****

Jenna's gaze shifted left to right on the computer

48

screen. Half a dozen instances were highlighted in Angie's email of AnaStone ruining a prediction. Every action ran as normal at first glance.

Claudine sauntered by and winked. A torch lit up in her chest.

Hayley strode to her desk, holding two plastic cups. "How did the meeting with Sebastian and Sandeep go?"

"I don't know the cause of the errors. They've been happening for over a month, and no one noticed. Thank you for sticking up for me." She opened University of San Francisco's projection.

"Of course. I am protective of our team." Hayley sat at the edge of the desk, sliding a cup.

"I can't imagine a better boss than you." She sipped the drink. Perfect. The way she enjoyed coffee when she drank it on rare occasions—no milk and sugar. Caffeine beckoned her. Today was going to be long, and she wouldn't have a spare hour for a lunchtime gym class to re-energize. Tracing a finger over the screen, she read each step on AnaStone concluding to sell stock.

A bitter taste traced the inside of her mouth.

"What's wrong?" Little lines formed on Hayley's forehead.

Jenna pointed to the display. "If the software followed the steps, Stone Corp would've bought into University of San Francisco. The system was on the right path, then in an instant, changed directions."

Hayley crossed her arms. "Strange. Maybe a bug. The best technology has issues."

"I'm cookie dough and haven't finished baking." Jenna double-clicked Homelander's trail and etched a finger at every action to show Hayley. Similar to the previous example, at one point, the system altered the conclusion. She tapped the screen. "The same problem occurred."

Hayley stood and rolled a spare chair beside Jenna. "Go through every suggestion one by one. I'll sit with you."

Jenna spent the next hour sifting through the case studies. Hayley confirmed her answers.

Frowning, she searched for bugs although she removed them over a week ago. None. The coding was perfect.

Her boss pinched the bridge of her nose, closing her eyes for a split second. "Who has editing rights to the software?"

Jenna racked her brain. "I'm the only one with full access as the creator. Basic editing privileges...you, Vanessa, Claudine, Sebastian, Angie, Sandeep, Tina from accounting, and Nathan from IT. The people who need it for their role."

Hayley straightened her back. "This means two possibilities."

Jenna leaned closer. A roaring echoed in her ears. "The system is broken and requires a complete reboot—"

"—or someone is hacking into the software." Hayley's eyebrows shot up.

Jenna's throat squeezed like someone had locked her in an invisible chokehold.

This wasn't good.

Chapter Six

The clouds outside the office windows had long turned gray. A dark vast blanket hung heavy in the sky, suffocating every building. Rain sprayed against the glass, trickling down, and pounded against the walls.

The weather replicated Jenna's mood. She switched off the computer. Claudine strode out of the bathroom. Leggings hugged her firm calves. A red helmet and backpack dangled off one slender hand.

"Don't tell me you're riding home in this weather?" Jenna packed away a notebook and reports into her personal cabinet.

"Keeps me fit. Only a fifteen-minute ride."

Jenna frowned at the wind rattling the trees. "You'll catch a cold." She checked the clock on her phone. More than enough time to collect her daughters from after-school care and prepare Marco's dinner. "I'll drive you home. I usually take the BART, but I read the weather would be bad this afternoon."

"Wow, you're organized. I'm fine, though," Claudine said. "Riding is my happy place."

A hot silver streak split the sky. The windows banged, and the temperature in the room dropped.

"See. You can't go out in the storm." Jenna beckoned a hand outside. "The mom in me has to be organized and also insist on taking you home. Don't want you sick throughout the weekend."

"Okay, if it's not any trouble. Will my bike fit into your car?"

"I drive a seven-seater. When my eldest was born, I had a crazy idea I needed more space. Your bicycle will squeeze in the back if I push the chairs down."

"Thank you. My bike's in the basement. Be right back." Claudine left her helmet and backpack on Jenna's desk and headed toward the stairs, swishing her peach-shaped bottom.

The week was finally over although she'd still fret about AnaStone throughout the weekend. Jenna ripped out disinfectant wipes from the tub and scrubbed the table—part of her pack-up ritual.

The elevator's "up" arrow lit up, and the doors sprang open. Claudine strode out, wheeling a bicycle. "Ready?"

"Let's go. I'm parked to the right of the entrance. We'll get wet, but the drenched look is sexier, anyway." Jenna's nose scrunched as she passed the helmet and backpack to Claudine.

"Better wet than dry." Claudine winked.

They walked to the elevator.

Jenna swallowed. Claudine stuffed the helmet into a bag.

Throughout the elevator trip, Jenna didn't utter a word. The walls squeezed them in tighter and tighter. Jenna examined her nails, breath caught in her throat. Once Jenna and Claudine exited the building, the true extent of the deluge hit.

"Let's run." Claudine grabbed Jenna's hand, wheeling the bicycle with her other.

Rain smashed against Jenna's clothes, the drops like bullets on downcast faces. Trees thrashed in the powerful gust, sending leaves dancing and swirling in the icy blast. Jenna's shoes splashed in water pools formed on the pavement as she sprinted.

Together they leaped over a puddle. Claudine skirted the bicycle, avoiding water. Hair clung to Jenna's face and wrapped her neck. They dashed into the underground parking lot. Jenna puffed out light and fast breaths before she burst into giggles.

"We look like drowned rats." Water dripped from Claudine's hair to the off-white T-shirt. A pine-green lace bra peeked through the now transparent material.

Jenna's heart flipped like a fish caught in a net, her hands twitching to unhook Claudine's bra and slide the straps down her smooth shoulders. Claudine would have the most beautiful, perky breasts.

Jenna clenched her sweater, squeezed water out, and pointed to the light gray SUV. "My car's over there."

She whipped out her keys and clicked the "unlock" button. Her gaze snagged on the keychain displaying a picture of Jenna, Marco, and the kids in tutus at the ballet studio years ago. Little paper cuts stung her heart. Since Eve gave her the present, no way she'd take it off because the picture included Marco. Nope, nothing to do with her heart aching every time she attempted to remove it.

Walking faster, she gripped the keychain. Finally, at the vehicle, she opened the back door and urged the seats down.

Claudine squeezed the bicycle inside. "A perfect fit." Her eyes twinkled.

An undercurrent zapped between them. Tiny licks of fire simmered through Jenna's body. Definitely her imagination. Only one other time in her life she might have felt a spark with a woman, but that was a non-issue too.

Jenna hopped inside, settling in the driver's seat. "Which way?" she asked as Claudine slid into the passenger chair.

"Go straight at the highway."

"Works out well. You're on the way to my kids' school." She snapped on the seatbelt and drove out of the parking lot. Claudine's sweet vanilla scent danced through their space. More delicious than any air freshener.

Claudine rummaged through her backpack and whipped out a plastic container. "Do you mind if I eat? I'm starving."

"Of course not." Jenna clicked the windshield wipers.

"Banana or melon?"

Jenna spluttered on her own breath until she spotted Claudine tilting a fruit box. "I'm fine."

"Besides a croissant this morning, I've been too busy to eat. What's your favorite food?"

"Can't choose. I enjoy every cuisine." Jenna tapped on the steering wheel.

"You must prefer one over others…hotdogs or tacos?"

Jenna gasped and drifted to the other lane. Every word Claudine uttered sounded provocative. She swerved her car back. "Umm…hmm…a tricky one."

"I love tacos." Claudine popped a melon piece into her mouth.

Heat radiated throughout Jenna's body. She envisioned Claudine's wet, swollen folds flushed deep pink and blossomed wide open. Staring straight ahead, she concentrated on the road.

"Any ideas on catching the handbag thief?" Claudine broke the quiet few minutes.

"I've been preoccupied today with the crap going on at work and barely considered the robber."

"Yeah, Hayley mentioned the issues before she left. I'm sorry you're going through this." Claudine's right leg jittered like she had too much coffee. "I'll keep a lookout for suspicious activities."

"Hardly your fault." Jenna sighed. "Not sure I can enjoy the weekend with this black cloud over my head." She pointed to the stormy sky. "Pun intended."

The car rang with silence. Claudine fisted her hands on her knees. Surely, she wasn't involved in AnaStone's catastrophe. The errors began weeks before Claudine started. And only an idiot did sketchy stunts when brand-new to a company.

"I hate someone taking advantage of you and Stone Corp." Claudine's words had an edge. "You've done too much for me."

Jenna exhaled. Claudine worried about her wellbeing. Jenna was paranoid for no reason. She signaled a turnoff at the approaching ramp. The rain fell heavier against the windows.

She increased the wiper speed and changed the subject. "I have no clue how to bring the thief down."

"He attempted to target you again in a similar area and time of day. Maybe he doesn't stray far."

"Do you have an idea?"

Claudine stroked her chin and half-laughed. "We can roam the region carrying a bag displayed wide open until we find him."

"It'll take ages. He may never appear again."

"Can you track your stolen cell?"

"I tried, but he disabled the app." Jenna gripped the steering wheel tighter. "I locked the contents, though."

"You didn't erase?" Claudine pointed ahead. "Exit here."

Jenna eased off the "accelerator" pedal and signaled to depart. "No, I always had some hope I'd claim my phone back. I have tons of family photos stored in it."

A car cut in front of her for the exit. Jenna stomped on the brakes, jolting them in their seats. She wanted to wind down the window and flip him the bird.

"Some people need to retake their driving test." Claudine sat up straight. "Let's trace your phone again when we're back in the office. He might be nearby. Turn right at the lights."

"Can't hurt. I'm furious he's getting away with his shit." Jenna's blood scorched under her skin. She was jumpy for weeks after he snatched her belongings. Bad people always won in the end. No barriers stopped him from stealing another woman's possessions.

"You and me both. I hate him already." Claudine's voice laced with venom.

Jenna inclined her head. Their gazes collided, and mutual understanding formed. A wicked grin spread across Claudine's face. Two scorned women plus a common enemy equaled a deadly combination.

****

Tonight was Marco's make–or–break moment. The first time his family organized a get-together over a meal in a year. Hopefully, this occasion wouldn't be their last. Every second must be perfect. His heart

56

jumped into his throat. He would remind Jenna they were amazing together. How special they were as a family. But his insides split open continuously. He couldn't fix himself, let alone a relationship.

Clutching a paper box of scones, he marched toward the front door. He grabbed the handle. A bang erupted outside. He yanked his hand away. Sharp needles pricked his skin. The room's gravity dragged him down. His chest hollowed and caved.

Bright headlights shone through the front windows' gray curtains. The thud was a car backfiring. His breathing slowed. He spun. Stumbled a few steps. Collapsed onto the couch. Sweat covered his hands. He couldn't keep a strong grip on the dessert box. It slipped through his fingers, falling to the soft cushions beside him.

He'd never be able to go out to dinner like a normal person. Darkness had grown roots inside him, niggling against his chest. He'd end up hurting Jenna…and his kids. All he was good at. Maybe if he continued therapy, he wouldn't have PTSD issues. Then again, the quack he visited was useless.

The phone pinged. He blinked, too slow for the action to be normal. The message might be from Jenna, canceling tonight. His body itched like little insects crawled over him. Hands shaking, he snatched the phone from his jeans pocket.

—*Good luck, Marco. Remember, you deserve your life to go right. Wishing you a wonderful birthday with your family. Bluebell x*—

He barked out a laugh. Bluebell was a true friend. They had met through a friend of a friend and bonded through mutual army experiences. He didn't chat to other people since he cut off his former team members from his life. No bother. He had no energy to talk to anyone.

He typed a quick response.

—*Cheers.*—

Bluebell always predicted when he was acting stupidly. She was a good person, and he hoped she'd reconcile with her wife despite her parents setting them up. The dinner invitation was the first good thing to happen in a long time. No chance he'd blow this and go back to barely speaking to Jenna again. The image of his daughters' smiling faces and dimples tugged his lips into a smile.

Like a bear emerging from winter hibernation, Marco thawed in the warmth his family gifted him. His edges softened, and his body perked up. He loved Jenna. He needed her. The times with family were the only moments he felt happy. Nabbing the white box, he jumped from the couch and sprinted out of the door.

****

A knock resounded on Jenna's front door, breaking her thoughts on the car ride with Claudine and someone messing with AnaStone. She lowered the stove's heat. Garlic beef mince sizzled on the pan.

"Daddy, Daddy, Daddy." Keisha hurried past her, holding a bright balloon displaying the number thirty-five, and opened the door. Eve and Scruffy trotted hot on her heels. The three wore matching pink bows in their hair.

Jenna wiped her hands on the apron before untying the strings and hanging up the purple polka-dot material. She braced herself to board the Marco Kravitz express. The destination might be disaster.

"Did you look through the curtain first? I could've been anyone. Nice balloons." Marco hugged Keisha and then Eve, who still had one eye glued to her favorite cartoon on the TV.

"I knew you were coming." Keisha rolled her eyes. "Happy birthday."

Jenna laughed under her breath. Her daughter exhibited a teenager's sass. Marco had always prioritized safety. Years ago, he installed a security camera at the front and back of the house plus alarms inside. He also insisted on teaching the girls and herself self-defense. A point she supported. Everyone needed to learn the basics.

Marco tickled their eldest daughter. "Better to check first."

Keisha shrieked and ran with Eve toward the TV. Jenna needed to act on their idiot box consumption. They should enjoy fresh air or read. She relaxed the one–show–a–day rule when their father moved out because guilt consumed her.

Marco walked to Jenna. A flicker shimmered through his eyes before he pecked her cheek.

A little taken aback, she stiffened. There wasn't a handbook on greeting your ex-spouse.

"Happy birthday." She didn't know what else to say.

"For you." He gave her a paper box. His top hugged his shoulders and tapered at his waist. She predicted when she looked at his face, the wood-brown T-shirt would bring out the color of his eyes.

And dammit…yes, it did.

Scruffy stood on her hind legs, sniffing Marco's gift.

Jenna giggled and nudged Scruffy down. She took the white box and opened the lid. Four scones sat inside with a jam jar and a side of cream. The scones were from her favorite bakery on the other side of town—almost as delicious as her family's secret recipe, but the raspberry jam was beyond special. Fruit chunks sat inside the glass.

Maybe Claudine baked scones in her spare time. Claudine dreamed of owning a café. She shook away the image. "How thoughtful. You would've driven for two hours to buy them in rush-hour traffic."

"The bakery was on my way home from work." He scratched the back of his shaved head, a sheepish grin spreading across his face.

She warmed, touched by his gesture. The scones transported her back to childhood. After church every Sunday, her mom baked them at her grandparents' house, and they used this exact jam. Her heart had shattered when her grandparents passed away within days from each other. The doctor said Grandpa died from a broken heart.

She clutched the box to her chest.

"I should've done more for you while we were together." His gaze held hers. He shifted his weight on the balls on his feet.

"Hey…you took out the trash once."

He did more than she let on. Throughout their relationship, he was never the typical roses–and–chocolates type of guy. However, sometimes he surprised her with a token unique to her or them, meaning more than all the flowers in the world.

"Your grandparents meant a lot to you." Marco squeezed her hand.

Seconds later, she gripped him back. She relaxed. His eyes reminded her of swirls of melted chocolate. Time and time again, she got lost in those deep pools. She bit her bottom lip. Their electricity was still there. In the past months, she'd elbowed him to the back of her mind. He was the first man she'd loved, and it scared her she might never find this connection again.

Tracing her tongue across her teeth, she faced the kids. "Who wants to give Dad his present?"

"Meee," the girls chorused, both holding the gift out as they ran to their father, eyes shining.

"Is this for me?" His eyes widened, and his Adam's apple bobbed. He turned to Jenna. "You didn't have to."

She shrugged. "Keisha and Eve's idea." She did not know why she gave the impression she had nothing to do with the present. Not inappropriate to give him a birthday gift to extend an olive branch as friends.

"Now, what could this be?" Marco lifted out the jigsaw puzzle of the girls ice skating and ran a hand over the image.

"It's us, Daddy," Eve shrieked.

"Do you like it?" Keisha asked.

"I love it. It's perfect." Hugging the girls, he kissed them.

Jenna's eyes filled. A raw, intense ache choked her, a buildup of painful memories. He had once belonged to her. His musky scent drew her in.

"Mommm. Can we eat now? I'm hungry." Keisha tugged at her arm.

Jenna jumped. Her gaze settled on her daughter. "I'll be right there, sweetheart."

She endured life without him for the past year. And

she kept surviving. For her sake and the rage she still had within her.

Drinking in the sight of him, she filed the image away. Throat too tight to speak, she plastered on a smile and headed to the kitchen.

Chapter Seven

At the dinner table, Jenna tossed her head back and roared with laughter. Tonight felt like old times before their separation. Before the trauma. Before the mistrust and the ever-widening gap of silence became part of their lives.

"This guy I work with, Rob, got told off by the manager today for swearing. Someone walking by overheard and complained." Marco leaned forward. "He was too quick, though. Pretended he had Tourette's and spent the whole afternoon cursing and cussing to prove it."

Jenna laughed so hard she choked on kombucha. He had a way of turning a funny story funnier.

"What's Tourette's?" Keisha stuffed a mushroom into her mouth.

Jenna was lucky her kids enjoyed healthy foods and didn't even have to bribe them. The body was a temple, and everything started internally. Although she didn't oppose the occasional treat, such as scones.

"A disorder where the person might experience tics out of their control. Sometimes it makes them use bad language, honey," Jenna said. She and Marco explained topics to their kids. Ignorance didn't equal bliss. Their children had to be ready for the world, safely. One reason they didn't shirk around the truth of their separation.

Keisha chewed and nodded. "Yes, I think someone had twitches in a movie."

"You're right. We watched the film years ago." Marco stirred the zucchini pasta. "This meal is as I remember."

The dish had always been a favorite. He loved the walnut and tomato flavors over the softened vegetable, spiraled to resemble spaghetti. Pleasure slinked through her body. She'd always enjoyed cooking for the family.

"Can we watch a movie over dinner?" Eve sipped her freshly squeezed orange juice.

"Don't you want to talk to us?" Marco poked her small button nose. "Maybe after dinner."

Jenna gawked. With the kids, she was the bad cop most the time. Nice to relax for a change. Maybe during their split, he had matured.

Marco's gaze penetrated deep inside her, promising a change. An ache speared through her chest. She averted her gaze to the food.

Twenty minutes later, Jenna and the family packed up the dining table, and they sat on the sofa. Eve giggled when the animated animal appeared on screen. She never grew tired of this story. The first movie outing as a family. Marco had embraced the day by buying popcorn and drinks decorated in the film's merchandise. Jenna still had the holographic cup crammed somewhere in the cupboard.

"Dad. Can we have ice cream with scones?" Keisha sat at the end of the sofa next to Marco.

"You'll explode if you eat more sweets. Like literally *kapow*." Marco shot his hands in the air and waved. "Green goo will splatter everywhere."

Eve's hand flew to her lips. "You're silly. Humans

aren't green."

The characters on-screen burst into song. The girls mouthed every word. They loved the film had two sisters.

"I'll grab the dessert." Jenna stood.

"Do you need help?" Marco brushed his fingers against hers. Heat raced through her body like flames on a gasoline streak.

"I'm fine." She made her way to the kitchen. After she searched for an unsalted and unbuttered popcorn packet, she tossed the bag into the microwave. The savory scent wafted in the air, every second filled with mini explosions.

While waiting, she removed scones from the box and set them on a plate. As she spooned cream onto each one, a scandalizing image entered her mind. The cream might be heavenly on her breasts as Marco licked it off. Tilting her head back, she closed her eyes. A soft moan fled her lips.

The popping slowed. Her eyes fluttered open, and she blew out a cleansing breath. She tugged on the microwave's handle and emptied the popcorn into a bowl. Grabbing the snacks, she exited the kitchen and plonked the food on the coffee table. She sat next to Marco.

Her skin tightened at her seating instinct. Every Saturday, they used to enjoy a family movie night. They were tightly knit once, with many shared traditions. A dry, silent sob yanked her back to the here and now. No, she was right to end their relationship.

The girls had cozied up to each other, and Marco wrapped his right arm around them both. Too easy to slip back to a comfort zone. To forget the past never happened.

Marco patted her knee. "You always get choked up at this part."

She blinked. The movie was at the scene when the main character felt completely alone. Choosing not to correct him, she grabbed a handful of popcorn. Her guard had dropped several times tonight. Here, all together…every feeling, every emotion, every memory resurfaced.

****

"Do you want tea?" Jenna held up a transparent container filled with leaves. The kids had gone to bed— only the two of them now.

"Please." He strolled to the shelf and picked up a book. His arm muscles rippled as he flicked through the pages, biceps with tattoos peeking beneath the sleeves.

He had been working out more than usual. His jeans hugged his butt. A chemical reaction inside her set off like a bomb.

Marco strode to the kitchen table. Averting her gaze, she faced the sink. They had been together for so long she almost forgot to appreciate his rugged handsomeness, enough to steal anyone's will away. No doubt the prostitute's face turned shades of red when one year, three months, and two days ago he betrayed her. Jenna clenched a hand on the kettle handle. The past was in the past—no point dwelling on negative thoughts. She topped up the ancient kettle with water that always took a long time to boil.

"Thank you for letting me join you and the girls tonight." Marco sucked his bottom lip. God, she yearned to be the one doing that. He wasn't this overwhelmingly sexually when they were together.

"Couldn't let you spend your birthday alone." She grabbed two mugs from the cupboard and fumbled for honey. Her emotions escaped her when alone with him. Time to get a grip.

Marco closed the distance between them. "I've missed you." Tenderness softened his eyes. He clasped her hands and tugged her to sit at the table.

She didn't know where to look. Her gaze bounced in different directions until settling on his chest. The T-shirt molded against every contour of his body, and a V-neck accentuated his strong jawline. A sudden urge overcame her to slip her hands under his shirt and find out the extent he had been working out. Jealousy nibbled inside her. Someone else shouldn't reap the benefits of his firm muscles.

She stood and hunched her shoulders. "Easy to say you've missed me."

Planting her feet on the floor, she refrained wrestling him—either from anger or lust. Her legs were as weak as overcooked noodles. Sure, she was on the biggest sex drought of her life since she'd told Marco to leave. Maybe loneliness caused her hormones to act disobediently—first Claudine and now Marco. Perhaps one last time with her ex might set her straight.

"I have missed you." His smile was warm and soft and inviting. When the spark reached his eyes, her resolve withered.

She rested a hand on his tight pecs. The thought of the naughty toys in a cupboard and putting them to good use goaded her. After the week she had, she needed the release. Jenna licked her lips in anticipation—tonight, she wanted to forget.

"You miss me?" Wrath stomped through her body.

She shoved his chest.

He didn't stumble back, but his eyes glowed with desire.

"Prove it." She bumped him again before clasping one hand at the back of his head. This was about getting her rocks off.

Marco didn't hesitate. He wrapped his muscular arms around her and took the two steps necessary to back her against the wall. "Is this proof enough?"

A hard erection strained against her belly. Their lips hovered inches from each other's, a mingled breath away. His mouth fell against hers in a fast, hard swoop.

No holding back.

Familiar but exciting. His tongue surged into her mouth, licking and nipping her lips. A pulse shivered between her thighs. Maybe the adrenaline of doing whatever the hell she wanted. And she wanted him. Stuff the consequences.

She fisted his T-shirt. "This is sex. Not reuniting."

His smile faltered. "Okay."

"Fuck me." This was for her. For too long, she'd considered others. To her detriment.

Tugging his shirt, she lifted the material over his head. An eagle tattoo in a Celtic style spread across his upper body, the artwork a combination of little knots, crosses, and spirals. She marveled at his granite-like abs, each line like they had been drawn on. His hips had ridges pointing south toward his groin, hidden in jeans. Sucking in a breath, she traced the valley of his chest with a single finger.

Multiple yellowish bruises lingered on his stomach. She frowned. "How did you get hurt?"

"Don't worry. There are more urgent things to do."

He unbuttoned her cardigan, but after the first couple, he hauled the knit top over her head and flung it behind him. His mouth seared a pathway along her exposed neck.

She forgot his injuries. Instead, she wished she wore fancier panties. Maybe the teddy, rather than a comfortable beige bra. But by the way his gaze flared, the outfit didn't faze him one bit.

"There are many wicked ideas I've contemplated." She had been with him for almost two decades. Sometimes the sex turned a little vanilla—A goes into B which equaled C.

She always felt too awkward to voice her cravings. But tonight was the "new" Jenna. The "take charge and demand pleasure" Jenna. Zero to lose. They weren't together anymore. No complications, right?

He brushed his lips up and down her neck. "I've wanted you for so long." Reaching behind her back, he unclasped her bra and threw the cotton to the floor. "Oh, God." He cupped her breasts. "I've missed these."

The heat of his palms spread to her core. Worried she might wake the kids, she suppressed a gasp. But they were deep sleepers after a movie and wouldn't stir if a firetruck roared next to their ears.

The kettle hissed on the stove.

She rubbed his cock through his jeans in slow, sensuous strokes.

Groaning, he thumbed her nipples, hands squeezing and kneading her sensitive mounds.

"Don't stop. Harder. Until my skin stings." She groaned, long and raspy. The discomfort drew out an intense yearning. Tightening her grip on him, she continued the fast motions.

He placed more pressure on her nipples and pinched the tips. Instant flooding between her thighs had her ramming her hips against his hardness, begging for release.

A half-savage expression appeared on his face. "We still have a lot to learn about each other."

The heady mixture of pleasure and pain left her speechless. Fumbling for his jeans button, she shoved the denim down. He stepped out of the legs, standing in boxer briefs. A snake tattoo in subtle tones wrapped his right leg, eyes sly and menacing. Arousal tensed his shorts, stretching the material in urgent need. She'd almost forgotten how much he turned her on.

Primal. Intense. Ravenous.

The feelings overflowed back with erotic clarity. At this moment, she was his, and they both accepted it.

His big hands grabbed her waist. Picking her up, he laid her on the table. The cold wood rammed against her bare back, but she didn't care. He planted kisses along her jaw, his firm, soft lips putting her under a spell. His tongue trailed down to her breasts, each lick leaving a buzzing sensation on her skin.

"No romance. Quick and dirty." Jenna raised her breasts closer to his face. A drawn-tight tension sat in her rigid body.

He lifted his head, scowling. "I hear you loud and clear."

"Do it, then. I've been very bad and want it hot and rough." Her voice wavered at her boldness. Never in her life had she uttered filthy words like this.

"At your service." He drove down his boxer briefs.

Drool lining her mouth at his full glory, she leaned on her elbows.

Marco shifted forward, poking his hard length between her breasts.

Eyes wide, her body froze for a moment at the unfamiliar territory. Her breasts swelled.

"I've always wanted to fuck your tits." He ground his cock against her breasts in a slow rhythm, pre-cum sliding across her skin.

"Why?" Her heart galloped. She used her forearms to drive her full breasts together, squeezing him tight.

"They're the perfect size…" Marco placed his hands above her on the table and growled. "…to stick my dick between."

She mewled, her nipples tightening. He thrust back and forth. Something naughty about this. Taboo. A fast, hard tremor shot through her. Using her hands, she hugged her breasts inward. He prodded his full, hard length.

The kettle hissed louder in the background, replicating the old-fashioned steamed trains.

It felt so good to be bad. The naughty act spurred every wild fantasy. She arched her back, embracing his stiffness.

His tip drizzled, mixing with her sweat. He stepped back. The loss of contact sent her reeling. He yanked her skirt to her waist, revealing boring baby-blue panties.

"You're sexy as hell." He slid the cotton down her legs, in a painfully slow motion, until they dropped to the floor.

Electrical senses hummed over her skin. "Remember, this isn't anything."

"You've made your point, woman." He lifted her from the table in a single swoop—easy with his six-foot frame.

Her arms draped around his strong neck. She nipped his bottom lip.

He squished her against the wall. "Are you still on the pill?"

"Yes. Are you sleeping with anyone?" She never stopped the prescription because the medication helped control her skin breakouts.

"No. You're the one for me." Marco's hand grazed between her legs. She was wet and hungry. He eased a finger inside her, and Jenna moaned at the glorious sensation of that one digit.

"I forgot how tight you were." His voice was like gravel. "You feel so fucking good, babe."

Another finger joined the first, stretching and preparing her for his rock-hard cock.

Jenna pined for more. "Please. Now, Marco."

Elevating one of her legs, he wrapped it around his waist and thrust deep inside her in one mighty push.

"Oh. My. God." Her eyes rolled back as his length slid in and out.

Her wet heat clenched him, her fingers digging into his shoulders. He drove greater still. Her moisture soaked him. She crushed her legs against him. He plunged harder and faster. Gripping her tighter, he licked up and down her neck while she raked his back.

The water from the kettle gurgled, a sign of a big explosion nearing.

She grabbed his shoulders, adjusting her position until his solid length rubbed her swollen clit. Her muscles contracted, drawing him deeper inside of her. Strands of black hair clung to her face and tumbled over her eyes.

He thumbed the lock away. "I want to see you when you come apart."

A fluttering pinch shivered between her legs. His body replicated pure masculine architecture. Every limb out of a hardware shop. She rested her knees on his waist to support herself and ground against him.

Liquid from the kettle sloshed the glass, intensifying her lust and excitement.

Her thighs scraped the skin of his hips. The friction burned her flesh. She wanted more of him, filling every inch of her. A fireball built in her chest. She tried to keep her eyes open. But he watched her with such intensity and adoration. Her eyes jammed shut to shake away his expression. She would not feel for him again.

Her head thumped against the wall. Working her fast, then slow, he sped up again. He pinned her up farther alongside the wall. She gulped for air. Pleasure sprinted through her body. Incoherent cries fled her lips.

He placed a hand over her mouth. "We need to keep quiet."

Her eyes shot open. She understood his reference to the children. She covered his lips in return. They stared into each other's eyes, hands over the other's mouth. His gaze darkened, his hot mouth and quiet grunts searing into her palm. She licked his skin. Their bodies crashed, slick with sweat and desire.

His pupils dilated. Burying his face into her neck, he thrust. His mouth covered hers, soaking up her moans and cries.

The water in the kettle bubbled over and over to the point the glass might break.

His ravenous groan spurred her and hastened her

breathing. A sheen of sweat dripped down her temples. She scrunched up her face, and her toes curled, cramping her feet.

His body grew rigid. Crying softly into his mouth, she bucked against him.

When her gaze settled from her explosion, Marco gaped. A dreamy smile curved over his lips.

Reality hit. Her breaths slowed, and body limpened. Unwrapping her legs from his waist, she stumbled to the floor. He held onto her arms to steady her. Satisfaction spread across his face. He tugged her disheveled hair into place.

Dammit. He had no right to look at her like this.

No, no, no. He was breaking their "no strings" rule. A disaster. No taking their dirty deed back. She wished she'd kept him at arm's length. The atmosphere had changed.

She yanked her hands away. "Thanks for the D."

Flinching, his body wobbled back as if blown by a sudden gust. Her sweet words for his dick rivaled poetry.

A heavy tension crammed the room. The gurgling in the kettle slowed and whistled, signifying the finish.

Chapter Eight

Last night was an unexpected defining moment. Marco's steps were lighter. Shuffling around the apartment, he shrugged on a jacket and fumbled for his keys on the coffee table. He and Jenna had plans to watch their daughters' ballet class—an outing they did every second week. He assumed the catch–up hadn't changed.

Maybe he could win Jenna over. No turning back after their night of utter bliss. Whenever he was with her, calmness washed over him like a secret passageway opened and beckoned him into safety. Into a happy place jam-packed with warmth and an explosion of color where the rest of the world didn't matter.

Even though Jenna had insisted the intimacy was a "no strings" arrangement, there was more there. He only had to convince her.

Whistling a merry tune, he grabbed the car keys. Body looser, he stepped out of the front door. Today was going to be a good day.

****

Jenna's daughters stretched on the barre in their ballet class, adorable in tutus and stockings. Keisha stood on one side with the eight- and nine-year-olds while Eve practiced with the fives and sixes.

Jenna and Marco sat on the benches against the

walls. She was surprised they occupied the same room without ripping each other's clothes off after last night's stellar banging. At the same time, guilt weighed her shoulders for using him for sex.

Marco hadn't uttered a word about their adult time while she could barely look at him without the heat of a thousand splendid suns rushing to her face. Maybe she read too much into the situation and needed to relax and have fun. An orgasm a day might take her work worries away. She had zero clue on fixing Stone Corp's issues.

"Look at me, Mom." Eve waved as she stretched her leg on the barre. "Dad, I'm getting good."

Jenna and Marco waved back.

Eve stood alongside the other little girls, practicing grand pliés. In unison, or as close to unison as kids could, they bent their knees toward the floor and lifted their heels like waddling ducks.

Jenna locked her job burdens into a mental safe. Her problems were for Monday. Today was about family.

Marco leaned in and dropped his mouth below her ear, his hot breaths spreading goose bumps on her neck. "Can we discuss last night?"

Jenna sighed. Wishful thinking he wouldn't bring the topic up. She became aware of every molecule of space between them.

Marco's hand grazed her right thigh so lightly the contact could be a breeze.

"What's to say?" The heat from his touch simmered her chest. She twisted her body and snapped a photo of Eve and Keisha on her phone.

"Plenty." Marco stretched his legs out, jeans hugging his quad muscles.

Unwilling to discuss their sex life within earshot of other parents, she shuffled down the bench. Marco followed suit.

"One night can't erase our problems." She smiled at Keisha who flapped her arms for attention.

"I know, but I'm willing to work on us."

"Easier said than done."

Marco's eyes grew hazy. "Don't tell me that wasn't the hottest sex ever? I haven't stopped replaying it in my head."

The images of Marco's long, hard cock pounding into her caused her bloodstream to burn. She let her thick, curly hair cover her face.

"I knew it. You want this." He growled, low and intense.

Crap…even his face turned her on and would look better between her legs. A part of her wished to let loose and enjoy. Last night was all about her. She had some making up to do. But this was Marco…the father of her children. The dynamic involved complications.

Yet she had been the good girl for too long. Her problems at work weren't going away, crushing harder on her shoulders. Damn the rules. Every part of her craved to crawl across the bench to him. But she didn't love him. Not anymore. Nope, definitely not.

Her teeth skated her bottom lip. "If we're going to do this, we need boundaries." Her practical side couldn't let anyone get hurt.

"Go on."

Their legs grazed together. Her breath caught at her throat. His thighs did magic when he rammed her against a wall.

She waited multiple beats until her blush subsided.

"Rule one. The girls can't find out. I don't want to get their hopes up. Hard enough when you first moved out."

"Agreed."

"Rule two." She held out her right index finger. "No sleepovers or we may as well still be together. Break my bed but not my heart."

"I can live with those terms." His husky voice had more bass than seconds ago. "We won't be the same as when we lived together. You've never moaned like that before."

Last night sparked their passion. They'd changed and were different people. Two sensual strangers ready to explore. The sex was so head-bangingly awesome even her neighbors might've needed a cigarette.

"Three. We won't be a regular schedule. Only whenever the mood strikes." Her voice came out flirty, the complete opposite to her intended firmness.

"Yes, ma'am."

"Number four." Jenna took a deep breath, bracing herself. "We can see other people."

No commitment—not fair if he waited for a connection to never happen.

The air became thick. A silence fell over them like a heavy blanket.

His shoulders curled, straining his muscles. "I don't want to share you."

"I'm not yours to share."

Marco's cheek ticked. His hands quivered and clenched on his lap like he tried to control them—clench, clench, relax, clench, clench, relax. "Fine."

"Are you sure? I don't want to hurt you." He had already been through enough in his life.

"Okay."

Their gazes crashed together. He held hers with a fiery intensity. An inferno of lust.

Slowly as though she had a stiff back, she turned her attention to the kids' class. At least now she had one aspect in her life sorted.

****

Jenna sucked air in her lungs as she ran on the gym's treadmill. The smell of sweat engulfed her. Weights and dumbbells clanged together, and footsteps thumped the floor.

Marco had taken the girls for frozen yogurt after ballet. She had an hour to workout. Her shorts clung to her legs. She didn't get the ass she desired by sitting on it.

What a week. First, the confusion with Marco and Claudine, then someone hacking into her employer's system. Her core shook. A software she worked hard on for years might crumble because of some buffoon.

"I'm dying." Her brother, Josh, jogged on the neighboring treadmill. His speed was half hers—never the athletic type. He groaned whenever the elevators broke, and he took the stairs.

She grabbed the water bottle from the cup holder and drank small sips. "Your sweat is your fat crying. Make it rain. Less than a minute. Remember, your audition for the lifeguard role is this Thursday. How was your tryout the other week for the play?"

"Fine. I received a call back." Perspiration drenched his bright-red face. Stumbling, he clutched his chest in mock despair. "Oh, my God. I can taste blood, Jenna. My lungs have burst."

Lucky he had a naturally fit-looking physique.

Jerk.

The treadmill's timer counted down. Five. Four. Three. Two. One.

"Let's start our cool down." She clicked the button to slow her speed. Sweat trickled down her temples. Lifting a towel hanging on the handle, she wiped her forehead.

"Thank God." He tapped the buttons with a fever she had only witnessed as teenagers when he chased a bus because he left a doughnut behind.

When her breaths steadied, she stopped the treadmill. She stepped off and sat at the edge of the ramp.

Josh plonked on his own treadmill. "Is your stress out of your system?"

"Not quite." Stretching her legs, she leaned over, gripping her toes. "How can someone manipulate AnaStone?"

He pinched his waist, puffing. "Follow the logic, I guess. Cozy up to everyone with access."

"The idea disturbs me. You know I don't like most people."

"You gotta do what you gotta do." Josh tilted his head left toward the mirror and raked a hand over his hair, flattening the strands sticking out.

He was vain but a good-looking son of a bitch. When younger, she felt like the ugly duckling compared to his big shiny eyes, smooth almond-colored skin, and unruly hair which proved more popular with the girls. Her characteristics were the same, though.

Standing, she wandered to the weights.

"Spot me." She attached fifty-pound plates to each side of the bar.

Groaning as he stood, he walked behind her. "Why would someone employed at Stone Corp deliberately lose them money?"

Settling on the black bench, she gritted her teeth as she pushed the bar up in a gradual movement. Her arms burned. "They might have their own investments. Everyone needs money."

Nathan Singh had spoken on the phone the other week to his girlfriend Desiree who also worked at Stone Corp. Screeches racketed from the other end on "needing" hair extensions, fake nails, and the day spa twice a week. Perhaps the pressure had sunk into him, and he refused to let her down.

Josh hovered his hands over the bar as she lowered the metal. "Maybe look at your team members. They'll know the system better than anyone."

"Nah. Vanessa's one of my closest friends, and she'd never rip off her boyfriend. They're too sickening in love. And Hayley helped me go through each case study."

"Maybe to throw you off the scent."

She inhaled. He had a point. Sometimes the person you least expected surprised you.

"What about Claudine? She's new." Josh nodded knowingly like he often did.

She shook her head. "No way. Too obvious. Plus, the problems started before she joined. Claudine's a good person and stopped someone stealing my bag."

"Is there a way to receive a notification when someone's completing live updates?" Josh asked.

After her eighth bench press, Josh lifted the bar from her and secured the heavy metal on handles.

She sat up straight. Her mind raced. "You're

cleverer than you look. I have to tweak a little behind the scenes, but your idea might work."

He grinned, holding out a hand for a high-five. "I've always been the smart one in the family."

****

First action Monday morning in the office, Jenna clicked through the software. She checked the fingerprint of everyone who had accessed AnaStone the past week. The obvious suspects. Sebastian, Angie, Hayley, Vanessa, Claudine, Sandeep, Tina, and Nathan did minor tweaks. Standard procedure. She had logged in the most.

Angie, Sebastian's assistant, walked across the room, stopping by every desk to offer a homemade zefir—Russian dessert resembling pink marshmallows.

Pausing at Jenna's desk, she held out the plate. "I prepared them last night."

Jenna didn't enjoy sugar in her body. You are what you eat. But she saved calories for Angie's delights that melted in your mouth—priorities.

"Thank you. This is exactly what I needed." She picked up a larger piece.

"You're welcome. They're Sebastian's favorite like my son's. Sebastian has been pulling his hair out under the pressure. He deserved a special treat. Cheers my son up whenever he's in pain." Angie sat at the edge of the desk. Her teenage son had Parkinson's disease. Rare for someone his age. "You look stressed as well. Must be something in the air."

Jenna's heart dropped at the confirmation Sebastian was worried. She was leaning toward blind panic.

"I'm not figuring out AnaStone's issue." Jenna

sighed. Sandeep's threat to let staff go tempted her to shove his face into a swollen-pink baboon's butt.

"Are there any updates? Sebastian asked me to check." Angie slipped on the table before she steadied herself. She reminded Jenna of the female version of the Penguin from Batman—tight ringlets, pale skin, and wide hips.

Jenna shook away the naughty thought. "The software is right. No errors or bugs. Only…"

"Only what?"

"Appears like someone's hacking the system."

Angie narrowed her eyes. "Super-duper bizarre. I don't think anyone here takes part in illegal activities."

"I wasn't sure at first either, but every sign leads to the conclusion."

"I'll raise your suspicions with Sebastian. He may report the crime to the police. Is there any job I could help you with?"

Jenna bit into the zefir. The airy texture danced on her taste buds. "Not unless you have a magic wand. I'm set up to fail."

Angie gave a tight smile. "Sebastian is a reasonable man, and others are looking into the software concerns. He's not the type to be cruel."

"No, of course not. I'm stuck on solving the problem." She regretted her previous words as soon as they left her lips. Angie was loyal to Sebastian and defended him on the rare occasion anyone uttered a negative word.

"I'm sure Sebastian will provide you every resource for success like with everyone. Hayley and Sandeep are in charge of investigating. He catches up with them regularly." Angie stood from the desk. "Do you want me to set up a meeting? He might offer advice you may not have considered."

"Yes, thank you." She didn't like the chances. Not to toot her own horn, she was more experienced with the software and her field than anyone in the business. Unlikely someone or the police could help. Then again, Sebastian knew his company inside out.

"He doesn't have a thirty-minute time slot until three weeks. I'll send you a calendar invite. You will be okay." Angie patted her shoulder and took the plate of treats to the next person's desk.

Jenna closed her eyes for a second. Maybe they'd figure out a solution. Intelligent people worked in this organization. Determined, she checked the moment AnaStone's process changed to recommend the wrong direction for Homelander. There must be a solution among the data. The screen switched over. She blinked at the pattern. Cold unease slivered through her body. The system had no footprint and showed a Romanian IP address.

She gritted her teeth. Someone overseas might be hacking into them for their gain. But every part of her sensed an inside job. Each step was too calculated, too convenient. Changing an IP address wasn't tricky. The actions had the sophistication and knowledge of an expert in the internal system.

Typing, she built a set of rules for a firewall to keep intruders out. Once finished, she checked the code again. The perfect firewall.

A sharp tension formed at the back of her neck. Solving this would never be easy, but it was proving impossible.

****

A group of teenagers shoved each other as they swaggered past Jenna and Claudine. The two lingered at the intersection packed with cafés, restaurants, buskers, and people in suits buying takeaway.

Jenna needed the break to clear her head after discovering the overseas IP address.

Claudine swung a wide-open handbag, purse peeking through. "Does anyone look familiar? I only saw the side of the thief's face."

Jenna bit her lip to stifle a laugh. Claudine was carrying through with the crazy idea she suggested in the car.

The gaze of one boy with braces met Claudine's. He stopped and glowed bright red before scurrying to catch up with his friends.

Not that Jenna blamed his reaction.

"I might not recognize him. Only his wide, trouty mouth. A hoodie covered half his face." Jenna grimaced.

"Recheck your phone. Has a trace come up?"

Jenna lifted her mobile to her face. Still no location on the old phone. "Nope. He might've sold my cell to the black market by now, along with my deep dark secrets."

A barista sauntered out of the café. "Espresso for Claudine."

Claudine raised a hand and took the drink. "Karma will get him one day."

"Hopefully, karma slaps him in the face before I do. How many times should we keep waiting around expecting him to turn up?"

"For as long as we're having fun." Claudine checked her delicate gold watch. "I have a meeting in ten minutes. Let's go."

She grabbed Jenna's arm, and they strode toward the office.

In truth, Jenna adored spending time with her colleague. A magnet drew them together. Claudine had a refreshing view on life from her stance on feminism to the hearts in her eyes when a loved-up couple kissed in front of them.

"I have a confession." Claudine's tongue poked through the left side of her lips.

"Don't tell me…you have a war against standing and replaced the office's floors with lava?" Jenna leaned closer. Claudine's long legs strode faster than hers. Not that Jenna was a petite woman with her curves and at five-foot-eight. But in heels, Claudine stood over six foot.

"Close, but no. I had a dream about you."

"Really?" Jenna's breath cracked in her lungs. She pictured them lying on their sides, facing each other, slithering one another's underwear off. "Was my hair okay?" *Ugh*…she replied any nonsense to steady her stomach's series of rises and dips, but why that?

One second ticked into two. Three. Then ten.

"My dream was inappropriate. Forget I spoke."

Jenna dangled at the end of Claudine's fishing line. "If it's inappropriate, I want to know more. I don't get offended easily."

"Okay…" Claudine's gaze didn't shift from Jenna's.

Gulping, Jenna bit down on her lip. Heat filled her like a kettle trying not to whistle. Her fantasy turned into kissing Claudine's pubic bone, hip, and then a long slow lick of her clit.

"You were the badass businesswoman you are." Claudine licked her lips. "You stood over my desk wearing sky-high red stilettos and growled, 'I'm ready to crack the whip.' "

Jenna ached for Claudine's heat to drench her fingers. A faint sheen formed over her face as she composed a sentence. "Uh…hmm…I'm not too bad, am I?"

"Of course not." Claudine hooked her arm into hers. The silk sleeve rubbed Jenna's skin. "You have a power few people exhibit. You fascinate me."

Surely, Claudine didn't have a deeper meaning. Jenna shook her head like someone forcing water out of their ears. Claudine respected her as a professional teammate. Jenna, as usual, read too much into the situation.

She limpened against Claudine and attempted a weak joke. "My day job will be a lot easier when everyone learns to worship me."

"Damn straight." Claudine purred and winked. "I'm not going to lie. I woke up a little hot and bothered."

Pure arousal slinked from Jenna's throat down to her nether regions. Another erotic image popped up— her mouth zeroing in on Claudine's pink nipple, sucking and tasting her. Shuddering, she dropped her arm from Claudine's. "Dreams are funny. I had one about my deceased grandmother. I turned into my brother before I flew away."

For the rest of the journey to work, Jenna chattered, voice high-pitched and tight, claiming strange dreams did not mean more.

Chapter Nine

The doorbell rang less than thirty minutes after Jenna arrived home from work.

Her body shook, too deep in thought about her work disaster. "Who could that be?" She switched off the iron. Monday was ironing day. Not that she was predictable or anything.

Keisha and Eve scrambled to the front window, yanking aside the curtain, craning their necks. They weren't allowed to answer the door unless she accompanied them. Scruffy barked in frenzied yaps at their feet.

"It's Daddy." They jumped up and down.

When she opened the door, Marco leaned against the doorjamb, his biceps bunching. "I have a surprise for you."

Her skin tingled. Sparks coursed through her veins. "What surprise? In case you're forgetting, we have two offspring."

"Which is why I arranged backup." He gestured a hand behind him.

Jenna's parents popped up, faces beaming.

"You're here," Keisha cried as she and Eve ran toward their grandparents.

Dad hugged Keisha while Eve wrapped her arms around Mom's legs.

Her petite mother embraced the girls and squeezed

past Jenna. "We're always too happy to look after our favorite grandbabies."

"Especially for you two to enjoy a night out." Dad's ebony-colored eyes twinkled as he followed Mom.

"You two are unbelievable." Jenna's stomach pinched. Her meddling parents stopped at nothing to reunite her and Marco. She didn't need their nosiness on top of job pressures.

"So how about it?" Marco's lips twitched.

Jenna placed her hands on her hips. "I've had a terrible day, and it's a school night." Hardly containing herself to not explode at her parents, her jaw tightened.

"We're more than glad to stay late." Mom winked.

Even though irritation seeped through her veins at Marco and her parents plotting, her heart still tickled at his thoughtfulness.

Keisha tugged Marco's hand. "Are you staying for dinner, Dad? I helped season the vegetables."

"No, I'm whisking your mom away." Marco's grin charged Jenna's body to life.

"Can we come?" Keisha glanced back and forth between Jenna and Marco. She was old enough for their separation to affect her and had become more chipper since Marco's birthday dinner.

"Maybe next time, sweetheart. We'll do a special date." Marco brushed his lips against Keisha's cheek. "You better stay home and look after Nanna and Pa tonight."

Dad picked up a blue jacket from a hanger, not matching Jenna's current green sweatpants and top. He shoved the coat into her hands. "By the Lord, go, go, go. You kids enjoy yourselves."

Jenna patted her clothes. "Should I change?"

"You're perfect," Marco said.

Dad forced Jenna and Marco out of the door and closed it with a thud.

Jenna let out a slow, controlled breath. "They drive me crazy."

Mom and Dad had nagged and guilted for their reconciliation. Funny how in a courtroom, reasonable doubt gets you off for murder, but in a separation, her parents didn't believe reasonable doubt was an excuse.

Marco lifted an eyebrow. "In a good way?"

"Up to the jury. Why did you plan tonight?"

"You want to potentially see other people. I'll keep your mind off the crazy idea." Marco's cheeks dimpled as he took her hand. He led her to the car's passenger seat and opened the door. "After you."

She bit her lip to stop a smile. He was making a huge effort, but a surprise outing was a fast-track to romance. It rebelled against every rule they had agreed to—no strings. Yet her pulse still raced, and she couldn't tear her gaze off him. Bracing herself, she hopped into the car.

He strode to the driver's side.

"Where are we going?" She clicked on the seatbelt and peeked out of the window for a clue.

"Secret." He stared straight ahead, not giving his plan away.

"I'm uneasy with not knowing. Especially your bombshells. Remember the time you bought my favorite chocolates? You ended up eating the whole box." She half smirked, half scowled at the memory.

"Trust me. The idea is good. I've noticed the little crinkle on your nose when you're stressed." He turned on the radio. The hosts discussed the best rock-and-roll songs in the world.

She twiddled her fingers. He still knew her too well.

They drove in comfortable silence. Of the intimacies she missed, she craved their shared quiet times the most. They used to sit for hours enjoying the simple presence of each other's company.

A soft rock song played in the background, almost a sweet melody. Even though she loved the girls with her entire heart, working full time and keeping them alive exhausted her. Her eyelids grew heavy. As her heartbeats slowed, she took a deep breath and closed her eyes. Marco's musky scent lingered in the small space, soothing her.

"We're here." He nudged her arm.

She opened her eyes and blinked. "Did I fall asleep?"

"For most of the ride." Jumping out of the car, he once again walked to her side. He opened the door and grabbed her hand.

"How chivalrous." She curtsied. His gestures reminded her of their teenage selves on their first few dates.

A familiar long and horizontal white building in the middle of Golden Gate Park greeted her. Seven rolling hills stood on top of the living roof, and palm trees scattered outside the gates. Stairs led up to the entryway, and a sign read, *California Academy of Sciences*.

"We haven't been to the aquarium since Eve's second birthday." Jenna quickened her pace. The sea and the creatures calmed her.

"I already bought our tickets." Marco whipped out two pieces of paper and presented them to the attendant.

They approached the floor–to–ceiling glass tank. Schools of rockfish swam among the coral and pillars. An octopus the size of Jenna's head drifted.

"Octopuses have always been my favorite." Marco stepped forward. "They change color within three-tenths of a second to mimic their surroundings. Smart. Maybe if I had the ability in the army…" He splayed his fingers beside him.

A rough grind scraped through Jenna like cheese on a grater. Little would console a man who had experienced hell. Perhaps humor might lighten his mood.

Grabbing Marco's hand, she twined her fingers with his stiff ones. "Imagine if you had eight arms. Oh, my God, you'd be all over me. We'd have some raunchy times." She waggled her eyebrows.

He threw his head back and laughed, hauling her into his body. "I wish I had eight arms right now."

"Kids are here." She giggled.

They looked over to the tank, Marco's arm still around her. A curious eel stared at them. She stood mesmerized by the blues and greens and browns of California's beautiful starfishes and reefs.

Marco led her to the ninety-foot glassed Rainforest Dome. The air, warm and humid, transported her to another place. Brazilian beauty leaves, West Indies mahogany, and dozens of shrubs surrounded them. Not to mention the Theobroma cacao—a small evergreen tree with flower clusters at the trunk and the plant creator of chocolate.

She traced her hand over a cacao pod, resembling a

giant mango. Bright butterflies in every color imaginable fluttered past. She held out a hand. A yellow and black one landed on her index finger but flew away in an instant.

"It's so peaceful here." The sweet, tropical scent engulfed her. The frogs' croaking packed the air. "I needed this."

"You work too hard. I'm in awe of you." Marco brushed his hand over her arm.

"You do a lot too." She basked in his words. "You're a great father." He did his fair share of pick-ups and drop-offs and prepared lunches when he drove the kids to school.

A green lizard scuttled in front, roaming free. Startled, she jumped. She almost stepped on it. "Bejesus."

Marco's eyes shone bright. The air between them thickened.

She swallowed. Once again, she must set clear boundaries. "What are you hoping will happen tonight?"

"What do you hope to happen?" The left side of his lips tipped up.

An ache pinballed through her body. "Do you see us going somewhere?"

"Like where?"

Blue birds chirped on trees above. A concert of humming, buzzing, and thrumming from other creatures enclosed them.

Glowering, she ducked under a tree branch. "I want to smack you. Are you going to keep answering my question with a question?"

His gaze twinkled. "I'm enjoying spending time

together again."

They descended to a lower level and walked through the transparent, flooded forest tunnel, under the water. To the right, cichlids in different sizes darted through the roots of a mangrove cluster. A giant gray-green arapaima glided within the water overhead in the plexiglass.

Her chest pulled tight. "Are you sure you're not expecting us to get back together?"

Three kids skipped by. They stopped at every corner, marveling at the creatures.

"Now, who's asking the questions? This is for fun." Marco paused at a long, silver freshwater fish. "With two kids, when do we score time to ourselves?"

They wandered out of the tunnel.

"True. You seem to have a plan for this outing," Jenna said.

"Besides getting freaky tonight, you mean?" He smirked. "I do, actually."

Her cheeks heated as she checked if anyone heard. People were too absorbed in the surroundings.

They left the Rainforest Dome and entered the Forum Gallery. Yoga mats spread across the floor. Couples and small groups stretched and chatted, waving their hands. Yoga was one of her favorite exercises. Lucky they both wore sweatpants. Joy dripped through her body at Marco planning the fun activity.

"Hatha yoga starts in five minutes." The instructor at the front tapped a watch. "Find your places."

"You're dedicated to health and fitness—your way of de-stressing." Marco led her to the back of the room and sat on a mat. "Nice to do yoga in a different atmosphere."

The lights darkened. A custom-designed space projector highlighted the walls. Planet and star images spun in each direction, an explosion of magical color. Every detail replicated riding on a spaceship and floating through the sky.

A soothing piano and guitar tune filtered through the air, in slow and soft rhythms. Her muscles relaxed.

"You hate yoga, though." Jenna sat next to him and stretched. "You prefer lifting weights any day."

"For you, I will. Plus, hatha is a more physical version."

Her vision blurred from a glassy layer of tears. This man...she had never expected a sweet gesture from him again. After many years, he still stunned her. She blinked the dampness away.

Without thinking, she leaned over and pecked his cheek. "Thank you."

His gaze collided with hers. The air pulsed with unsaid words. They held the moment, two broken hearts building a small bridge back to each other.

He patted her hand. "Worth every moment to see the happiness in your eyes."

****

Marco walked Jenna up the five steps to the front of the house. At the door, they meandered outside underneath the white arch. Medium-sized black cylinders held fern and china doll plants on both sides of the doorway. He stood trapped in the heat of her gaze. God, she was beautiful.

Shivering, she fumbled for keys inside a handbag. Two hard points of her nipples tented her silky cardigan. He had fought the urge to pop open the six small buttons the entire night. His dick strained against his pants.

"Thanks again for organizing tonight." Jenna's voice was a raspy whisper.

"Thanks for coming." His words hung between them. When their gazes met, he leaned in to capture her mouth. His tongue sought hers, and he sighed when he found it. She probed and stroked his in return, and he thrust her against the door with a growl. His chest flickered.

The door creaked open. Marco and Jenna sprang apart. His pulse spiked.

Her mom and dad peeped through the gap.

His mother-in-law took the two of them in. Beaming, she nudged her husband. "Don't mind us. We were just leaving." The older woman grabbed her handbag from the hallway table and dragged her husband along. "The kids are in bed."

Jenna's dad peeked over his shoulder multiple times before they left without another word.

"Well…not awkward in the slightest. Do you want to come inside?" Jenna chuckled, low and carefree. How he missed her laughter.

"Fuck yes." He followed her into the living room.

"Take a seat. I'll make tea." She tottered to the kitchen—a sign she might be nervous.

Relaxing onto the sofa, he rubbed his eyes. He hadn't stayed out late in years, and his temples pounded. Crowds overwhelmed him these days, spinning his mind like a hamster on a wheel.

He shouldn't be happy and off doing normal activities considering his mistakes in Afghanistan. A memory of his men on the ground shuddered him to the core. He wrapped his jacket tighter.

From the kitchen, the kettle bubbled, reminding him of their steamy sex. He lay down, resting for a second. Breathing heavy, he opened and closed, opened and closed his eyes.

****

The fresh acrid gunpowder stung Marco's nasal cavities. A bitter wind swept the hillside, blowing dust and dirt. The land stayed quiet, now a graveyard for the unburied.

He motioned a hand to the small boy with dark curls. "We can't leave him here alone."

"He's the enemy." Colin, the tallest in the army group of six, thinned his lips.

The others nodded in agreement.

A rain of bullets fired from a distance followed by shouts and cries.

The child's big, brown eyes peered up at him.

An ache speared through Marco's chest. "He looks the same age as my youngest daughter. Let's bring him."

Colin's jaw ticked. "Fine."

"Keep moving." Marco pointed to the kid and hurried toward the approaching helicopter. He stepped over the ash-like crumbled stone. The ruins and debris didn't compare to the destruction inside his soul.

No small footsteps shadowed him. He pivoted, searching for the child.

A loud noise reverberated like a thunderclap. His body flung back and crashed to the ground. The bright flash blinded his eyes. A fiery yellow ball billowed outward, and smoke rushed out.

When his vision cleared, he scouted for his crew. No sign. Blood and guts splattered the soil. Blue fabric from the boy's shirt peeked through the rubble. Colin lay among the chaos, his eyes open, a bloody smear where legs should be. Three other men sprawled nearby.

"Please God...let them not be dead." His limbs weighed him down, like every drop of blood grounded him. He reached a hand to the youngest man, opening and closing his mouth like a goldfish.

Smoke pricked Marco's eyes, and the back of his nose burned. Everything decent in the world lay smashed, stripping away his last thread of hope.

****

Jenna found Marco asleep on the couch. Neither were used to being out on a weeknight. Instead of hot, passionate sex, maybe with bondage toys, he'd dozed off. She drank a chamomile tea, contemplating plausible ideas to fix her work dilemma.

The lines around his eyes softened as he slept. His crinkles weren't there before deployment. Even his discharge didn't diminish his haunted expression.

Maybe she should wake him. Rule two was no sleepovers. They weren't asleep in bed together. The situation technically didn't count.

Marco stirred, his mouth twisting. "No. We can't."

She stood, rooted to the spot. Since he returned home for good, he tossed and turned in his sleep. Unlike her, he didn't enjoy retiring to bed early. Perhaps the nightmares visited, and there was no escaping his head.

His face contorted, sweat trickling down his temples.

Jenna didn't think. Her gut reaction to comfort Marco took over. Kneeling, she gently shook his shoulder. "Marco, wake up. It's okay."

"No, no, no. Get away." He thrashed, his forehead and neck bathed in sweat.

She ran a hand over his damp forehead, his skin hotter than boiling soup. "You're fine. It's me. You're home."

Jolting awake, Marco's eyes sprang open. Mouth in a hard line, he peered around the room. "We have to leave."

"You had a nightmare. We're all right." She stroked his cheek with the back of her fingers. Sympathy pierced her heart, sharp as a dagger.

"I wasn't dreaming. Let's go." He grabbed her hand, taking shaky, shallow breaths.

She nudged him to rest on the couch and kneeled beside him. "Calm down. You're fine. We practiced yoga tonight. Keisha drew you a picture of our vacation in Australia. We stood outside the Sydney Opera House. She left the sketch at the coffee table."

He faced the artwork, breaths steadying. Sweat lined his upper lip.

"Shall I call Gabby?" She kept her voice low and soothing. Marco had two older sisters but had the strongest bond with Gabby, closest in age.

He stared at the drawing without blinking and shuddered.

"Daddy, you're here." Eve appeared in the room, rubbing her eyes. "I needed to pee and heard shouting."

He blinked twice at their youngest daughter. "I was telling a funny story." Sitting up on the sofa, he forced out a soft, weak chuckle. He had three different laughs—when he poked fun of someone, of pure and utter joy, and a defense mechanism. This laugh fell into the last category.

"Go back to bed, baby. You usually always sleep through the night." Jenna didn't shift away from Marco in case he needed her. "Remember, you have a school trampolining excursion tomorrow. Save your energy."

Eve's eyes brightened like she just remembered. "Yes, the sooner I sleep, the sooner I'll be there." She skipped to her room.

Marco stood and grabbed the wallet and keys from the edge of the couch. "I didn't realize the time."

"Do you want to talk?" Jenna followed him to the door, brows furrowed. Surely, he wasn't in a fit state to drive.

"Yeah, sorry. We didn't have time to get down and dirty tonight." He winked.

Her fingers caught with his. "No, I'm referring to your dream."

"Don't remember. I probably dreamed of polka dots. You know my irrational fear." Again, the same fake laugh tore from his lips.

Marco hated dot patterns from bandages to designs on clothes. She often joked that if he accidentally cut himself, he'd prefer to bleed to death rather than accept a spotted plaster.

"Might help to voice your thoughts." Ready to kiss his problems away, she stood on her tippy-toes. She fell back onto her heels. Not her job anymore.

His gaze didn't meet hers. "I have an early start tomorrow."

Leaning over, he pecked her cheek and opened the front door.

He trudged toward his car like he struggled to walk. Jumping in, he sped off, not once glancing back.

She ached to go after him, but he might wish to be alone. A knot of worry screwed tight in her stomach. If she displayed more compassion and had the skills to help him, they might not have developed problems. Perhaps their separation hadn't been solely his fault.

Chapter Ten

The words "FUCK YOU" were written in white text on one side of the black baseball bat Marco clutched.

"Yeah, yeah, fuck you too." He grabbed a glass beer bottle from the carton of fifty by his feet, tossed it high into the air, and smacked the useless object—hard. Adrenaline flooded into his blood at full pelt. The bottle landed on a pile of glass and other bits and pieces scattered across the far end of the "rage room."

His relationship with Jenna took a backward turn last night, and he wanted to…well, break stuff. Whoever invented an anger room the size of two parking spots was a genius. He should learn to better manage his emotions rather than running off because he had a big, bad scary dream. No better way to let off steam than to spend twenty dollars on a space designed to destroy random items for half an hour.

Thick, voluminous heavy-metal beats from the sound-system engulfed the room. The gruff, slurred vocals resembled a demonic outburst with the growls, moans, screams, and rumbles. He snatched another bottle and smashed the fragile object. Glass exploded into a hail of jagged splinters against the brick wall, flying everywhere. Bouncing on the balls of his feet, Marco's muscles tingled.

The attendant at the front counter tapped on the

plastic window on Marco's left, placed his index finger to his thumb to form a circle, and mouthed. "You okay?"

Marco gave the thumbs–up sign. The employee twirled and returned to the desk.

He shouldn't have freaked out. Maybe he could pretend he hadn't snapped when he texted Jenna hello. Sweat trickled into his eyes. Lifting the plastic face protector, he wiped his skin with the back of the thick glove.

The drums in the song sped up. Aggressive riffs and off-beat rhythms thumped like a patient trying to escape from an asylum.

He should be a man and address the situation, but he didn't know how to explain. Somehow, he didn't believe, "Hey, Jenna, sorry you married a basket case" excused him. She didn't deserve his extra baggage—the very reason for their separation.

In the song, an electric guitar wailed from the speakers, a sinister voice distorted and ragged with accented and ominous notes. Marco stomped on a lone ceramic plate near his boot. Dropping the baseball bat, he stormed over to the heap and seized an old television set. Every single one of his limbs moved on their own. Lifting the TV over his head, he threw the screen onto the ground.

His heart wanted to beat free of the cage. As he kept trashing his surroundings, sweat became a welcomed addition, energizing him. Perspiration dribbled down his back like condensation on a windowpane. He yanked off the gloves and wiped his palms on the thick, white coveralls.

When the music ended, he stood over the mountain

of rubble. The tension in his body melted, although he took shaky, shallow breaths. He set his jaw in iron-clad determination. Jenna appreciated honesty and deserved the trait at a minimum. She'd always said a simple apology often overruled fancy gestures. He must contact her and ensure he hadn't ruined his chances— no way he'd let the love of his life slip away ever again.

****

The dazzling winter sunshine provided an electric thrill even when the wind bit into Jenna's skin. A pine needle scent floated in the breeze from trees positioned like soldiers, stiff, upright, standing to attention. They reminded her of Marco.

She lingered outside Stone Corp, squished beside Vanessa and Hayley. Hayley needed a break to rest her eyes, and Jenna was happy to tag along. She was lucky she didn't need glasses even though she spent every day in front of a computer screen.

Last night's date—no, they weren't on a date— with Marco went amazing until they returned home. He was more troubled than she realized. She didn't know what to do. He was far from okay but would never go to counseling—too proud.

Vanessa's lips tugged up. "You have a faraway look on your face. How's Marco?"

"Fine."

Vanessa wiggled her eyebrows. "Only fine?"

"Okay, we've gotten along better than usual." Jenna's ears grew warm. Her mind slipped to their kitchen escapade almost a week ago. He respected her wishes and kept their relationship slow and casual.

Annoyingly slow.

After yoga, she craved for him to rip her clothes

off, bend her over a table, spank her, and have his way with her. An act they had never indulged in before.

"Oh, my God." Hayley's eyes widened. "You're banging your husband."

"I...uh..." She racked her brains to find the words, but no sound came out.

"You are, and you didn't tell me." Vanessa clutched her chest in mock hurt. "I confide in you with every small secret. I feel so betrayed."

"Early days. We're not together." At the aquarium, she pretended to believe Marco's insistence they were having fun. Her heart shrank to an icy pebble in her chest for leading him on. For the first time since their split, singledom didn't overwhelm her. Maybe a certain raven-haired beauty swayed her new attitude.

"Sounds like you're snagging hot and kinky sex, you sly old dog." Hayley nudged Jenna's shoulder. "About time a shower crashed down after your drought."

Vanessa bit her lip to suppress a giggle. "Sometimes, I wonder how you get away with the stuff that comes out of your mouth. Especially as our manager."

"How was the first time you 'reunited'?" Hayley lifted her fingers in air quotations, ignoring Vanessa.

"We only 'reunited' once." Jenna's breath puffed in vapor clouds. "The sex was better than ever."

Marco had surprised her. Her body still flushed at the memory of his shaft thrusting between her breasts. If someone told her a few years ago they'd engage in a racy sexual act, she'd laugh. The man she'd met when she first got braces had her raging with desire. But dammit, she longed to do him again.

Vanessa hugged her side, the warmth comforting her. "You deserve the very best."

Hayley whistled. "You must share tips on whatever wild deeds you've done. You're glowing like you've had a facial. Justin and I have been in a rut for years."

"Maybe Marco gave her a full-service facial. They might be into weird kinks." Vanessa smirked.

Hayley's lips twitched up into a wicked grin. "Eww gross, Vanessa. When did you get inappropriate? I must be rubbing off on you."

They snorted together. Hayley rested her hands on her knees until she straightened, dabbing a tissue under her eyes.

Jenna's stomach ached from laughter, but she welcomed the feeling.

"How is AnaStone's research going?" Hayley checked the time on her cell.

Jenna's smile disappeared. "Not well. I've investigated every idea for weeks. The IT team have hit a dead end too."

Vanessa's eyes shone with sympathy. "What are your next steps? Don't put so much pressure on yourself. Sandeep is the head of the department. Figuring out the problem is more his job."

Jenna slumped onto the wall. "I know, but he doesn't understand the software as well as I do. I have a few leads. The problem is trickier than I thought. Whoever is altering the software…they're smart and already hacked the firewall. I've set up a notification whenever someone is live on the system. The external consultants aren't having luck either."

"A shame." Hayley's gaze averted. Tight lines developed at the corners of her mouth.

"What?" Jenna studied her boss. Hayley often offered a million and one opinions. The new quietness flared a panic in her stomach.

"Forget I said anything. We'll chat at our catch–up this afternoon." Hayley shook her head, her voice low.

"No, speak now. I'm happy to discuss in front of Vanessa." Jenna would go nuts awaiting a terrible meeting.

Vanessa patted Jenna's shoulder. A quiet reassurance. "We'll stick together and figure out the problem."

Hayley sighed. "I didn't want to worry you. Sandeep has been on my case. He hasn't been able to figure out the issues. Neither can I. Since the software is your primary role, and Stone Corp's losing money from it, you may not have a job if we can't figure out the challenges. He hinted the consultants might replace you."

Time blurred as Jenna cruised along, conscious of voices, but not quite hearing the words. She came to life, one second at a time…she might lose her job.

God…Sandeep again. The only sound she ever enjoyed from him was when he shut up. Anxiety wormed and slithered through Jenna's core. Stone Corp was her home. She didn't know another way of life.

"Don't stress. I'm doing every action to not let this happen. The police are investigating the hacking. Hopefully, they'll figure out the culprit. Not all on you." Hayley's words tumbled fast, not loading Jenna with confidence.

Jenna's body cracked in half from the weight in her chest. A chalky, bitter taste filled her mouth.

Vanessa shuffled closer to Jenna in a protective

stance. "We've got you."

"I doubt it'll come to that. Sandeep is overdramatic. He's black and white." Hayley's voice softened. "Over my dead body you're leaving."

Maybe Jenna should put her foot down so it wouldn't end up in Sandeep's ass. Years of hard work, overtime, and sacrifices might be for zilch.

"I appreciate you both backing me. It may not be my sole responsibility, but because AnaStone's my creation, I feel responsible." Perhaps she wasn't good enough to solve the mystery, and she should've concentrated more on family like her traditional parents requested. The kids attended after–school care half the week, and her parents looked after them the other days. Guilt weighed on her shoulders for not being there for Keisha and Eve more often. She'd find a job with no overtime.

Potentially getting fired was a sign. She had misplaced loyalty in Stone Corp. Her employer was willing to let her go after over a decade of immaculate work and devotion.

****

Jenna followed Vanessa and Hayley into the office, her feet scraping the gravel pavement. Sandeep wishing her gone caused her to crawl inside her shell. Dammit, she was good at her job. He had no right to judge. She had worked in the company for way longer than him and would stay well after.

"Vanessa and I have a meeting with Nathan from IT." Hayley turned left, the opposite direction to their desk pod. "Meet you back there."

Vanessa lingered behind and squeezed Jenna's hand. "Please don't worry. You're too valuable to leave. I'll speak to Sebastian before anyone lets you go."

Her heart warmed. "You're a good egg, but don't use your personal relationship to help me."

"I won't be. Everyone needs you."

"Thanks." Jenna appreciated her friend's support, but she doubted Vanessa's position as the CEO's girlfriend could save her. Not if board members or investors started breathing down Sebastian's neck.

"You'll be okay. Who's the most obvious suspects?"

Uneasiness slid through her body. "When Claudine joined the team...the hacking ramped up. Do you think... Oh, never mind."

Vanessa sidled closer. "What's going on between you two?"

"What? Nothing?" The walls swayed beside her.

"I see the way you look at her."

Heat inflamed Jenna's cheeks. Powerless to talk like her tongue had swollen, she shook her head.

Vanessa clasped Jenna's shoulder. "I know your family is strict and religious. Don't let bias morph into suspicion and push Claudine away."

"I'm not doing that. Or maybe..." Apprehension overtook her attraction toward Claudine. Perhaps desperately hoped for something wrong.

"The time a stunning server flirted with you, you were taken aback." Vanessa let go of her shoulder. "Don't get stuck in your head too much. Look at Hayley. She doesn't give a shit what anyone thinks of her being pansexual."

Hayley twirled from a distance like she had heard her name. "Vanessa, you coming?"

"Yep." Vanessa gave Jenna a quick hug. "Chin up."

Vanessa hurried to catch up to Hayley.

Jenna stood there, unable to move. Vanessa's logic was sound. Maybe she thought the worst in Claudine. But she would've known she was bi or pansexual, right?

Shaking her head, she started walking. She had to concentrate on who was infiltrating the company's system—fast. Still too many possibilities and she hadn't narrowed down the list.

Sweat beads formed on her hairline, and her throat closed. The sounds in the office faded into the background. Another role scared her. She knew everyone well, and stepping into the building daily provided comfort. A panic began like a cluster of sparkplugs in her stomach. Clasping a hand to her mouth, she ran toward the bathroom five feet ahead.

Andy, a business development manager, paused at the meeting room's door. "You okay?"

Jenna pretended not to hear. Once she burst through the bathroom's entrance, she stumbled to the sink and opened her mouth. No bile. Taking deep breaths, she twisted the tap and splashed cold water onto her face.

Her phone beeped from her pants pocket. She fumbled—maybe Sandeep informing her not to bother returning to work.

Marco's name displayed on the screen. The shaking in her shoulders subsided.

—*Sorry for my weirdness last night and rushing off. Some moments for me are better than others. Thank you for a fun evening.*—

Still queasy, she slipped the cell back into a pocket, noting to reply later. Concentrating on the sink's smooth ceramic, she traced a finger over the cool tap. Marco's openness was a massive turning point. It must have taken genuine courage to admit to vulnerability. He was brave, so she should be too.

Every movement stiff, she straightened her shoulders. Her eyes were a little red when she glanced at the mirror on her way out. Work wasn't the entire world, and she had savings. She had other priorities in life and could find another job. Definitely. Maybe.

One step in front of another, she stumbled down the hallway, a throb piercing between her temples. She hadn't experienced an emotion resembling a panic attack since her early teens with her parents' strict rules and beliefs. A far cry from the successful, put-together woman she had become.

Jenna paused by the water cooler. She tugged on a plastic cup, filled it, and chugged the entire contents. Desiree's desk sat unoccupied, emails on display. Ironic because Desiree worked in the policy and advocacy team, and company policy stated to lock the computer every time someone left their seat.

Jenna walked to lock the screen. Then she considered Desiree's big loan for a fancy schmancy new house. Desiree bragged her parents gifted her the entire deposit, proving her not capable of saving a single cent.

She rooted on the spot. Now was the perfect time to peek at Desiree's contents. The current AnaStone tracking methods didn't work. She peered around. No one loitered nearby. The closest person sat a few pods away and banged on a keyboard, occasionally cussing.

Wobbling forward, she rested on Desiree's chair, hands trembling. Guilt wedged inside her chest, but the tightness eased when she remembered Desiree condescending Jenna's small house.

Shrinking lower into the seat to stay hidden, she scrolled through Desiree's emails. And as she suspected, Desiree was borderline illiterate. The messages consisted of meeting acceptances from co-workers, a fire warden's responsibilities, and requests for updating new policies online.

One subject line read, "REMINDER OVERDUE NOTICE," from Bank of the People.

She clicked the attachment. The PDF asserted Desiree's home loan stood in arrears, and she hadn't paid one dollar since she bought the house.

The document stated, "Please contact us as soon as possible, or you will be referred to our legal department."

Jenna gulped. An eviction loomed over Desiree. Maybe she lived above her means and fell far behind on bills. Desiree often sported designer shopping bags whenever she returned from a lunch break. People did silly things when they were used to a particular lifestyle.

Her heart thumped against her ribcage, but doubt seeped into her mind. Desiree wasn't tech-savvy and once asked how to save a Word document. Doubtful she hacked a complicated software.

Jenna minimized the email, clicked to the web browser, and opened the history tab. Her jaw dropped. Many AnaStone articles Jenna had written appeared—how the software worked, frequently asked questions, and troubleshooting issues. This program wasn't part of

Desiree's role, and she had never shown interest in anything besides her mirror reflection.

Jenna typed "AnaStone" on the computer's search bar. The software's red "A" icon on a stone surfaced. Her breaths came out short and erratic. They said some people "played dumb." Desiree might have been ripping off Stone Corp the whole time.

Footsteps thudded in her direction. She skidded the seat back and stood. Her heart leaped in her throat. Scrambling away, she raced the several feet toward her desk.

Desiree's computer history proved no wrongdoings, but everyone had secrets.

Jenna veered around the side of her cubicle.

Dark, glossy hair and a curvy body occupied her chair. Jenna froze. Claudine hunched over and peeked left, then right.

Jenna stood confused like someone had randomly thrown paint onto a canvas. At least the screen was still locked. A sour taste crept across the back of her mouth as her new friend snooped.

She stalked over and crossed her arms. "What are you doing?"

Chapter Eleven

Claudine jumped in the seat, and her eyes opened wide, almost childlike. She faced Jenna, and a slow, shy smile spread across her lips. "Waiting for you."

Jenna's brows furrowed. "Why?"

Claudine stood and brushed her fingers over Jenna's arm with a feather-lightness. Sparks shot through her. Claudine picked up a paper box of protein bars from Jenna's desk. "To give you a thank you present. I should've done this sooner."

Jenna blinked tentatively, stepping forward. The tension between her shoulders diminished, but her posture remained guarded. A Post-it Note on top read, *I'd be homeless without you.*

Jenna burst out laughing. She lifted the lid, and the box displayed a variety of flavors. "Protein bars…how sweet."

"Healthy snacks aren't the cutest token of appreciation, but you eat them every day."

Did Claudine only wait at Jenna's desk to offer a gift, or did she have other motives? Suspicion overcame her, but Claudine actually had a present, and the hacking started weeks before she joined the company. Stress triggered Jenna's paranoia. Vanessa was right. She projected negativity onto Claudine. She should be more like Hayley and block out everyone's opinions.

Jenna hovered a hand over the box and opted for

her favorite banana flavor. She indicated for Claudine to choose too. "A woman after my own heart."

Claudine selected the peanut butter. "Are you free to catch up over wine tomorrow? You've been good to me since we met. I owe you."

"You don't owe me, but I enjoy bribes."

"Seriously, I do. I have much to learn from you. You're smart and gorgeous. Unfair to the rest of us mere mortals." Claudine leaned closer, her cherry lip gloss intoxicating Jenna.

"Such a charmer." Jenna's cheeks heated like a stove. She unwrapped the packet. Claudine trickled into her thoughts more often than she liked. Maybe Claudine had the same inklings, whatever they were.

Her colleague pouted her lush lips. The painted-on dress she wore hugged her hourglass body. "Please. We'll brainstorm how to catch the bag snatcher."

Was Claudine asking her out on a date? A gallop tore through Jenna's chest. No, the invitation was an outing as colleagues. She let out a shuddering breath and bit into the snack.

"Sure, I'll check if someone can look after the kids." Jenna slid her cell from her pants pocket and straightaway clicked to Marco's name. Funny how he became her go-to person.

—*Hey, can you please mind the girls tomorrow night?*—

Unsure of her desired answer, she held her breath. Seconds later, a reply.

—*I'll be happy to see my favorite daughters.*—

"Yes, their dad can watch them." Jenna tossed the phone to the desk, half excited, half terrified. If she accompanied Claudine, she might have to face her

115

attraction for the woman. Her fascination toward the same sex was very unlike her.

"You're the best." Claudine brushed her lips against Jenna's cheek and strutted to her desk.

Jenna finished the rest of the protein bar. Claudine was a beautiful person, and yet Jenna still eyed her with suspicion.

****

"Man up and put your money where your mouth is." Marco tapped his fingers on the wooden table. He picked up a tumbler and sipped the smooth scotch on the rocks.

"Fine." His eldest sister, Maria, rolled up her olive-green sleeves and placed white chips in front. She tucked her chin-length dark, curly hair over one ear. Her home was beautiful. High-coffered ceilings and cypress floorboards. Not to mention an impressive alcohol selection on the shelf against the wall to his opposite.

He laid two cards on the table. "Full house."

Maria groaned and threw cards at him, landing on his tall pile of multicolored chips. "How did you win again?"

"I'm sure you're cheating and have cards up your sleeve." His other sister Gabby ruffled her thick, long hair she permanently straightened. She gathered up the cards and shuffled before passing the deck to Maria.

Maria slid the three of them two cards each. "Any headway with Jenna?"

"We had a sorta date last night at the aquarium, and she texted me to look after the girls tomorrow. She's never asked me before." His heart ballooned with hope. He separated the reds, blues, and whites and allocated everyone their amount.

"Very promising." Gabby lifted the corners of the two cards and popped them down. She gave Maria the small blind button and Marco the big.

"I'm not sure. She's still insisting we won't be together and adamant we should see other people." His voice was low and tight, coiled like a snake ready to strike. The heat from the richly carved fireplace embraced him. A faint pine fragrance sifted through the room.

"Convince her otherwise." Gabby dropped two red chips. "I call."

Marco reviewed his cards. Pocket aces—one heart, one diamond—but he chose not to give away his position. "Check."

Maria burned a card and positioned the flop on the table, one at a time. Two of spades, seven of diamonds, and queen of hearts. "Check too. Marco, check or bet? I second Gabby about Jenna."

Damn...these cards didn't help. Wishing he wore sunglasses to disguise his poker face better, he grabbed five white chips. "Bet. Any ideas about Jenna, then, genius?"

"You're bluffing, but I've got nada. Fold." Gabby slid the cards to Maria. "Remind her she's missing out. Get her hot and bothered. Make her scream. Keep your relationship light and fun. Show her you're irreplaceable."

"Geez, Gabby, we don't require info about our little brother's sex life. He needs to be more secure. Become the person Jenna could be sure of without a doubt. Trust is a big issue between you two." Maria matched his chip pile. "I call your bluff." She burned a card and turned over a king of hearts.

Still no ace. Marco shifted ten green chips. "You gotta risk it for the biscuit."

Maybe the solution to win Jenna back—risk his hand, or he wasn't worthy of her. Right now, he wasn't proud of himself. He must be a better man. She wouldn't take him back with amazing sex. But when they made love, the world felt right.

Maria's eyes widened as she shoved chips forward. "No way you have a king."

She burned a card and flipped over the river—ace of spades.

His heartbeat turned into a rapid staccato. He drove his chip stack into the center. "All in."

He must go all in for Jenna too. Hooking up together offered his first glimmer of optimism. Maybe he should reconsider therapy, but the one session he'd attended hadn't helped. Based on his sisters' advice, he should be easy-going and fun but also reliable and contented at the same time. A lot of pressure.

****

In bed, Jenna flicked through the book pages, blanket wrapped around her body. Although the thriller was a page-turner, her mind kept flickering to her job at stake. Not to mention Claudine's intentions for their catch-up tomorrow night. Throughout the day, she half-hoped Marco would message to cancel minding Keisha and Eve.

The cell pinged from the nightstand. Marco's name zoomed over the screen, and her lips tipped. They had texted many times today after his apology, and her heart knocked in anticipation whenever her phone lit up.

—*What are you up to tonight? X*—

Her fingers flew across the typing pad. —*Getting ready for bed. You should go to sleep.*—

She turned the page. Way too long since she last enjoyed a novel, even though she loved reading. With two kids and a full-time job, she often fell asleep by the time her head hit the pillow.

His reply flashed a minute later. —*Who says I'm not in bed?*—

—*You're a night owl who catches up on chores once everyone's asleep.*— She adjusted the lamp to shine more directly onto the paperback.

—*Maybe I'm taking a leaf out of your book. You've always been the smart one, and I miss our routine.*—

He shouldn't be missing her. At the aquarium, she reminded him they were friends. She waited a beat to consider a reply. Marco delayed going to bed as long as possible. Staying awake was unlike him.

—*You're in bed? I call BS. You're probably checking the stove's turned off for the millionth time as usual.*—

He always took safety to another level. Perhaps part of his military training.

Placing the novel on her lap, she grabbed the hand cream. Mandarin fragrance filled her nostrils. She rubbed the lotion on her fingers and up to her elbows, dreading going to sleep. The sooner she slept, the sooner work arrived.

The phone chimed. An image preview displayed on the screen.

—*See, in bed.*—

Marco was in bed all right, but his washboard abs stared back. Her gaze trailed south. The V line of muscles disappeared.

Laughter tripped out of her mouth. Wishing he lay next to her, she lifted a finger to trace the lines across his stomach. He sure was one fine-looking man. Adrenaline surged through her veins. She tapped two fingers to her lips. You only lived once.

She stood and locked the bedroom door. Returning to bed, she whipped off her top and flicked the mobile's camera to face her. Raising her phone over her head, she adjusted her body and pinched her nipples until they were hard buds. Her boobs looked amazing. From different angles, she snapped multiple times. A nervous giggle caught at her throat.

She lowered her arm and skimmed through the photos. Hovering her finger over the best topless image, she hit the "send" button before she lost her nerve. She trusted Marco with the picture despite his past mistakes. Her breath hitched, waiting for the three little dots to appear on screen.

Nothing.

The phone rang, a generic tune, in her hand.

"Yes?" she answered, voice light and innocent. "What's up?"

"You know what," Marco growled, causing a current to ripple through her body. "What are you doing to me?"

Her heart jackhammered in her chest. "Did you like the picture?"

"Fucking hell I did."

"What are you going to do?" Her dirty mind ran through every possibility.

"Well, I'm in bed alone. There's self-lovin' as an option." His voice lit up. "Unless…"

"Unless…" she repeated in a breathless whisper.

"What are you wearing?"

Squirming, she patted her blue flannel pants. Maybe she should exaggerate a sexier nightwear. But she was topless.

Instead, she told the truth. "The same PJ pants I wear most Tuesdays."

She had set pajamas Monday to Wednesday and another outfit Thursday to Sunday.

"Always floated my boat. Rest one hand on your stomach."

Every single hair at the back of her neck raised at his commanding voice. His military training came in handy for a situation other than protecting the country.

She put Marco on speaker and plonked the phone beside her. He needed the control after his traumas, and she'd gladly give it. She trailed her belly button. "Now what?"

"Cup your right tit and squeeze your nipple. Imagine I'm doing it."

A warmth pulsed between her legs. Picturing him on top, she obeyed his order. Her nipples hardened, and her breasts became full and heavy.

"I'm sucking on your nipple and licking in small circles." His low voice reverberated through her bones. "Are your nipples erect?"

Closing her eyes, she arched her back. "So hard."

"Slide your hand down your pants but leave it above your panties." His voice embraced her.

She glided her hand. Heat beneath the cotton seared into her palm. Wetness seeped through, and her body tightened. Up and down, she rubbed over the material. A soft moan fled her lips.

Marco inhaled a sharp breath. "Slide two fingers

underneath your panties and rest the tips on your clit. Don't shift your fingers."

"But I'm hot and wet and horny as hell." If he wanted to play, she'd play. Unable to keep from rotating her fingers, she fidgeted.

"You're forbidden to massage yourself. Keep your fingers still," he barked, deep and low. "I'll know if you defy me."

"You can't tell me what to do." Her fingers trembled, keen to stroke her swollen nub.

"Do you want to come to the sound of my voice or not?" His tone was gentle but firm.

She had always fantasized about submitting to someone's every whim and the kinky metal balls and rope. More importantly, she yearned to return some power in Marco's life and take his mind off his agonizing memories.

A tremor sprinted through her body. More moisture dripped onto her panties. In her imagination, Marco was at the end of the bed, head between her widespread legs.

The other end of the line grew silent besides the occasional crackling. Was he still there?

"Marco?" Almost panting, she squeaked. Her clit pulsated. Absolutely delicious, relinquishing her entire self.

Static filtered through their connection.

"Good, you've shown restraint. I shall reward you." His voice lifted in amusement. He taunted her, but he didn't seem to care. "Glide your fingers over your clit. Slowly."

In an instant, she circled her nub in continuous, eager strokes.

"How does that feel?" He groaned, and she knew he had closed his eyes.

"Too warm." Although rules were rules, she longed to swirl her fingers faster.

"Keep doing that. Real slow, now."

A whimper left her lips. Was that animal sound from her? Her body inflated like a balloon, ready to burst. "But, Marco…"

"Keep going. Don't you dare come."

She rubbed in achingly slow motions. A high-pitched noise tumbled from her throat. If she kept going, she'd reach the top. She forced her mind to other activities—kids' laundry, a work data problem, her parents' walking in on her in this state. The only images in her head were of Marco on her, beside her, in her…

"This is torture. Are you touching yourself or only listening to me?" she croaked. Her hips writhed.

"I'll leave that to your imagination. Keep stroking yourself. Now, with your other hand, slither a finger inside your sweet heat at the same time." The desire in his voice rivaled hers.

Shuddering, she let out a bracing breath. Warmth trickled through her limbs. Hard enough doing the one task. She sank a shaky finger inside her, sliding along her sensitive flesh. Her body contracted. Wetness enveloped her finger. She was burning and slick and drunk with yearning.

A primitive groan resounded from his end. "Fuck yourself with your finger."

Moaning, she let her finger thrust in and out, in and out, in slow, deliberate plunges. Using her other hand, she caressed her clit with each pass.

"How do you like that?" Marco asked.

Jenna gasped, barely able to talk. "I'm hot. Wet."

"Hold this pace. Don't orgasm yet." The authority of his voice wavered like he was as turned on as she was.

"Marco…please…" Her finger was well and truly soaked. Pulse thundering beneath her skin, she bit down on her lip. Fully aware at any moment she might explode, she stalled her actions.

"Patience. Worth it in the end." He chuckled.

Ripples of awareness coursed through her. His words made her hotter. Her stomach fluttered, and her toes curled every few seconds. Too easy to hit the sweet spot. He'd never know if she kept quiet.

But she enjoyed the game and wanted him to feel protected.

"I'm close right now." Every time she was almost at the brink, she paced herself. Pleasure flipped up and down like a seesaw.

"Okay. Let go. Now." A raw edge infiltrated his tone.

Her mouth watered. Finally, she earned her prize. She massaged faster in rotation. "Oh, God, come with me, Marco." He needed a release more than anyone.

"I want to. I'm rock hard. I'm pumping my cock and picturing you here…" His voice broke. "I'm tasting you before I pound you until the sun comes up."

Her eyes scrunched closed. His dirty words took her over the edge into a fierce eruption. Breaths wild and ragged, her entire body shattered. Gasping for air, she arched her back. The top of her head grazed the bed frame. Spreading her hands across the mattress, she clutched the bed sheets.

Marco let out a strangled noise. She missed the

sounds of his release. Every sigh of pleasure, his deep sexy voice, the way he groaned. A masculine roar sounded through the phone.

Sweat coated her hairline. Her body sank into the mattress.

"Well…" Marco's breathless voice turned husky. "That was…fuck…" He chortled. "Different."

The room cleared as her vision focused. The line fell silent. When her euphoria lowered, a shyness overcame her. Her cheeks burned. Vulnerable, she tugged the covers over her body. She tangled her fingers together. They hadn't had phone sex before. He must be as flustered as she was. Maybe she should reply with any small talk to fill the awkward moment.

"Yeah, good job, buddy."

Nailed it.

Groaning, she grabbed a pillow and covered her face.

Chapter Twelve

The entire day at work, Jenna had a permanent smirk on her face, and heat rolled off her in waves. A bit of dirty fun last night was a welcomed distraction with potentially losing her job. But she'd have to plan her next words to Marco. Trusting him completely, she had let her walls down. He needed their risqué phone sex as much as she did and be in charge at every step.

She rubbed the back of her neck, her warm touch reassuring her. Maybe she'd have to reset boundaries yet again. Standing from the desk, she walked toward the kitchen to heat leftover salmon and steamed cauliflower for lunch.

"Give me more time to finish the report." Sebastian's assistant, Angie, spoke into the phone at a desk, wearing a Santa hat. Way too early for Christmas outfits considering now was the first week of December. "I can't manage on such short notice. Fine, will do, Scott."

Jenna laughed. "This is why you should set the standards low, so people expect little from you."

Angie jumped in her seat. "Sorry, you scared me. I was off in my own little world. Every request is always urgent when you support the CEO, though."

"They will have to learn to wait." Tina Ly from accounting appeared beside them. She removed the glasses from her round face and rubbed her eyes. "You can't please everyone."

"I think I'll lock myself in the meeting room no one goes into on level twelve. Smash out my work. Worth the flickering lights." Angie took Tina's hand, brows furrowed. "How's your day, doll? You look tired."

"I'm exhausted. I was on the phone with the bank this morning." Tina popped back on the spectacles.

"How annoying. Sometimes I'm on hold for so long my cell battery dies," Jenna sympathized. She got along with Tina well, and they had the occasional lunch. Tina experienced the ups and downs of single parenthood, but her child had special needs. If Jenna found her life difficult, Tina's experiences rocketed to another level.

Tina placed her hands over her face. When she lowered them, her eyes were red.

Jenna's mouth parted. She stepped toward Tina, but Angie jumped from the seat and wrapped an arm over her.

"What's wrong?" Angie squeezed her—always the first to offer comfort when someone had a bad day.

"The bank won't lend me extra money for Kelly. They said I can't afford more. What do I do? Expenses keep coming for schooling and care. Kelly had a fall the other day when her sitter left her alone for one second." Tears ran down Tina's face.

"Hope your daughter's okay." Jenna ripped out tissues from the box and pressed them into Tina's hands.

Angie tugged Tina to sit at the spare seat. "I'm sorry. Banks are ruthless. Can you try another provider? Does your insurance cover any part of the accident?"

"That was the fourth bank I contacted. I doubt I'll have luck elsewhere. Our insurance won't cover additional costs. They claim the sitter was negligent even though she stepped into the kitchen to fetch Kelly's lunch." Tina blew her nose on a tissue.

"Sounds accurate. Insurance companies cry when they open their wallets." Jenna wheeled a chair for the three women to sit in a triangle. "Do you have family members to help?"

Jenna's heart went out to Tina. Guilt outweighed compassion when distrust nagged her. A parent gave up the world for their child. Maybe Tina corrupted Stone Corp out of hopelessness. She was one of few people with AnaStone access. But then, Tina still applied for loans. Perhaps she corrupted the system to gain from the shares until she secured lending.

Tina shook her head. "My parents aren't well off, and my ex's family aren't in the picture."

"Caring for a child with a life-term condition is stressful. I hate seeing my son vulnerable. Can't wait on the sidelines." Angie patted Tina's shoulder. "We'll go to payroll and request an advance on your bonus. It'll tide you over while we think of your next step. I'm sure Sebastian will approve given the circumstances."

Tina nodded, eyes glassy. "You think so?"

"I know so. You're a hard worker, unlike others in the office. I've had issues with Claudine, for one." Angie helped Tina out of the chair. "Let's go."

They waved goodbye to Jenna, who mulled over the conversation. Claudine always appeared competent, but Angie had problems with her.

Tina must be frantic. Jenna's throat had already seized up at possibly losing an income with two hungry mouths to feed. Tina's situation was a thousand times worse although she didn't strike her as disloyal. One time, Tina found a purse on the sidewalk and reported the designer item to the police straight away. But desperate times called for desperate measures.

****

Jigsaw puzzle pieces scattered across Marco's small, round dining table. The kids asked to put his birthday present together when he collected them from school. Suited him fine. After last night's dirty talk with Jenna, he barely concentrated on other topics. Her voice told him she had freed her guarded heart, and maybe, just maybe, they might build back their relationship.

Keisha picked up a puzzle piece from the opened box and added it to the image of her and Eve ice skating. A perfect fit. They had almost finished. She patted Scruffy's head, who sat at her feet. Today was also the first time the little dog accompanied the girls. Another step in the right direction with Jenna.

Holding a piece in one hand, Eve hovered over the puzzle. "Will you move back home, Daddy?"

Marco's hand froze mid-air. "Why do you ask?"

"You and Mom have been talking more. I miss you."

His heart melted. He missed seeing his daughters every day and the early morning cuddles. He lowered his hand to a puzzle piece of a white fluffy jacket he recognized as Eve's. "There are no plans."

He refused to get their hopes up. When he moved out, he packed his belongings while the kids were at school, so they didn't watch him leave. Hours later, Keisha called him, sobbing.

"I hope you do." Keisha gave a half-smile. A

knowing smile. She sure didn't miss a beat for someone her age. Her brows pinched together when she concentrated on the puzzle.

Eve pouted as she leaned forward on the wooden chair, attempting to slide in a jigsaw piece that didn't fit.

His cell rang. Scruffy stretched her front paws on his thighs as he stood. He patted his clothes for the phone—always losing his stuff. Spotting the cell on the kitchen bench, he grabbed it. Connor's name—the one who organized his illegal boxing matches—flashed on the screen.

"I'll be right back." He strode to the barely furnished bedroom, closed the door, and answered. " 'Sup, Connor."

"Ready to rumble again, dickhead? You took quite a beating." Connor's voice boomed into the phone like he ruled the world. In the combat realm, maybe he did.

He bit the inside of his cheek. "I won't be stepping into the ring again."

A silence fell over them. Marco squared his shoulders in an alpha dog stance, staring at the flaking cream wall.

Connor huffed. "Fuck off. You've had more than enough time to recover."

"I quit." With Jenna back in his life, he felt whole again. He didn't desire the adrenaline or alcohol anymore and committed to do better. Be better.

"People have already bet over one hundred thousand dollars on you, a'ight."

"Not my problem."

"Daddy, where does this piece go? We're hungry." Eve's small voice called out, faint outside the room.

The smell of roast chicken, squash, and sweet potatoes in the oven wafted through the apartment.

Marco strained his neck toward the bedroom door, aching to be out there with his daughters. Every second with them was a gift. Using one hand, he covered the speaker. "I'll help you in a sec, sweetie."

"Sounds like your kiddo needs her father. Lucky you're around." Connor's snarl vibrated Marco's bones.

He clenched the cell in a white-knuckled grip. His pulse tripped through his temples. "Are you threatening me?"

"No. I'm a family man too." Connor's softened tone didn't remove the edge from his voice. "I'd never let harm bestow them."

"What do you want?"

"I have a fuckton of money on your fight, bro. Since we're friends, I'll let bygones be bygones if you compete one more time."

Marco's chin jutted out. The knot of fury in his stomach screwed tight at Connor's crooked shit.

Laughter burst from the living room followed by Eve's squeal. Keisha was probably tickling her as usual. His heart launched into his throat. He couldn't let them get hurt. Connor was stone cold when taunted.

"Do I have your word the next fight will be the last?" Every muscle in Marco's body wound tight like a spring.

"Yes, I may not be much, but I am honest." Connor answered straight away.

He examined Connor's tone for a lie. His voice didn't stiffen, nor did he speak measuredly. Connor was a straight shooter, and hopefully the trait hadn't changed.

"Fine. Text me the details." Marco ended the call. His stomach thrashed like a washing machine. Stretching the kinks out of his shoulders, he took deep breaths and left the room.

Keisha and Eve squinted hard at the puzzle. The younger one whooped.

"We finished, Dad." Eve clapped her hands.

They'd completed the entire jigsaw. His daughters' smiling faces beamed back. A mist clouded his eyes. Despite the phone call, here, right now, was a perfect moment with his family. One person was missing from tonight's activities—Jenna. Longing immersed him followed by fierce protectiveness. His lungs squeezed. First, he must keep his family safe before he could reconnect them.

****

Jenna fished the strawberry from the sweet cocktail and ate the juicy fruit. She hadn't had a drink in months, but she committed to drowning her work sorrows. Although tonight was a friendly outing between two colleagues, her heart had kicked into overdrive when she left work with Claudine to walk to the pop-up ice rink.

"This is nice. I'm glad you suggested here," Jenna said.

An adorable tinsel-trimmed ice rink displayed a flight of stairs below the bar's glass barriers. Inside the bar, snowflakes and spray-on snow sparkled from the walls, reflecting the candlelight from each table. Magical.

The setting might be the perfect date night with Marco…wait, no…she had no business thinking about her ex. Thinking led to feelings which led to deep trouble. Her complete submission had left her exposed. Yet they drew closer together.

"Beautiful, and since now's nighttime, we're not surrounded by little kids. A bonus." Claudine picked up a toothpick with olives attached, tilted her head back, and slid them into her mouth.

Jenna often pictured those scarlet lips on her breasts, wrapped around her nipples. Claudine's every movement appeared erotic. Her fire-engine-red cardigan accentuated the smoothness of her collarbone.

Sweat gathered at the nape of Jenna's neck despite the cold. Grabbing the daiquiri, she downed the entire contents. "How are you finding Stone Corp? Want to assassinate anyone yet?"

"Nope, I have amazing colleagues."

"True, except for whoever's hacking AnaStone." She eyed Claudine for a reaction, but not an eyelash flickered.

"Terrible. I'll keep a lookout. Any gossip or info to tell me?" Claudine leaned a few inches closer. Not good—a few inches between them were dangerous.

Jenna's heart knocked against her ribs. "Not really. There's hardly any office romances I'm aware of. Except for Nathan and Desiree, and Sebastian and Vanessa, of course."

The conversation reminded her to chat with Hayley about Desiree downloading AnaStone.

Claudine rolled her eyes. "Yes, Vanessa's the envy of half the office. Women act like horny teenagers around our CEO."

"He's the kind of attractive where you drool and trip over yourself to get under him."

"Ha, he's not my type." Claudine crossed her legs

and smiled in a way that should come with a warning.

Jenna's eyebrows shot up. Even the men in the office admitted Sebastian was handsome. "Sure. Most mere mortals wish to ride off in the sunset with him and be part of his happy ending."

"I don't swing that way." Claudine's penetrating gaze stripped her bare.

Jenna shifted in her seat. Claudine's response confirmed her sexuality. Anxiety grew from a kernel in Jenna's chest. Surely, Claudine didn't think they were on a date. No, Jenna was being ignorant. Just because Claudine was gay, it didn't mean she was attracted to every single female she had ever met.

Claudine's cheeks dimpled, just a bit, when her grin spread. "More specifically, my type has always been women with dark, curly hair and smooth bronzed skin. Have you met anyone like that?"

The space between them thickened—a miracle Jenna still breathed. Her mind wandered to them in a sixty-nine position, Claudine's moans pulsing against Jenna's folds. Her body tightened like a bowstring. She changed the subject. "Did you always know you were gay if you don't mind me asking?"

"As a child, I played kiss-chasey, and I yearned to grab Angela from class. Getting close and personal with the boys didn't interest me." Claudine's husky laugh caused Jenna to bask in her glow.

Maybe Jenna was bi-curious. When younger, she had no interest in girls. "I love you're one hundred percent yourself. You're so cool ice cubes are jealous."

"I can't deny who I am." Claudine's gaze held a deeper meaning.

Jenna blinked, the intensity taking her aback. The

way Claudine looked at her, she saw right through Jenna. Unable to convey a semi-intelligent response, she cleared her throat. "Are you ready to skate?"

Claudine tossed back the last drops of the dirty martini. "Let's go."

Jenna and Claudine grabbed their skates and walked down the stairs to the gate. After attending to their footwear, they entered the ring in slow shuffles. In weeks, work would break for the holidays. She must uncover the software problems. No way she'd spend Christmas agonizing over AnaStone.

"I skated twice as a kid. I'm not exactly an expert." Claudine held on to the edge, hobbling along. "Have you done this before?"

"Yeah, I did ballet and then ice skating for fun." Jenna's cheeks were still a little warm from the alcohol and Claudine's confession. Claudine entered her mind multiple times a day, but she wasn't ready to act upon temptation.

She skated farther ahead and sprang into a flying spin, her legs soaring in a scissoring motion off the ice.

"Show off." Claudine let go of the rail and stuck her arms out to balance. The first time she had appeared anything but sophisticated and sexy.

Jenna met her halfway, holding out a hand. "You can do this. The first steps are the hardest."

Claudine reached out, brows furrowed.

Their fingers grasped. Electric thrills skittered over her skin, turning her legs to jelly.

"Gotcha." Claudine smiled in triumph.

Jenna opened her mouth to speak, but no words came out. Quelling her nerves, she took a deep breath.

Claudine tightened her grip. "Don't let go. Please."

She kept peering down at the ice like she was afraid to fall.

A toddler whooshed past them, twirling three times in a row.

Claudine's head shot up. She eyed the child, cursing under her breath. "Oh, come on."

Jenna muffled a laugh. "We'll go around slowly."

They skated at a snail's pace, circling the tall Christmas tree with tiers of lights and a gold shiny star on top. Jenna brushed a branch aside. The few kids in the ice rink lapped them repeatedly. But she enjoyed taking her time, relishing the fake cold snowflakes falling on her cheeks and the warmth of Claudine's hand. Upbeat music about snow and winter played in the background. She was a kid again. Not a grown woman in a complicated relationship with her ex, two dependents, and a career on the line.

Claudine still frowned, pouting a bit. The look hadn't left her face since they entered the ice rink.

Jenna hesitated before she spoke. "Can I ask you something?"

"If the question is whether I can skate myself, the answer's *no*." Claudine's laughter jingled. "But, okay, shoot."

"When you came out to your family, how did they react?" Jenna's parents might not accept her knowing a woman enticed her. They were strict but also loving, teaching her and Josh ice skating.

Tight lines formed around Claudine's mouth. "They kicked me out of home when I was sixteen."

"Oh, my God. How awful." She pursed her lips, stopping insensitive words. Claudine's parents were too cruel to their flesh and blood. Not in a million years, she'd ask Keisha or Eve to leave. She and Marco didn't mind who they loved as long as they were a good person.

With her religious upbringing, Mom and Dad might've done the same. No, surely not. When she was a teenager, her mother had arrived home one night exclaiming she met the most charming gay shopkeeper who helped her choose home decorations.

"My family issues are in the past. I stayed with my older cousin for a year. We sorted out our differences when my brother and sister refused to talk to my parents until they reconnected with me." Claudine's fingers tensed in Jenna's hand, either from fear of falling, or the tension of reliving her experiences. "They were shocked. I was Daddy's little girl, and we played soccer together. We were close."

"Are you okay with them now?"

No wonder Claudine had a certain air of strength after her abandonment.

Claudine raised a shoulder in a casual shrug. "Yes, we have a family dinner every Sunday. My parents prefer not to know my dating life, though. They're under the impression if no one talks about the issue, I'm not gay, and eventually, I'll grow out of it."

"How absurd. Someone can't choose their sexuality and switch attraction off like a tap." Unease crept into Jenna's chest. Maybe she was a hypocrite. She kept dismissing any fascination she had with Claudine.

"Yes, but I won't receive more from them." Claudine straightened, skating closer to Jenna.

The mood between them dropped. She didn't expect to go into such heavy territory on a fun

137

excursion.

A couple skated past them holding hands, not going over thirty seconds without sneaking a kiss. Envy crept in Jenna's chest. To be in love again.

Claudine yanked on her hand, stumbling and skidding. Jenna's hold loosened. Her friend slid back, slipped out of her hand, and fell onto her ass.

Claudine sat still, blinking in a daze. Bursting into giggles, she placed her palms on the ice. "I'll never be good at skating. I don't like the cold or snow."

Jenna held out a hand. "You're not tripping over. More having a gravity check. Why did you suggest ice–skating, then?"

"You like it." Claudine tugged her down.

Jenna toppled over, reaching for the ice to slow her fall, and sat beside Claudine. Still, the landing was more graceful than the other woman's. Laughing, Jenna lightly punched her arm. "Last time I help you. Wait. How did you know I love ice–skating?"

Claudine's mouth twisted into an awkward smile. "I checked you out on social media."

"Checked me out, huh? You stalker. We could've gone somewhere else if this wasn't your idea of fun."

"You're still here." Claudine fluttered her long, butterfly eyelashes. Pink splattered across her nose from the cold.

Jenna's heart raced an entire track. Mist puffed out of her mouth. The surrounding people blurred into the background.

Claudine's gaze drifted to her lips, then to her eyes. A mirror of mutual longing.

Jenna inhaled. Blinked. Exhaled. Licked her lips. Parted her mouth. Cleared her throat. Up close, her colleague had perfect skin—creamy and delicate. Jenna wanted to suck on her skin, to check if it was as hot as it appeared. Her nipples strained against the fabric of her bra, reducing her to a puddle of want.

"Look. Mistletoe." Claudine pointed to the printed pattern on the ice rink's barriers.

Jenna tilted her head. "Pictures don't count—"

Time distorted. Those plump lips edged toward her like the drumroll before the main act.

Their lips met. Claudine's, a silk cushion soft, but in charge. Pins and needles rushed through Jenna's body. Claudine's vanilla scent enveloped her as she clutched onto Jenna. Skin feverish, Jenna rested her palm behind Claudine's head. The woman urged her on. She relaxed into the kiss, far exceeding expectations. Claudine's tongue dipped into her mouth, nipping her lower lip.

Delectable tingles sprinted through her. Fire spread across Jenna's body, her skin sensitive. Claudine's heated touch should be illegal—her existence too much to bear.

Surely, it was acceptable to jump Claudine here and now with little kids around. A chuckle wedged in her chest. No, she did have some common decency.

"Get a room," a snarky male voice drawled.

They sprang apart.

Jenna recoiled. Claudine still held her hand, but it was like she touched someone else. Her skin numbed.

A group of teenage boys sniggered six feet away. One whistled. Claudine shook her head, offering Jenna a reassuring smile. Not everyone displayed her level of poise.

Jenna's esophagus jammed, making it difficult to

inhale or gulp. She wanted to wipe the stupid smirk off the boys' faces. They lived in San Francisco for God's sake—no one cared when two women kissed.

But she'd have to answer to her religious parents if their chemistry grew. She had no clue how to explain to Marco, let alone her daughters. A fling or silly crush wasn't worth the trauma.

"This was a mistake." Not meeting Claudine's gaze, she stood.

"We're fine. They're kids. No one ever reacts like them."

Jenna ignored her, skating away. The speed created a gust of wind, licking her hair.

"Let's talk. Jenna, please," Claudine called after her, her voice raised in hurt.

Jenna needed distance and to escape. Her gaze stayed glued to the exit.

Tumbling out of the ice rink, she changed her shoes and fled before Claudine stopped her.

Chapter Thirteen

Throughout the morning, Jenna sat imprisoned at her desk. Restructure whispers had floated through the office, putting everyone on edge.

She must figure out AnaStone's issues with a deadline of yesterday. The police, Sandeep, or Hayley hadn't progressed either. Even though the software emailed notifications when someone was live on the system, no untoward actions had happened. She opened the program. Strange. Yesterday AnaStone had recommended Stone Corp invest more in Titans Pharmaceuticals. The company was in dire straits financially. She bit the inside of her cheek. The situation kept worsening. The hacker had broken through the firewall.

She checked the code again. Whoever was on the other side must be smart. Typing an email, she informed the IT team with Hayley and Sandeep cc'd about the fraudster's level of technique. Maybe they could help strengthen the security and block all hackers out.

On the plus side, Claudine had sat in meetings most of the Thursday after ice skating—thank God. Jenna's neck constantly strained from peeking over her shoulder. Now Friday, she only spotted her colleague in passing. Each time, Jenna averted her gaze. On an immaturity scale from one to one hundred, she was sixty-nine.

On her desk calendar, today's word of the day was, *audacious*. How ironic. She rejected the situation with Claudine like there was no *I* in *denial*. A pressure built in her throat at the memory of their kiss. She yearned to kiss her again, but more intimacy would rock her life.

The weekend couldn't come fast enough.

Tempted to text Marco, she stopped herself from picking up the cell for the thousandth time today. Marco had no obligation to lift her from the pit she'd dug.

Sighing, she flipped the phone display to face the desk and tightened her jaw. He wasn't her comfort source. Maybe she needed to stretch her legs to clear her head. Standing, she shrugged into a camel trench coat and strode toward the stairs—three flights to the ground. It amazed her when people rode the elevators for a short distance.

Halfway down, she met Claudine racing up the other side. Their gazes collided. Jenna's breathing rose high in her chest. She fastened her top two shirt buttons—any higher, the blouse would cover her face.

A shadow clouded Claudine's expression. Still, she oozed so much sex appeal she could fog up a professor's glasses. The tension was like water dripping into a shower—little by little until the floor overflowed. Her body heated. Too damn hot in here. Her underwear could peel off like the material was burning paper.

If only she could rewind time and go back to normal. Alas, no such device existed. She sidestepped to the left at the same time as Claudine. They almost crashed. She shifted to her right, and Claudine mirrored her actions.

"Sorry." Jenna hurried past, racing down the stairs like an express train with no brakes.

Once outside, she gulped air. Damn…bumping into her was more awkward than the moment someone realized they're chewing on a borrowed pen.

The sky, crowded with gray, had a watery glow illuminating thin patches of blue to brilliance. Trees shivered in the harsh wind. Candy canes and gold bells hung on naked branches. Twig bundles stooped and bent in every angle.

Closing her eyes, she pictured the safety of Marco's embrace. An intimacy she still found soothing. Her eyes fluttered open. She rolled her shoulders, backward and forward. Giving in to temptation, she removed her cell from her pants pocket.

—*Hi, Marco, can we catch up tonight?*—

A reply flashed in two seconds.

—*Of course.*—

Beaming, she stuffed the phone back into a pocket. She started walking, darting between the crowds of people in sharp business suits and stressed expressions on their faces. Building strips extended above her, the windows alight from within. The Financial District sure had beautiful skyscrapers. Baroque and gothic ornamentation to terra cotta exteriors.

The street glistened, and the gravel crunched underneath her footsteps. Entering Union Square, she glided past high-end designer shops with fake frost and snowflakes on the windows. One day, she might live like the one percent with no money or pesky job problems.

A woman with a long amber mane, most likely hair extensions, pointed at a boutique jewelry store's window. "The ring looks a little cheap."

Nathan Singh, Stone Corp's IT Analyst, hunched his narrow shoulders. "Ten grand isn't cheap, Desiree."

Jenna patted herself on the back for no longer reacting to Desiree reminding her of Marco's friend, Bluebell. Her steps slowed. Nathan was one of few with AnaStone access, and Desiree had the software on her computer. She still hadn't shaken nor proven her idea they had tampered with the system.

"My friend Stacey has a one point five carat ring, the grading rated excellent in every area. Her husband loves her more than his own life." Desiree tucked a lock of hair behind her ear, revealing shimmering sapphire earrings. Undoubtedly real.

"Stacey married a trust fund baby. Let's use the money for our own place or to help pay off your home." Nathan raked his fingers over his slicked–back black hair and stroked her arm. "You'll look stunning no matter what."

Jenna's hand twitched. She hid behind a tree, aching to slap Desiree. Banks chased after the idiot who worried about bling size. When Marco proposed, a ring from a cereal box would've pleased her.

"I'll wear an engagement ring for the rest of my life." Desiree scrunched up her paid–for nose. "Not unreasonable to expect a nice one."

"Diamonds are expensive."

Yes, put your foot down, Nathan. Go you. Crossing her arms, Jenna sent him a silent telepathic message.

"You promised you'd treat me like a princess. I grew up with peanuts." Desiree pouted, not a single line forming around her mouth. Her immobile face was as expressive as a mannequin's.

Nathan's expression lost the resolve. "Okay, I'll find a second job."

Shoulders sagging, he kissed his girlfriend briefly on the lips. Probably dreading the zero sleep he'd receive giving in to Desiree's every whim and demand.

Jenna shook her head. She wasn't saying Desiree was a gold digger...more someone who loved money and shiny objects. Massive pressure for Nathan. Maybe he'd go to extreme illegal lengths to keep her happy.

Desiree and Nathan turned and strolled off.

Startled, Jenna jumped back and hurried away. Not looking where she was going, she crashed into a trash can. The can tipped. A plastic cup with fries, a banana peel, flyers, and more junk spilled onto her. A rotten food smell occupied the space.

Gasping, she wiped the red sauce from her pants.

Nathan and Desiree twirled.

Jenna's ears burned hotter than an iron.

People whizzed by, without a second thought of helping.

"Jenna? Are you all right?" Nathan rushed toward her, scooped the rubbish into the can, and stood it upright. Desiree followed him in slow steps and halted a healthy foot behind.

Jenna wiggled out of her coat. "Yes, I enjoy creating an obstacle course wherever I go."

Nathan patted his jacket and trousers before turning to Desiree. "Do you have a tissue?"

Desiree unzipped a designer handbag and produced a packet. Grimacing, she handed the tissues to Nathan.

"Are you sure you're okay? We can run into a shop and grab you a change of clothes." Nathan ripped out tissues and passed them to Jenna. Gratefully, she accepted and dabbed them over her top and pants.

"I still have a pulse, so I must be fine." Jenna gave a tight smile. The prices in these stores were astronomical. No chance she'd buy an outfit from this strip. "How's work for you two?"

If she kept the conversation casual, Nathan might let information slip about money worries, or Desiree with AnaStone.

A little boy pointed at Jenna, tugging on his mother's sleeve. "Can I play with the trash too?"

"I bathed you an hour ago." The woman twisted her lips in apology. She nudged her squirming son away who kept charging for the can.

Jenna's face warmed, imagining her skin an uncooked steak color. How she wished to hide behind the garbage.

"Not much ever changes with me," Nathan replied.

"How's every little thing going on in your life, Desiree?" Jenna flashed a big, phony smile. Okay, the tactic might be a tad obvious.

Desiree scoffed. "I wish I didn't have to do a lot of jobs. Everyone wants a piece of me. I work until midnight every day."

Jenna rolled her eyes so hard she could see her brain. Desiree always acted like she was busy even when merely converting oxygen into carbon dioxide. "Well, AnaStone can lighten your workload."

A silence draped over them.

Desiree's cheeks reddened. "Yes, Tina is mentoring me to be involved with numbers and strategy. Did she tell you?"

Jenna's jaw dropped. "No, I didn't think you were interested in analytics, though."

Desiree had a ninety-year-old's tech savviness.

"When you're as senior as me, you're expected to know every area." Desiree huffed and tilted her head back, basking in the invisible sun. "I have a busy day ahead. Nathan. Come." She waved a hand to summon him like a puppy. Twirling on her heels, she headed the other way.

Jenna's brows drew together. "What was she on about?"

Nathan leaned closer. "Desiree's manager set one of her KPI's for technology improvement. Don't tell her I told you. She's embarrassed."

He hurried to catch up to his girlfriend. Well…this explained why Desiree read AnaStone articles. She'd confirm with Hayley.

But Desiree was late on mortgage payments and might ask someone to infiltrate the software. Someone like Nathan. He was lovely but under the thumb. Desiree wasn't worth doing illegal stuff over—either to assist her or to afford a ring.

People gave her quizzing looks as they shuffled around her. Covered in gunk, she stood still in the middle of the sidewalk, not looking at anything. She was a terrible spy and should stick to her strengths.

****

A quarter mile away from Marco, the yellow bulldozer lowered the sharp-edged wide metal blade, scraped the ground, and lifted the hard-packed earth. A power saw screamed like a banshee and vibrated, slicing into the wood for the school's half-completed outdoor swimming area. Workers raked the gravel at the bottom of the large, six-foot deep rectangle pool placement.

Five teenagers, some in midriff–baring sweaters and low-rise jeans, sauntered outside the school's gate. Marco wanted to tell the late teens to put some clothes on. The frigid air winnowed away his body heat.

Damn…he must be getting old. At their age, he ran wild in a tank top and shorts to show off his muscles. Teammates catcalled the women even though their boss had already given a warning.

"Dayumm. Nice legs."

"What's your number?"

"Where you going?"

Two girls giggled, one smirked. The rest ignored them and strutted off, their heads held high.

"Shut up. Some of you are old enough to be their dads." Gritting his teeth, Marco shoveled the ground. "Or grandads." He would hate if creepy men subjected Jenna or his daughters to this kind of harassment, no matter their outfits.

One girl shot him a grateful look.

"Only having fun, dude." His colleague, Adam, called out.

"Have fun without disrespecting anyone," Marco grunted.

"I agree with you, Marco. They're tools. But you still need to chill out more." Douglas dropped the shovel on the ground. "You're always on edge. Follow me."

Eyebrows knitted, Marco settled the shovel to one side and followed Douglas to the gate. Many people strolled past. "What are we doing here?"

Chuckling, Douglas crouched and pointed ahead. "See the fiver on the ground?"

Marco ducked to his level. "Yes. Why is money

148

there? And why are we hiding?"

"Watch."

A middle-aged guy with a blond man bun stopped and did a double take at the spot on the pavement. He stooped and attempted to pick up the note, frowning when he couldn't lift it.

"What the hell," he grumbled, trying again. Still stuck.

"Glued the note down with epoxy. That bitch is never coming up." Douglas hugged his middle in laughter.

Struggling to yank the money out, the man's face glowed bright red. With shaky shoulders, he stood and spun, checking for spectators. Marco and Douglas slumped lower as he sped away.

A tickle wedged in Marco's throat. "You have way too much time on your hands." He clutched his chest, chuckling soft at first, stopping and starting. His laughter rumbled from deep inside his stomach, and tears trickled from his eyes.

He turned to Douglas and placed a hand on his shoulder.

"All good, buddy." Douglas's eyes shone with understanding. Although he had never experienced the army, he suffered hardship growing up with a drunk, abusive father.

Marco hadn't laughed like this since Afghanistan.

****

After work, Marco grabbed apples and dropped the bag into a basket. He hummed along to a Christmas pop song playing in the brightly lit supermarket.

His cell buzzed. He patted his jeans pocket. Empty. Instead, the phone lay in the shopping basket. He always misplaced his belongings. Whipping it out, he hoped the message was from Jenna. His heart sank at Connor's name.

—*Your fight is at 10 pm next Thursday.*—

Sighing, he stuffed the phone into his pocket. The sooner the night arrived, the sooner he'd be free. He prayed to God Connor would keep his word.

Today on site, he belonged in the crew—the first time since his army team. Douglas helped him more than medications ever did. But when he had headed to the supermarket, a group of guys behind a pub window laughed over a beer. His lungs spasmed, forcing out the little air left. He was alive, and his fallen friend wasn't.

As he picked up onions, a small boy with dark hair and big brown eyes scuttled by in a blur.

The wheels in his brain ground to a halt. "No, you can't be."

The child from Afghanistan was dead.

His mind took him back to digging up the rubble until he found the boy's body. The metallic smell of blood suffocated him, and his men's whimpers didn't stop.

He quickened his pace. The kid paused at the candy section. His mind played tricks on him. Of course, this child wasn't the same, but he needed to be sure.

Marco stepped closer. Now, face-to-face with the transparent ghost of the Afghani child, wearing the same torn blue T-shirt and black jeans. Blood smattered across his torso.

Marco stumbled back. "You're not real." His grip tightened on the basket's handle. Hot moisture covered his body. His hallucination was punishment for forgetting his army friends for a moment.

The boy raised his right index finger to his lips. "Shh."

Marco's vision blurred, darkening at the corners. Squeezing his eyes shut, he counted to ten...one Mississippi, two Mississippi...*he's not there, he's not there, he's not there*. He opened his eyes. The boy still hadn't budged.

Marco dropped the basket, landing with a clang. His clothes strangled him, digging into his ribs. "What do you want from me?"

A thinness in the air amplified every sound—the scanning at the checkout counters, a wailing baby, and the stacking of yogurt tubs.

The boy gave a nonchalant shrug, tilting his head.

Customers glanced at Marco. He bottled up his emotions and buried them. As long as he appeared calm on the outside, the boy wouldn't beat him. Life was short. He should embrace every good day.

"You don't scare me." He spat the words out like they tasted of sewage. The last few weeks with his family flashed through his mind.

Jenna...his center of gravity, the only woman tying him to this earth. Without her, he'd float into the sky, a balloon with the string sliced off.

Picking up the basket, he clenched his jaw. Ice chips scraped his throat despite his bravado. He finished shopping, not once peeking whether the boy's spirit still lingered.

****

As soon as Jenna arrived home, she whipped up a tuna and quinoa salad for dinner and set the kids to do homework at the dining table.

She had texted her mother to look after Keisha and Eve tonight. Mom's response half amused her, half riled her, and half exasperated her. That equaled three halves, but she didn't care.

—*Of course. Another hot date with Marco? ;)*—

Groaning, she wondered how Mom learned the winking emoji.

The doorbell rang.

Jenna rushed to the front, Scruffy at her heels. She opened the door. "Hi, Mom. Dad."

Scruffy wagged her tail frantically. Mom and Dad patted her.

"Hi, yourself. Where are you off to this fine evening?" Mom's long dark braid brushed Jenna's arm as she let them both inside.

"I have errands to run. Thanks heaps for doing this, especially with my late notice." Jenna grabbed a handbag. "Bye, girls. I'll be back soon."

Before they asked more questions, she quickly closed the door. They'd badger her, and she was in no mood to entertain. She drove out of the driveway, brainstorming solutions for the Claudine situation. For a start, she must stop avoiding her colleague.

The keychain photo of Marco and the kids caught her gaze. She should change the image but was always too busy. Even though she and Marco were no strings attached, her insides lurched at potentially hurting him by kissing someone else.

Light rain splashed onto the windows. She switched on the windshield wipers. After a few miles, she clicked the turn signal, veering left into the gas station. Getting fuel was one of her least–favorite activities. Her anxious mind didn't let the tank lower more than a quarter. At least she had a buy one, get one free coupon for a small yogurt tub snapped as an image on her phone—a perfect dessert at Marco's place.

Opening the car door, she picked up one nozzle and pumped the gas. The entire time, she pictured Marco filling her deep inside. Lately, everything reminded her of sex. Liquid overflowed the compartment. Gasping, she yanked the pipe out, plonking it back onto the rack.

She closed the gas cap and walked inside the station. Shoulders sagged, she grabbed two yogurts from the fridge. Claudine might never speak to her again based on her childishness. She snatched a mint pack, headed to the cashier, and dropped her items on the table.

"Any coupons or reward cards?" The guy in his late teens or early twenties yawned. Long, blue-streaked hair half-covered his eyes.

She'd like to trim his bangs—such a mom urge.

"Yes." She rummaged through her bag, removed the sunglasses case and a notebook, and slid out her cell and a fifty-dollar bill.

The attendant's gaze lingered at the small television in the shop's top corner. On the screen, a man kicked a ball into the goalpost.

"Goooal." The cashier lifted his arms, hopping.

She flicked through the camera roll's images. The screenshot yogurt coupon appeared. An audience member's dark shiny hair flashed across the TV. She silently yelled at the universe for sending Claudine reminders.

Flustered, she stuffed the pens and notebook into the bag and handed over her phone. "Who's winning?"

"The right team." He scanned the items one by one. "I've never paid much attention to soccer."

The guy's wide-eyed gaze snagged on her cell. Raising the screen to his face, he did a double take. The gadget slipped a little in his hand.

He cleared his throat. "Are you sure you meant to give me this picture?"

"Yes, the photo's specifically for here." She eyed the clock above, twitching to be in Marco's arms, safe and sound.

His cheeks flamed beetroot red, glancing between her and the cell. "Oh. Well…umm…thanks, lady."

Her eyes narrowed, an eyebrow raised.

"Did I give you the wrong coupon?" She grabbed the phone and looked at the screen. Blood drained from her face. Her cheeks burned hotter than a desert sun. The topless picture she texted Marco stared back— boobs out on full display, lips a slight pout. Just her luck keeping the screenshot coupon close to *those* pictures.

Sweat formed at the cashier's hairline.

Jenna's legs refused to budge. Averting her gaze, she wanted the ground to swallow her whole and never spit her out. Technology was evil. She had flashed an unsuspecting victim. All because she let thoughts of Claudine distract her.

She scrambled the rest of her belongings into the handbag and placed the fifty on the counter. Every molecule in her body switched on high alert. "Keep the change."

Her breathing cut short. She shuffled her feet, her arms flapping like an uncoordinated bird. The guy stared at the ceiling, his face redder by the second. She bolted out of the automatic doors.

Chapter Fourteen

Moonlight shone through the gap in Marco's living room curtains. Outside, teens yelled the best places to score more alcohol. A reindeer headband hooked on the top of the television—his small Christmas effort.

Marco clutched one hand to his chest, laughing. "And then what happened?"

"I didn't acknowledge the topless photo and ran out faster than someone whose boss asked if anyone could stay late on a Friday." Jenna smacked a hand on her forehead, her face glowing as red as Rudolph's nose.

He gasped between bursts of laughter. "Poor boy. Actually, lucky boy."

The oven timer pinged. When his wife first arrived, her legs and arms didn't stop twitching. She baked muffins to eat away her mortification.

Jenna stood, walked to the kitchen five steps away, and opened the oven door. Her jeans pulled taut against her legs as she bent over. Steam rushed out of the oven, and a banana scent perfumed the air.

He strode over, grabbed the oven mitt, and slipped it on. "Let me. You're the guest."

He took out the hot dish and settled the tray on the cooling rack, removing the glove. His chuckle echoed throughout the room.

She ripped a chunk off one muffin, blew on the

pastry, and popped the morsel into her mouth. "I shall destroy you." She marched to the living room.

He followed her and sat on the couch. Her purple blouse hugged her firm torso when she leaned against the armrest, mesmerizing him.

"Aww...poor baby. You gotta admit...pretty funny." He grazed her forearm with the backs of his fingers and hauled her closer, wrapping her in a bear hug.

She lifted her head and glared like lasers could shoot out of her eyes. "I will end you."

He bit his lip, shoulders shaking in silent amusement.

Her lips tugged up. Giggles rolled out until she snorted. Tears leaked.

Little flickers ignited in his chest. Her laughter still sparked his lust.

"I blame you. If I wasn't coming here..." She rested her cheek on his shoulder, fitting perfectly against his collarbone. His heart stuttered.

He patted her thigh. "What can I do to make you happier?"

Jenna curled her hands into his waistband. "I have some ideas."

He removed her hands and switched on the television, clicking to their favorite action movie.

Her mouth swung open. "Huh? Don't you want to get busy?"

"I crave you, but I want more than sex. We haven't been friends in a long time." Palm opened, he held out his hand. "You're too important to me."

Their relationship must reconnect in every way— mind, body, and spirit—for them to work.

She stared at him. After several long seconds, she accepted his hand, and they settled into the couch.

****

When Jenna arrived home and tucked the girls into bed, she raced to the bedroom and rummaged through the bottom drawer.

Marco was a distraction from Claudine and work. A very tempting distraction, although he didn't budge on the damn film. Now alone the dark ball of pressure that burned inside her chest reappeared.

She picked out a leotard with a skirt and slippers and slid into each clothing item. Ballet had been in her blood since she was four—from the graceful way she walked and talked, to the moves instantly calming her. Few people understood.

She strolled to the rumpus room—the biggest in the house—featuring a treadmill, weights, and a spin bike on the right. Still holding onto the phone, she clicked the playlist and switched on a classical piano tune. The music danced through the space, circling above and around.

Energy swirled within her. Her skin prickled. Starting slow, she traveled in sequence, marked her steps, and twirled, slippers tapping the tile floor. Her shoulders loosened. It was not a big deal she kissed Claudine. The incredible kiss looped in her mind and shone in her heart like a beacon.

Her back straight, she lifted her head high. She launched into complex footwork. The tempo sped up. A shock of power ripped through her. Even though she often denied it, she desired Claudine. She always told her daughters they could be whoever they chose, as cheesy as the words sounded. Damn…she sure gave sound advice. Yet she couldn't accept she ached for Claudine.

She raised her arms. Sweat coated her skin. The air thickened with magic. Rhythm rose inside her. One foot slid along the tiles before lifting and brushing the air. With her supporting leg, she launched off the floor. This leg met the other, assuming fifth position. She landed with a plié.

Claudine also sashayed with a cat's elegance, and her touch was so intense Jenna lost her train of thought. She had Marco too. Doubtful she had feelings for two people. She missed her footing. Maybe the universe delivered Claudine into her life to push her beyond any comfort level. Claudine was her mirror, revealing her worst parts.

Stretching farther, she turned faster. Her eyebrows pinched together. She was a hypocrite believing people couldn't help their physical attraction but not accepting the idea. As idiotic as someone who said they're a vegetarian but could still eat chicken. Whenever two people of the same gender walked down the street holding hands, no one batted an eyelid. Meanwhile, a simple kiss tied her in knots.

Her jaw set. Claudine made her feel good. Adventurous. In a life of uncertainty, she must be true to herself. Relief washed over her at coming to a decision. Beginning tomorrow, she'd no longer be a wuss and sort out her lure to Claudine.

****

Keisha peered at the paper Eve scrawled over. Scruffy napped on the couch. They had been sitting quietly and writing at Marco's dining table for almost an hour after Jenna dropped them off at nine in the morning.

Keisha pointed to Eve's work. "The word 'grateful' is spelled with an *a*, not an *e*."

"What are you two doing?" Marco lowered the stove's heat, simmering the chicken noodle soup. He strode over.

Keisha lifted her head. "Writing letters through *Your Soldier*."

A frisson of warmth shimmied down Marco's back. "Why?"

Your Soldier was a program where military men welcomed letters from people they never met. Many recipients didn't have family and were quite isolated.

"My teacher mentioned the idea." Eve's brows furrowed at the note. "We didn't want anyone to be lonely."

"You two are good girls." Sliding a seat between them, he wrapped an arm over each daughter. Moments like these softened his war experiences.

"Will you read my letter, Dad?" Keisha's shy gaze flicked to him as she slid the paper across the table.

"Absolutely." With one finger, he traced her neat handwriting. She took after her mother's tidiness.

Dear Hero,

My name is Keisha and I'm 9. I have the best mom and dad, and my little sister is okay too. Thank you for keeping us safe. I can go to ballet because of you. Time away from family must suck. I missed my dad when he was in Afghanistan. Hope you can return home for the holidays.

Merry Christmas,

Love Keisha

A lump formed in Marco's throat. "Perfect." He

tugged his daughters close and relished the sweet orange scent in Eve's hair. "What shall we do today?"

Keisha leaned into him. "Go shopping. Our ballet friends are going. We haven't seen them since class last week. Our concert is tomorrow."

The kids from their lessons were performing a Christmas show for the parents. He had looked forward to the play for weeks.

"We can't let that happen, then." He laughed. "Everyone needs time to have fun with their friends. Your mom and I only stay home."

Eve finished the last of the letter. "Mom's visiting a friend today too."

"Who?" The word cannonballed out of his mouth. His nails carved sickles into his palms at the idea of another man.

Keisha folded the letter and slipped the paper into an envelope. "She didn't say."

Jenna's friend might be no one, but she stressed she might date other people. His insides were raked out, his skin a series of open wounds someone had rubbed salt into. A bitter taste filled his mouth. He might have lost her for good. If there was a new guy, maybe he gave her happiness. She deserved the best.

Shaking his body like a wet dog, he pulled himself together. Whether or not someone else was in the picture, he must up his game.

****

When Jenna stepped off the BART, she headed toward Claudine's house. A Frisbee flew over her head at Dolores Park. Downtown San Francisco displayed proudly at the end of the park's slope. She always enjoyed the walk. Many couples strolled arm in arm, cozy in beanies and puffy jackets.

Red and gold hues stretched far and wide in the sky, the sunset as brilliant as a fire hearth. Street food—corn on a cob, chargrilled chicken wings, and noodles—beckoned her.

She must speak to Claudine before she lost her nerve. Claudine might not react to her visit favorably. Last night, she texted Claudine she was coming over and didn't receive a response. She took the no reply as a "yes."

"Jenna?" A female voice called behind her.

Spinning around, she found her colleague, Tina, wheeling her seven-year-old daughter in a chair. She had met Kelly several times at Stone Corp's family days and learned more on cerebral palsy.

Tina gave her a quick one-armed hug. "I thought I saw you. What are you doing this side of town?"

"Visiting a friend." Jenna shifted on her feet. Tina knew Claudine. This might lead to complications.

Tina stroked her daughter's black hair resembling her own. "Kelly, you remember Jenna, don't you?"

"Yes...I d-do." Kelly spoke in a breathy voice, tilting her head.

"Keisha and Eve would love to see you again soon. Let's schedule a playdate in the coming weeks."

"Co-cool. Coo, cool, cool." Ducks waddling across the grass snagged Kelly's attention.

Jenna faced Tina. "How did you go with the advance on your bonus? I'm still mad the banks declined you."

"My request got approved. Funds went into my account the other day," Tina said.

A guy in his early twenties bumped into Jenna as

he caught a ball. "Sorry, miss."

Jenna rubbed her arm, wincing. "It must be a huge relief. You seem a lot happier."

Stone Corp's issues were still happening. Now Tina had money, and she had no reason to hack the software. Jenna's limbs loosened, becoming more fluid. Maybe she should still check payroll on Tina's bonus status to rule her out. They probably kept staff information confidential, though.

Tina beamed. "Yeah, my luck has changed lately. I bought Titans Pharmaceuticals shares ages ago. They shot up since Stone Corp acquired more."

Jenna's muscles braced. Stone Corp had many stocks in the company, and AnaStone recommended the wrong action in purchasing recently.

"Real lucky. How long have you kept the shares?" Jenna crafted each word as though they were fine china. Maybe Tina had input in AnaStone's problems. She had a lot to gain and more to lose.

"Years before I started at Stone Corp. I thought they were a write-off. Now Kelly and I have breathing space."

A screwdriver drilled Jenna's stomach, her heart strapped to an explosive vest. Economists stressed Titans was under financial strain—a huge coincidence Tina gained from the investment.

Kelly nudged Tina. "I'm r-ready for...for...for dinner."

"Okay, let's go." Tina patted her daughter's head. "I better get this one some food. Catch you Monday. We'll do lunch next week."

"Sure...see ya," she muttered, not paying attention to them leaving the park. Her gut feeling over Tina had turned into diarrhea—a huge mess.

****

Jenna stood outside Claudine's pale gray condo. She raised a hand to knock but backed away. Admitting to liking women was a huge step. She had her job to deal with, especially with Tina's new information.

No turning back once she tapped on the tall wooden door. Claudine's alluring nature captivated her—pure magic. Jenna took deep breaths, striking the door three times in a steadiness surprising her. She shoved Marco in a delicate box inside her heart…for the time being.

The door creaked open. Claudine's dainty face poked through the gap, her luscious dark locks toppling over one shoulder. Her brows inched up. "I thought you didn't wish to see me."

Jenna's ankles wobbled. Invisible wires bound her legs tightly together. Now or never for the truth. "I wanted to see you. Too much."

Claudine's mouth parted. "You better come in."

Jenna stepped inside. Medallion vintage moldings lined the ceiling, and a three-seat velvet sofa stood on a leather rug. Silence drenched them. The moment slowed into their own surreal bubble. Jenna stared at Claudine like a gobsmacked tourist.

"Why are you here?" Claudine's bright blue eyes had purple and silver specks up close. Another jolt tore through Jenna's body.

"To apologize and have more courage." Jenna stumbled back into the tree-shaped marble coat rack.

"I see. Take a seat." Claudine picked up a tray from the kitchen bench and placed it on the coffee table's wooden top. The rustic base resembled a birdcage. "Please don't run away again. Whenever you're confused or anxious, we'll work the problem out."

Jenna collapsed onto the couch. "I'm sorry. I was a child."

"Apologies you were uncomfortable I kissed you." Claudine's cheeks tinted a rosy red. "My gaydar must be off."

"You weren't wrong. This is new territory for me. I didn't fully realize...I mean...I...I wasn't attracted to both women and men until you. I had an inkling, though." Jenna covered her face. Her brain was full of marbles—loose and scattered. "I'm not sure if I'm making sense."

Claudine sat on the opposite end of the sofa. "You're making perfect sense."

"I'm tired of pretending to be someone I'm not." She grabbed a cookie and stuffed the treat into her mouth. "This is delicious. Snickerdoodle?"

"Thanks. Yes, correct." Claudine sidled closer. "So...what do you want from me?"

A tremble scurried through Jenna's body as she chewed. "I like you. You're audacious and intelligent and beautiful, but I'm a mess."

"You're pretty special yourself and put together."

"I'm not. Who in their right mind has a weird friends–with–benefits arrangement with their estranged husband?"

Claudine's eyes widened. "Will you get back together?" A note of steel embedded her voice.

"No. Nope. Nup. Too much broken trust."

Many beats slithered by. Claudine gave her a quizzing look.

Jenna raked her gaze over Claudine's body, her ruffled hair, lush lips. She yearned to trace a finger over Claudine's face and slip her tongue into the seam of those plump lips. The sweet vanilla perfume distracted her, banishing every thought.

"I enjoy spending time with you," Claudine said.

"To be honest, you captivated me from day one. But I'm not ready to be in a relationship with anyone."

A chuckle slid slow and easy from Claudine's lips. "I recently ended an eight-year-long relationship with my fiancée. I'm not suggesting a marriage proposal."

"Oh. What do we do?"

Claudine patted Jenna's thigh, leaving tiny fire bursts. "I'm more than happy to be friends. Let's take whatever this is one day at a time."

"I'd like that."

"Friends suit us better. Sort out your head." Claudine held out a hand. "Capeesh?"

"Fair point." Jenna grinned, shaking her hand. "Capeesh."

Their fingers connected. Heat clambered up her arm like a vine. She stilled, terrified she'd lose the sensation, that this moment didn't exist. For too long, she had denied her lust, and now she confronted her feelings head on. Even though they decided not to pursue their connection, the noise in her head over others' opinions had now quietened.

Chapter Fifteen

The stage's burgundy curtains flung open to display living room props and multiple windows with red drapes. Two stairways met in the middle. Marco sat to Jenna's right and her parents to her left. They clapped, cheering alongside the audience. Her children had practiced hard for the stage show. Now the day had come to demonstrate the skills they learned the past year.

Violins played an uplifting melody and a bouncing beat. Keisha and Eve stood in party dresses among other kids in front of a tall Christmas tree.

Jenna took out her phone and snapped multiple photos. As a child, she had performed the same play.

Her mind was tired from the hours of conversation last night with Claudine. Despite the initial awkwardness, she looked forward to seeing her again. But here, sitting next to Marco, her heart deflated like a balloon. She still cared. Deeply. Like Claudine, he deserved an honest conversation.

Trumpets increased in volume.

She leaned into him. "There's something I need to tell you. Can we talk later?"

Her chest pulled tight. The room shrank into a tiny pocket of space with only the two of them. Although she was insanely attracted to Claudine, they were friends. But the kiss should be out in the open for her and Marco to have a healthy relationship.

The grooves on his forehead scored deep. Tilting to her, the bands of his bicep muscles shifted. "I promised the girls I'd take them and their friends out for hot chocolate."

"Tomorrow after work, then?"

"I have to prepare for…" He cleared his throat, his right eye twitching. "I have an errand."

In puffy skirts, their daughters twirled and floated to the middle, interacting with the other kids. The music rose in a series of fast crescendos. Jenna took more photos.

"Like what?" A pressure itched deep inside her brain. His right eye twitching revealed he hid details.

He schooled his features into a statue. "If our chat involves you seeing someone else, don't tell me. Not unless you've chosen him."

A hole burned in her stomach. He was close to the truth. "Marco, I—"

"Shh." Mom nudged Jenna and raised a finger to her lips. "Plenty of time to gasbag later."

Jenna faced the front. Keisha completed a triple pirouette. Mom was right. She should watch, but Marco's secrecy bothered her. Hopefully, he wasn't in trouble.

"Don't worry, Jenna. We don't need a serious conversation." Marco took her hand. Their fingers entwined, fitting perfectly with one another. "Let's just sit here and be with each other."

Well, she'd respect his right to remain ignorant. As her two girls glided and spun across the stage, her shoulders relaxed.

****

"Can you send me the photos from Eve and Keisha's play? I'll show them to my church friends." Mom sipped a tea, sitting with Dad and Josh on the floral couch.

Straight after the performance, Jenna followed her parents home to set up the new smart TV. A huge white Christmas tree displaying silver and gold baubles stood proudly next to the television. On the shelf above, rows and rows of snow globes in different shapes and colors shone. Every time her parents ventured anywhere, they bought one as a souvenir. Jenna and Josh used to love giving them a light shake and admire the snow sprinkling down—magical.

"Sure." Jenna whipped out her cell and hesitated. No repeat of flashing someone a topless photo. Definitely not family. Clicking through the pictures of the kids—she had taken hundreds—she allocated the ones from today in a separate album. She triple-checked they were in the right folder. Not that she was paranoid or anything.

She handed the phone to her mom. "Here you go. Which ones do you want?"

"Link them to the new TV, please. We ought to make the most out of our money." Mom removed her glasses and rubbed her eyes. "I can't view photos so small."

"Your brother missed the play. He needs to see the pictures too," Dad said.

"Sorry, Jenna, for not coming." Josh picked up the remote and turned to their parents. "See the red button. This switches on the TV."

"Stop apologizing." Jenna opened a phone app to replicate the TV's setting. "How often does my little brother audition for a massive Hollywood producer?"

"See." Josh's voice came out razor sharp. "Jenna doesn't mind."

"Your nieces noticed their favorite uncle missing," Mom tutted.

Josh waved his hands in a fed-up motion. "I'm their only uncle. Besides, Jenna said they were distracted talking to the other kids afterward and barely spoke to you guys."

Jenna laughed. The phone's images synced to the TV. She clicked on the first photo of Eve dancing in unison with ten other kids, accidentally facing the wrong direction.

"The TV's colors are vibrant. I can almost touch her." Mom shuffled forward. "They both looked and danced like angels. We're blessed."

Jenna clicked to the next photo of her parents enjoying the show.

Mom winced. "Move along. I look terrible."

She tapped through twenty more pictures. The cell vibrated. A message from Marco flashed on the screen, and to her horror…also on the TV.

—Your breasts looked amazing in your top today. I want to fuck you again until you scream.—

Dad squinted. "What does the text say?"

Jenna fumbled to exit the message, but today of all days, she had fat fingers.

"The message is from Marco. Your breasts loo…" Mom bunched her long dark hair over one shoulder and fanned her face. "Lordy Lord."

Josh clapped his hands together. "Naughty."

Dad shifted in his seat, averting his gaze to anywhere but her.

Jenna grabbed the remote and hit the power button. She wanted to hide her face or run to the car and never return. Ducking her head, she opened her mouth to speak. No words.

Mom covered her mouth. "Jenna? Why did he text such explicit language?"

"We don't need to discuss this." Dad grabbed the coffee table book—*Food Delicacies Around the World*—and flicked through the pages, not lifting his head once.

Cheeks burning, Jenna let her hair drape over her face.

Josh clutched the edge of the sofa, choking on his own laughter. "Yes, we do."

"Wait, does the text mean you and Marco are back together?" Mom's eyes widened. "Incredible news. When is he moving back home? You'll be a family again."

Jenna shook her head. "We're not in a relationship."

"You obviously seem...umm...friendly," Mom squeaked. "What's the issue?"

"We have a lot of history." Marco had his demons. His mystery at their daughters' performance was suspicious, and he often had unexplained injuries.

"Faith can move mountains." Mom's eyes glimmered. "I love him like a son. Exciting. Like old times. I can't wait to tell everyone you're reuniting. Have another baby. You're quite old."

Mom rattled off her hopes and dreams for them. Jenna sank into the seat, hands over her face. Her parents were like their old TV—might have to hit them a few times before they got the picture about Marco.

Half-hoping the conversation would divert back to the sexting, she wished and wished her mother was more fluent in silence.

****

On Monday, Jenna kept smiling shyly at Claudine. Whenever Claudine asked for help, she brushed against Jenna. Accident or not, she enjoyed the easy interactions.

Jenna fumbled over the desk for a stapler to bind a report. For some strange reason, staplers disappeared like planes and ships in the Bermuda triangle.

She strode to the stationery closet and rummaged. A paper stack buried a black object on the third shelf. Victory. At least one part of work was a success. Hayley had confirmed Desiree's access to AnaStone, leading her back to square one. Although the IT team reinforced the firewall to block any unknowns, the hacker would most likely break through again.

The door creaked open behind her. A vanilla scent drifted through the room. Baby hairs at the back of her neck spiked up. She recognized the alluring fragrance anywhere.

Footsteps clipped toward her.

Closing her eyes, she pictured Claudine brushing her hair over a shoulder and soft kisses up and down her neck. Groaning, she turned. The room's dim light shone on Claudine's face. Her mouth tipped to one side.

"How are you this morning, Jenna?"

"I'm fine. Thanks for the chat." A low hum vibrated in Jenna's chest. "You've helped me a lot, you know? I know myself…better than I ever have."

Before Claudine, she had never acknowledged she was…bisexual? Hell yeah, she was.

"My pleasure. We didn't plan how we're catching the bag snatcher." Claudine leaned on the cupboard, and the pens, paperclips, and folders rattled. Her tall, curvy body radiated against Jenna's skin. She wanted to cradle Claudine's breasts in her palms and enjoy the shape and softness.

"I've been so distracted."

"Me too. You always smell exquisite by the way." Claudine's gaze made her tingly and warm like a dog receiving a belly rub. If only she could trace her hand across Claudine's soft and silky legs, and over to her firm, round ass.

A knock banged on the door.

Jenna jumped. Adrenaline zipped through her body like a live wire.

"Why is the door locked?" Angie's hoarse voice croaked from the other side.

Jenna cleared her throat. "Oh, we were looking for a stapler to mail a report."

"The door must have locked behind us," Claudine added.

"Slacking off again, Claudine? I need a USB stick for Sebastian. He's leaving the office in ten minutes." Angie huffed. She hated when someone impeded her looking after the CEO.

"One second." Jenna checked her reflection on the metal shelf. She didn't appear flustered. No sign she was tempted to get down and dirty. Was having sex at work even wrong? Not a single sentence in Stone Corp's guidelines stated the act was frowned upon.

She searched the shelves until she found a USB stick.

Claudine squeezed her hand. "I hope to talk more

soon."

Jenna opened the door to find Angie glaring. Beside her, a lanky teenage boy scowled. "Sorry for keeping you waiting, Angie. No idea how we got locked inside."

Angie raised an eyebrow. "You took your time. This is my son, Simon, by the way."

Sweat beads dripped down his pale face. He appeared to be in pain.

"Staplers are hard to find here. Can you please order more?" Claudine stuck out a hand to Simon. "I'm Claudine. Nice to meet you."

He stared at her hand and grimaced. Stalking off, his feet dragged every single step.

Jenna's jaw dropped. Teenagers were moody, but now she understood why some animals ate their young. She handed the USB stick to Angie. "Here you go."

Angie took the small device. "Thanks. Don't mind Simon. His Parkinson's disease is playing up, and he's in a nasty mood. I've let him take the day off school to rest. He's in the office in case I need to drive him to the doctor's."

"Poor kid. He'll be in a lot of discomfort." Jenna patted Angie's shoulder. She stressed whenever Keisha and Eve had a scrape on their knee—hard to avoid considering they practiced ballet.

"I'd give up my life for him." Angie bit her lip, her eyes moist. "I should check he doesn't make anyone cry." Angie spun, walking toward her desk.

Jenna's heartstrings pulled—must be hard to have a sick child. Remembering bumping into Tina and her daughter at the park, she noted to keep more tabs on her colleague. Titans Pharmaceuticals skyrocketing set off alarm bells.

"Poor Simon. Terrible for a kid to go through his type of illness." Claudine's lower lip trembled. "Do you want to grab dinner tonight?"

"Yes. Good timing. The girls have a sleepover." The pulse in Jenna's throat tingled. Even though they were strictly platonic, excitement still overcame her.

****

While Jenna worked, she kept peering at Claudine. The pull of the woman disoriented her like a stalker on social media, careful not to "like" any posts.

Claudine glanced over her shoulder and winked. Jenna flushed and reverted to the screen. Her body emitted enough heat to illuminate the entire office.

A message flashed on the phone.

—Hahaha. My bad.—

She shook her head at Marco's response to the aftermaths of his text popping up on the TV. He always found her public embarrassment funny. To her surprise, he didn't react to her almost disclosing Claudine. He must really want her back.

Recalling Claudine mentioning the bag thief this morning, she opened the app to track the stolen phone, not having checked the status in days. Guilt settled in her stomach at someone else getting robbed.

A red dot blinked on the map. Her previous cell was near Le Morning Sunshine. Breathless, she sprang from the seat and charged the four steps to Claudine.

Her colleague twirled in her chair. "Where's the fire?"

Jenna held out the cell and pointed to the flashing bright icon.

Claudine jumped up. "Oh, my God."

Jenna followed Claudine out of the office. The icy wind smacked Jenna's face. Realizing she forgot her jacket, she rubbed her arms.

"Shouldn't we call the police?" Jenna wished she hadn't worn heels with a winter dress today as she dashed past contemporary and historic skyscrapers.

Claudine grabbed her hand. They sidestepped a puddle. "Today is the first time the location on your old phone has turned on. By the time the cops arrive, the creep might be long gone."

"Fair point." She checked the cell again. The flashing mark traveled on the map. "Looks like he's heading toward the BART."

"Let's split up and corner him."

"He might be dangerous."

"Not in the middle of the day among crowds of people. He has only stolen in the past." Claudine pointed left. "I'll go this way." She hurried to the direction.

"Be careful." Jenna called after her. She halted for the Muni bus to go by and continued. Maybe Claudine had a point about trapping him. Last time, he disappeared down an alleyway.

Fifteen minutes later, she closed the distance between her and the thief. A tallish medium-framed guy wearing a black hoodie crossed the road. He might not be the right person. Many men fit the same description.

He slipped into a lane.

She rounded the corner. The guy walked to another man and held a phone. A star sticker displayed in the center. *Her* cell. Keisha had stuck on the hard-to-remove sticker.

"You have my phone, asshole," Jenna blurted

before she could stop herself.

The man turned, spotted her, and sprinted off.

The buyer's brows raised. "I did not know the phone was stolen."

She chased after the fleeing bandit. A foolish idea but she was determined to claim her property.

Claudine appeared at the end of the alley.

Trapped in the middle, the stranger twirled toward Jenna and then back to Claudine. His hood fell off to reveal wavy ash-brown hair and a face appearing in his late twenties.

Claudine stepped back. "Damien?"

"Hello, Claudine." Damien's wide lips tipped up to a smirk.

Jenna glanced back and forth between them. "You know this guy?"

"We worked at TMC Investments together before my layoff." Claudine's glare sliced through him. "Funny career choice, resorting to theft."

Jenna's eyebrows shot up, heart wedged in her throat. TMC was Stone Corp's rival company. "Did you target me last year?"

His face schooled to neutral, lips in a firm line.

Jenna stalked over and twisted his arms behind his back and forced them upward. The times Marco taught her and their daughters self-defense came in handy right now.

Damien yelped, "I'll lose my job."

She yanked him tighter to the point his arms might break.

Dampness formed at the back of his neck. "Fine. I heard you were developing AnaStone and you carried details on a USB stick."

Claudine pulled her phone from her pocket and grabbed Damien with her other hand. "I'm calling the cops."

Jenna frowned, her heart thrashing like a caged animal. Someone at work must have informed him she saved data on a portable device. "Who put you up to the thefts?"

Damien hesitated.

Tightening her grip, she forced more pressure into his arm. Meanwhile, Claudine held firm on his other arm and explained their location on the phone. People walked by and pointed. Jenna gave them her best, "there's nothing to see here" smile.

He struggled in her grasp. "I acted on my own accord. Thought I'd be promoted."

His inflicted tone gave away his lie.

Claudine lowered the cell. "The cops are coming in a few minutes. Two officers are having their lunch break nearby."

"Good." Jenna nodded. Before she had the chance to question Damien further, sirens echoed the alleyway. A police car rounded the corner, sped up, and parked in the lane.

Chapter Sixteen

"Cheers. We caught him. I'm still shocked he's someone I know." Claudine raised a wine glass.

Jenna and Claudine celebrated after work in the rustic, country-style bar. A gigantic American flag hung on the brick wall in front. In the far-right corner, diners clapped and whistled at the woman in her fifties wearing a baby-pink power suit riding the mechanical bull.

"I still believe TMC Investments pulled the strings. No way he acted alone." Jenna frowned, raising the red wine glass to clink glasses.

A huge coincidence Claudine had worked with the guy. Knowing the tampering occurred before Claudine had joined Stone Corp, Jenna was relieved. Today's encounter changed everything. Maybe Claudine was a plant. Through their fifteen-minute police interaction, they learned Damien had attempted to find AnaStone information on her cell. When his attempts didn't work, he did a factory reset to sell the device. Luckily, he hadn't completed the action properly, which allowed Jenna to locate the phone. The police had taken him away for more questioning. Jenna informed Hayley and Sebastian right away.

Claudine shrugged. "Probably."

A server in a black cowboy hat burst through the wooden saloon doors and marched toward their table booth holding a tray of sizzling chicken wings. Fat dribbled out of the pan and onto the tray, the chargrilled barbecue aroma wafting to her nose. He set the wings and a bowl of mac and cheese onto their table and asked if they needed anything else. She and Claudine answered, "No," in unison. He left.

Jenna's mouth salivated, not having enjoyed good old-fashioned southern comfort food in months. She spooned mac and cheese onto her plate. "Why did Damien risk jail time for a job? The whole situation is fishy."

"Agreed." Claudine shifted in her seat and stabbed a wing with a fork. "Anyway, tell me a story no one knows."

Claudine obviously changed the subject. Maybe she was a little shaken her previous employer went to risky lengths for their own agenda. Although they had a deep and meaningful conversation, and Claudine appeared direct, Jenna might not know her in the slightest. An unease settled in her stomach. "Are you okay?"

"Yeah, I'm tired." Claudine rubbed her temples. "Are you avoiding my question to divulge your intimate secrets?"

Claudine hid information. Definitely. She knew a thief working for their employer's rival. Possibly a coincidence but a big one.

"Umm…I have an irrational hatred for French fries." Jenna kept the conversation light and casual for Claudine to open up. You caught more flies with honey than vinegar. She'd speak to Claudine again later.

Claudine spluttered on her wine. "What? Why?"

"Fries' shape and texture remind me of long,

creepy fingers." Jenna shuddered. "What about you?"

"Well...I don't have any illogical loathing for foods most people like."

"A family memory, then." Jenna was curious, considering Claudine's parents kicked her out of their home.

Claudine picked at the chicken. "When I was younger, I asked my dad's permission to use the computer."

"Doesn't sound too bad."

"Within thirty minutes, Dad came into the room and said, 'I think you have had enough screen time.' Dad instructed me to unplug every cable, and he hid the computer somewhere."

Jenna's hand halted halfway between her plate and mouth, a chicken piece falling off the fork. "Hmm...umm..."

"You can say the words. My family's a bit strange. Who bothered to hide a whole computer? Especially since technology has always been one of my passions." Claudine laughed. "Whenever I wanted the computer back, I asked Dad's permission to be distracted for a while. My parents were strict."

Jenna's lips parted wide enough to post an envelope through them. For a man who acted so bizarrely over technology, it wasn't a far stretch to see why he'd booted his lesbian daughter from the family. "I...hmm..."

Claudine patted her hand. "Wow, the story has put a downer on the night. Don't worry. My family has their...quirks, but they've made me who I am today."

With the intensity of Claudine's gaze, Jenna was suddenly aware of every detail in the room. From the end of her dress swishing her ankles to the way her thought process hiccupped.

A wild cheer exploded through the pub. Jenna and Claudine turned. A middle-aged man had fallen off the mechanical bull.

A guy with a goatee wearing a light brown cowboy hat swaggered onto the stage. "Anyone else like to ride the bull? Last for over ten seconds and win a free drink."

People hooted, but no one raised their hand.

Claudine inclined her head. "You should volunteer."

"In this dress?" Jenna beckoned to her outfit. "No way."

Claudine raised her hand. "Chicken. I'm wearing a skirt." She stood. "I'll try."

The host pointed and nodded to Claudine. She sauntered to the front and elegantly swung one leg over the beast. Her skirt rose, revealing creamy legs.

Jenna followed for a better view. Her chest exploded in heat. This woman was fearless.

Claudine gripped the bull with her thighs and held out one hand, palm flat.

The cowboy tapped the stopwatch he held. "Starting in three, two, one."

The machine whirred to life.

Jenna's heart stuttered. Claudine rocked back and forth, back and forth, real slow. How she yearned to kneel in front of Claudine's legs, spreading her inner thighs to keep them open.

The host held out two fingers. "Two seconds."

Some male patrons leaned closer in their chairs, hypnotized like rodents before a cobra.

"Five seconds."

A surge of pride shot through Jenna's body. Claudine sure rode the bull well. The pace sped up. She hung on tight.

"Eight seconds."

Jenna's pulse tripped. Claudine slipped but swung back up, closing in on her goal. The bull jerked and thrashed, tossing Claudine and flinging her to the ground.

Gasping, Jenna climbed into the ring and helped her up. "I'm impressed."

Claudine winked. "If a little riding impressed you, you ain't seen nothing yet." She turned to the host. "Well? What was my time?"

The guy checked the stopwatch. "Ten point oh two seconds."

Claudine squealed, jumping up and down. Jenna clutched Claudine's waist, abandoning doubts about her friend's connection to the robber. Finally, someone had a win, even if the prize was only a free drink.

But Claudine gave Jenna reasons to doubt her. She needed a plan to finally prove her guilt or innocence.

****

"I had a fantastic time tonight." Claudine held Jenna's hands outside the restaurant. Wooden planks lined the exterior and a red neon sign glowed, *Southern Charm and BBQ*.

People lingered in a small group nearby, puffing cigarettes and chatting, saying their goodbyes. Jenna held her breath to prevent inhaling smoke.

"Come to my place for dessert?" Claudine stroked Jenna's hand with her thumbs.

Jenna's heart leaped, but the earlier capture of the

crook squeezed and pinched her stomach. She couldn't spend more personal time with Claudine or anyone else at Stone Corp without proving they didn't take part in illicit activities. "I better not. I have an early start tomorrow."

Claudine's face fell. She bit her lip and kissed Jenna's hand. "Totally fine. I'll see you in the morning." Walking over to the bicycle locked in front of the restaurant, she lifted the helmet and fastened it over her head. She had changed her clothes in the women's restroom.

Jenna's brows furrowed. "Will you be okay getting home? It's almost ten already."

"Absolutely." Claudine blew her a kiss before she rode off.

Jenna exhaled. Claudine was disappointed, but Jenna had too much information to dissect. She strolled to the curb to signal a cab. A tall, muscular man with a shaved head marched ahead.

"Marco?" She called out, hurrying to his direction.

The guy turned. Piercing blue eyes stared back at her. Marco's was dark brown.

"Sorry, my mistake." She shrugged in apology. The man smiled and continued.

The stranger jogged her memory. Marco guarded his upcoming activities at their daughters' play. Searching her handbag, she found her cell. When married, they had synced their phones' location and events. The app allowed them to coordinate the kids easier, and Marco often lost his cell.

Hopefully, the notification wouldn't pop up on his phone. An invasion of privacy, but he might be in trouble. Sometimes he had bruises underneath his clothes. He always shrugged off her questions and claimed clumsiness at work. Maybe someone was hurting him.

She opened the map. Her ribs seared with pressure at checking up on him. Marco's phone was three blocks away.

She raced, passing restaurants, bars, and shops. A familiar swagger and olive skin appeared. "Marco?"

He didn't turn or pause—must not have heard her. His feet dragged and shoulders sagged as he entered a slipway.

She followed. "Marco."

He strode through a black door. Cheers and hisses echoed from the other side. A bearded man with a beanie and a bullring between his nostrils stood at the entrance behind a counter. He served two guys with ratty, long hair.

Heaviness weighed in her stomach. She bought a ticket and braced herself for the night ahead.

****

The audience in the boxing ring scoffed and jeered, stamping hard on the ground in a fast and steady rhythm. Vibrations rumbled at the soles of Marco's feet. His heart thumped like a trapped fly as he circled Joaquin "Dippy Dog" Barker. He had cursed when he laid eyes on the other man in the ring. His opponent's identity hadn't been revealed until tonight. The crowd demanded a rematch, but Marco hadn't attacked yet and dodged every strike.

He didn't wish to fight anymore—too tired and his life was looking up. Maybe if he kept avoiding Joaquin, he'd bore him to sleep. No harm in wishful thinking.

Joaquin attempted a jab. Marco bent his knees and

185

shifted to the right.

The crowd heckled, giving the thumbs-down sign. "Boooo."

Joaquin advanced toward him, backing him into a corner. No escaping. The room revolved around Marco like a merry-go-round, his breath choppy.

As Joaquin's punch arrived, Marco delivered a sharp, lateral, open-handed blow to his enemy's forearm, deflecting the hit. Marco adjusted his rear hand to cross his body, rotating his stance counterclockwise. His straight punch landed on the other man's stomach.

Joaquin groaned and stumbled to his knees.

Marco hit again, then two, three, four. Drops of sweat flew off his face. As much as he hated to admit it, adrenaline still rushed through him with the satisfying thud of his fists striking flesh.

A man with a widow's peak hairline banged the cage. "Get up, Dippy Dog."

As if operated by a remote control, Joaquin staggered as he stood.

Marco cracked his neck left to right, bouncing on the balls of his feet. He held his clenched hands up, chin tucked in, one elbow protecting his ribcage.

"Marco." A familiar appealing voice had him spinning to find the source. The tone was frantic and hoarse.

He spotted dark curly hair at the seventh row. His chest wringed out like a lemon on a squeezer.

Jenna stared, her face performing robust gymnastics.

A loud smack settled on his jaw. He fell. The ground spiraled up to greet his head, and his vision faded into oblivion.

Chapter Seventeen

The spare bedroom in Jenna's house was blue. An ocean painting hung on the sky-blue wallpaper, the bed covered in navy-blue Egyptian cotton sheets, and little plants filled aqua-blue pots on the windowsill. The space induced calmness—the complete opposite of her current mood.

Her shoulders still hadn't lost the tension as she placed an ice pack on Marco's swollen jaw. "What have you gotten yourself into? Why do something so stupid and dangerous?"

He lay bare-chested on the bed. Despite the eagle tattoo on his upper body, his injuries won in the color department.

Luckily, the kids were at a friend's sleepover. Their father was in a terrible state. He had refused to go to hospital, claiming the injuries were bruises and superficial wounds. But the earlier revelations tonight…Marco beating the crap out of someone and getting pummeled in return.

Although BDSM fascinated her in the past, his fighting was on another level. She had gaped for minutes like someone burned by a hot pan, not registering the pain at first. Emotions swamped her tonight. First disbelief, then anger, and now confusion. He must be in worse emotional shape than she thought to compete in a vicious, illegal boxing match.

Marco winced, shifting on the bed. "Tonight was the last time. I couldn't quit without settling the score with the organizer."

She fluffed up the duck–feather pillows. "What possessed you to fight in the first place?"

"When I returned from Afghanistan, I was numb. I didn't feel emotion. Especially after I started antidepressants."

Jenna weaved. Her heart ached like someone scraped her against sandpaper. "Why didn't you tell me you were on medication?"

"Embarrassed, I guess. I didn't want you to think I couldn't look after you or the girls."

"You have been through a lot. I understand. No shame in receiving help."

He must've believed he had no one to turn to, bottling up his traumas. A screw twisted in her stomach. She was still his wife and hadn't aided him. Maybe she was an insensitive bitch.

"I thought I could handle myself." Marco stroked the back of her hand. "None of my actions are on you."

Her eyes pricked. She stared up at the ceiling, draining the moisture back down.

"I'll grab you more water and painkillers." Swallowing the lump in her throat, she picked up his empty glass from the ash timber bedside table. "Please rest."

She stumbled out of the room, her body rocking. Two warm trails from her eyes dripped to her jaw. He needed her while Claudine and her job distracted her. She was a terrible person. Although she couldn't be with him out of obligation, maybe she didn't deserve anyone. Wishing her life wasn't such a mess, she covered her face with her hands.

****

Marco and Claudine sat on the edge of Jenna's bed. Jenna stepped between them, wearing a quarter-cup royal-purple bra and matching thong. Black suspenders held up her sheer stockings.

She placed one hand on Marco's left shoulder, the other on Claudine's right. Tension gripped her body.

"Choose one of us." Marco stood, but Jenna nudged him back down. His bare torso glistened, and his chest, his glorious, tattooed chest, rippled beneath her fingertips. No other man displayed his level of pure masculine perfection.

"Surely you know if you desire me or not." Claudine slid her white lacy bra strap down her left shoulder. Her breasts overflowed from the cups held together by a tiny bow. Her lips were full, a slight dimple on the bottom. Jenna wanted to tug at that lip, to nibble on Claudine's flesh until she moaned.

"Is there a reason I can't have it all?" Jenna shoved Marco and Claudine onto their backs, one leg on top of them each. Heat and moisture rushed straight to her core.

Claudine's eyes glinted. "Good point. The more the merrier."

Marco flipped Jenna onto her back. "Triple the fun."

Jenna's heart slammed against her ribs. Her tongue snaked across her lips.

Marco stayed on her left side, brushing his lips against her neck. Claudine traced her fingers up and down Jenna's right arm. Together, they slithered down Jenna's bra cups to reveal her nipples. Her breasts peaked, her skin prickling. Sweat broke out on her top lip.

Her two lovers gave one another a knowing look before they faced her. They leaned over and sucked on a nipple each.

Their beauty dazzled her, shining brightly. Letting out a shuddering breath, she squeezed her eyes shut like she had looked into the sun. Her body thrummed. Fully prepared for a delicious night ahead, she arched her back.

****

Jenna woke with a start, gasping for air. Her heartbeat bounced like a jackrabbit. Over and over again. Her gaze adjusted to the darkness. She lay alone in bed, clutching the blanket in a white-knuckled grip. Sweat clung to the back of her top. Usually, her sole fantasy about two people at once involved one person cooking and the other cleaning.

Her mouth dry, she blew out a slow controlled breath. Marco was in pain, but she was orgasming in her sleep about threesomes. Swallowing, she tried to keep moisture in her mouth. She climbed out of bed and padded barefoot to the kitchen. Grabbing a water bottle from the fridge, she took big gulps. The cool liquid soothed her burning throat.

Too wired to sleep, she switched on the light and pulled eggs and butter from the fridge and dry ingredients from the cupboard. She set to work baking her family's scones, mulling over her problems.

Maybe she should start applying for jobs. She was in over her head. More importantly, tonight's illegal boxing match might not be Marco's last.

When the scones were in the oven, a terrified yell

erupted from the spare room.

She raced to Marco.

"Get out of here. A trap." Marco tossed and turned in bed.

She switched on the bedside lamp. His face twisted in angst. Sweat beads trickled from his forehead to his neck. "No. No. No. We're going to die. He has a bomb."

Jenna shook his shoulder, her heart bleeding. "Marco. Wake up."

His eyes opened, wild and lethal. He sprang up, thrashing on the spot.

Jumping back, she lost her balance and slipped to the floor.

His Adam's apple bobbed, his chest heaving in violent bursts. He'd had bad dreams in the past, but he was never this out of touch.

She clambered to her feet and shuffled onto the bed to face him. "You're dreaming. Take deep breaths. You're okay." Beckoning to her mouth, she inhaled visibly. "Breathe with me."

He copied her. They breathed in sync.

His shoulders quivered. "I was…back there. My fault. Every injury my fault."

Tonight was the first time he uttered his deployment horrors. Normally, he described the more fun times—a PTSD sign from the information she'd read.

She held onto his hands, brushing her thumbs against his knuckles. "Breathe. Think of our Vanuatu honeymoon. Remember Champagne Beach? The water glistened a deep blue. Palm trees swayed. We had grilled butter lobster most nights for dinner."

His gaze scooted around the room like he was deciphering his location. Raising a hand, he cupped her cheek. "Did I hurt you?"

"No, I'm fine. You suddenly waking up startled me, and I stumbled."

"I could've harmed you." He shifted away and hugged his knees to his chest.

"You didn't." She closed their distance. "Do you want to talk about your nightmare?"

Hesitating, he closed his eyes. She waited for him to crack a joke like he often did.

His eyes fluttered open, and he straightened his legs. "We found a boy in Afghanistan. Alone. I took the kid with us. He looked six or seven. I didn't realize he had a bomb."

Her chest chilled. No child had access to an explosive device. "Did someone force him into carrying one?"

"Who knows?" Marco rubbed his eyes like the story exhausted him. His right leg shook. "Colin was closest. He didn't survive. His wife is a widow, and his three kids will grow up without a father." He averted his gaze. "You can yell at me. Hate me. I deserve the consequences."

Jenna yanked him into a tight embrace and held him for a long minute, rocking him and stroking his back. When she tore away, she lifted his chin. "Not your fault. Do you hear me? Not your fault."

"How can you believe that?" His voice quaked out with raw emotion.

"You did your best. No one could've predicted the attack."

He had a permanent mask up since he'd arrived

home—must be exhausting to carry his burden for the last few years. While they were together, she tried over and over again to break through to him, but nothing worked. He had almost become a different person.

"I was in charge."

"Doesn't matter. You don't think anyone else would've trusted the boy?" She peppered his face with kisses, lips against the salty tears on his chiseled cheeks. "Beneath your tough guy exterior, tattoos, and muscles, you have the biggest heart. One of the first qualities I loved about you."

"Loved?" Marco's face fell, but he kept his gaze on hers with full intensity. "I made awful mistakes. Do you think you could love me again?"

Her mind sifted through every event that happened between them. In the past months, she had occasionally researched PTSD and appreciated his point of view.

"Not impossible," she whispered, unable to answer the question.

In reality, she didn't think she ever stopped loving him.

****

"What do you think of the psychiatrist here?" Marco sat in the family room, fiddling on Jenna's laptop. He dragged in a breath. Deeper. Tilted his neck side to side. Tested his pain. Sore and stiff, but he'd live. His hand trembled on the mouse.

"Of what? Will you be okay when I go to work, by the way? I'll cook dinner when I'm home." Jenna swung a blazer over her shoulders and slid the silver bracelet with a ballerina pendant on her left wrist. A pearl brooch fastened on her shirt collar. He loved watching her get ready. Every movement was elegant as she glided across the floor to the kitchen.

She picked up a bowl of muesli he had prepared. He used to do these small gestures when he lived here—have breakfast waiting—and he enjoyed spoiling her again.

Marco rubbed his eyes and rested his hands on his stomach, quelling the rising nausea from the computer's contents. "Of course. I'll pick up the girls from school if you don't mind. I have today off. Quality time with them always calms me to a better place."

"Sure." She walked over and peered at the screen. A website described trauma counseling. Her eyes broadened. "Are you seriously thinking of going? You never believed in psychology stuff."

He'd always laughed at the idea of professional help, claiming a good night's sleep or watching sports would fix him. What a dumbass. Last night was a wake-up call. His heart had stopped when Jenna tripped, and he spent the morning researching the other counselor his doctor previously recommended.

A tinge of hope simmered inside him at the positive reviews. Yet his chest still weighed him down at attending. The clinic offered after-hour appointments, though. No excuses.

"I wouldn't have been able to live with myself if I'd hurt you." He clicked onto the appointment's tab, choosing the six in the evening spot for tomorrow.

"Don't beat yourself up."

"I do."

She wrapped her arms around his neck. "I'm proud of you."

Her warmth soothed him. He hit the "confirm" button.

****

Chatter, footsteps, and ringing phones filled the office, drowning out Jenna's thoughts as she walked inside. She held a plate of the scones she baked last night—ended up with too many.

"Scone, Claudine? These scones are *the* family recipe passed down from my great, great grandmother, originally from England." She pointed to the pieces of heaven.

Claudine's eyes lit up. She picked one at the front and spooned cream and jam from the small compartments. "Finally." Nibbling at the end, she closed her eyes for a second. "Oh, my God. The scone is like eating sunshine. Tell me the ingredients."

"Sorry, Mom is insistent the method stays in the family." Jenna set the plate on her desk.

"Please, please, please."

"Mom's too scary to go up against." Jenna opened the proposal on the computer. "Did you hear any info about the purse snatcher yet?"

"Aww, I taste a spice I can't put my finger on." Claudine crossed her legs and took a bigger bite. "Not yet about Damien, you?"

"No." Jenna had waited by the phone for the police to ring, but no luck. She'd have to follow up. "How are you with the thief being someone you know?"

"A bit freaked out. We were friendly. It shows you never really know a person."

Jenna pondered the words. Maybe she did not know Claudine. Every time she dug deeper, Claudine never gave an inch. "Look, I'm in serious trouble with the AnaStone business. Do you have any clue who is infiltrating the system?"

Claudine's gaze flickered, and she leaned back. "I'll ask my previous colleagues about Damien. Keep you updated."

A snake curled in Jenna's stomach, tightening around her organs. Whatever Claudine's secret, she must find out. Fast. Even with less–than–savory means.

Hayley sauntered to their desk pod. "Can I grab you for a sec, Claudine? Andy requested clarification on the next steps for Bank of the People."

"Sure." Claudine plopped the scone on the desk and followed Hayley toward the elevators.

Jenna stretched her arms behind her back, eyes twitching from tiredness. When she asked the sky this morning if her existence could get any worse, it was a rhetorical question.

She checked her email. Angie had sent a meeting request thirty minutes ago titled, "Jenna and Sebastian catch–up."

In the body, Angie wrote:

"Apologies for the few reschedules. I hope the afternoon time on Thursday suits you. Please prepare an AnaStone update. Sebastian wishes to discuss your role going forward."

Jenna's blood frosted, her breathing rapid and disjointed. Angie's words had implications. Her throat constricted. She sat immobilized. When she glanced at the time, an hour had drifted by. She stood, needing to leave the desk. Perhaps a green tea might soothe her soul. Gaze unfocused, she hobbled her way to the kitchen.

Voices exploded inside the meeting room. She recognized Claudine's husky tone arguing with Angie. Jenna stepped closer as the volume raised.

"You can't do this." Angie's words rushed out.

"Watch me." Claudine snorted but somehow the sound was still ladylike.

Brows furrowed, Jenna's ear glued to the door. Angie had never been angry at work.

"You're nowhere near as smart as you think you are," Angie seethed. "What you're doing is wrong."

"We have different opinions on the word 'wrong,' then." Claudine sniffed. "You'll regret this."

Footsteps clipped toward the door. Jenna sprang away and hid behind the fridge. The door opened. Jenna peeked around the corner. Claudine's lips were set in a firm line, shoulders trembling. She headed to the stairs. Angie cowered in a chair.

Bile rose to Jenna's throat. Claudine threatened Sebastian's sweet assistant. She should call a mathematician because none of this added up. Perhaps Angie discovered information Claudine didn't want disclosed? Angie was loyal to Sebastian and Stone Corp and would hate for someone to not have their best interests.

Jenna clenched her hands. Jobs were at stake, and she must investigate every avenue. Maybe Claudine tricked her into securing a Stone Corp role. Befriended her to gain her trust or orchestrated the bag snatching to meet. The idea repulsed her. Hopefully, Claudine and Angie's problems were personal and had nothing to do with AnaStone.

Shoulders drooping, she marched back to her desk. She slid out the cabinet's bottom shelf and whipped out a USB spyware stick in case of an emergency. The plan was unethical, not to mention illegal. No turning back once trust was broken. Guilt roiled in her stomach.

Overhearing the conversation confirmed the next step.

She crept to Claudine's desk, turned her head left and right to check no one watched her, and stuck the USB into the computer slot. Her job had become worse than a toothbrush being in someone's mouth. No, she was equivalent of toilet paper.

A minute slinked by before she tugged the gadget out. Now, she'd not only see every action Claudine did on AnaStone, but also on her workstation. Lucky Jenna had been a tech nerd her whole life and gained the expertise to handle the software.

She couldn't believe someone's words anymore and must spy on the people with AnaStone access— Tina, Desiree, Nathan, Angie, Sebastian, Sandeep, Vanessa, and Hayley. She hesitated at Sebastian, the CEO. He had no motive. If he discovered she snooped on him, she'd be in serious trouble. Mentally, she struck him off the list. She considered her close team members, Vanessa and Hayley. Vanessa was a dear friend, and she had known Hayley for years. She must include them no matter her affections.

A silent cry burned her throat. Small devious device in hand, she walked to Desiree's desk to check she was away.

Chapter Eighteen

The door clicked open. Keisha and Eve climbed into the back of Marco's white sedan.

"How was your day?" Marco tugged up the jacket collar and wrapped the scarf tighter to cover his injuries. After the kids buckled their seat belts, he drove out of the blue metal gates. He was right this morning—their sweet faces swelled his heart.

"Okay." From the rearview mirror, Keisha fiddled with a braided friendship bracelet.

He switched on the heater. "Only okay? What did you learn?"

"Stuff." Eve leaned against the window, yawning. The cold weather brought out her lethargy.

"Wow, you've really painted the picture for me. I feel like I was right there." Chuckling, he slowed at the traffic lights and faced them. "Tell me a highlight, then."

"At school assembly, the principal asked us to think of one thing we're grateful for. So we appreciate our life." Keisha let out her long, dark locks from her high ponytail. His two daughters looked more and more like their mother every day. He'd have to be shotgun ready when they became teenagers.

"Great idea. What did you both decide?"

"I'm happy to see you more," Eve said.

He stretched and patted Eve's leg. Spending more

time together the last couple of months had been a blessing. His daughters were his best creation, and they still surprised him. He faced the front. The lights turned green. He eased on the gas pedal. "Very sweet."

"I chose Mom's cooking," Keisha said. "What is yours, Dad?"

Contemplating the question, he lifted his left hand and stroked his jaw.

They drove past a park. Smiling kids played on the swings while a golden retriever kept a watchful eye.

He had a lot to be grateful for, including the luxury of admiring the surroundings on the drive. His war experiences offered more awareness on life's small pleasures. He never considered his turmoil to be a positive. Often, he fumbled through the day like someone had switched off the light in his mind. Maybe he'd take a leaf out of the school's book and also focus on his blessings.

Glancing up at the sky, he murmured, "I'm grateful for the soft edges, faded colors, and all-out darkness. Now I can use every sense I have to navigate."

****

Jenna stirred the vegetables while Marco set the table. The rich smell of black bean sauce simmered through the house. It was good to be home after a stressful day. She enjoyed spending time with the family.

The kids sat on the couch reading books, absorbed in their own little world. Scruffy slept at Keisha's feet.

Marco wiped the table. "What's on your Santa wish list?"

Keisha peered up from a junior chapter book and rolled her eyes.

Eve giggled. "Secret, so my wish comes true."

"We'll set up the Christmas tree after dinner." Remorse rolled in Jenna's stomach. Too busy with work, she had neglected the tree decorating tradition on December first.

Her phone beeped. An email preview from Sandeep displayed on the screen. "Jenna, this is urge…"

Her cell screen blackened. "Dammit."

"What's wrong?" Marco lifted his head. Cutlery clanged on the table.

"My cell died, and my boss's boss is on the warpath."

"Can you ignore him? It's dinner time."

"He has some terrible habits. Existing is one." She added more ginger. "I better reply."

He strode over. "Is your work okay?"

Shoulders slumping, she exhaled, long and slow. He looked at her with such concern she confided in him again. "One colleague is hacking into AnaStone. I need to figure out who, or I may not have a job by the end."

Marco's brows knitted together. "Holy shit. What are your next steps?"

"Don't ask." Her insides flipped at resorting to the USB spyware, but her co-workers kept giving her more and more reasons not to trust them.

He secured a hand on her shoulder. "You're not alone, you know? I doubt you'll end up losing your job, but for the worst-case scenario, I've got your back."

Relaxing into his touch, she squeezed his hand. Of course, he'd support her and the girls.

He indicated a finger for her to scoot from the stove. "I'll take over the cooking while you handle work."

"Nah, I like the sauce prepared a certain way." She waved him off and tossed the food in the wok with a spatula. "Can you please grab my phone charger from our…the bedroom?"

"Sure." With a soft smile, he strolled away.

Slip of the tongue to say, "our bedroom." Frowning, Jenna chopped the chicken with more aggression than usual. Sandeep had found another reason to criticize. Her heart sank to her feet. She did every action within her power. Not her fault someone played the system.

No…she refused to check his email until tomorrow or she'd obsess over each word. Hopefully by the morning, she'd either have some answers with the spyware or she'd discover it was *International Slap Your Annoying Co-workers Day*. Her first order of business would be Sandeep.

Heavy footsteps entered the kitchen.

She faced Marco. "I thought you got lost. You took ages."

He clasped a black cable. "I had trouble finding your charger but discovered these." He held out a bag loaded with the whip, rope, handcuffs, and metal balls.

Mortification flooded through her body. Her hands twitched to snatch the bag. She lowered the stove's heat, grabbed his arm, and nudged him into the pantry. "Hide that before the girls see."

"I understand we agreed to date other people. But…actually, don't tell me." He stashed the bag on one shelf as though the contents were poison. "I…I hope he's no one I know."

"No." The single word shot out like a cannon. "I

need to tell you about the last few weeks, but you might not like it."

"What?"

She averted her gaze. No more secrets. Panic scraped her throat. She forced the words out. "I kissed someone else."

He stepped back. His eyes hardened. Air expelled between his teeth. "It's okay. You mentioned more than once we weren't exclusive. I kinda guessed, although it hurts for you to confirm my instincts."

Jenna let out a sharp breath. He was more understanding than she assumed.

His jaw clenched. "Who is he?"

Now was the moment to tell him. She broke eye contact, but she must be open and honest. Slowly, she met his gaze. "Actually, 'he' was a 'she.' "

Marco's mouth opened, then closed. Brows rose and fell. Eyes widened. "I wasn't expecting that."

"I know."

"No, I mean…must've been hard to explore another side of yourself, given your strict family." He leaned his forehead against hers. They stayed connected for several long seconds. She closed her eyes until he spoke. "Brave, beautiful girl."

"I didn't realize I was bisexual until this year. You're not weirded out?"

"I'm jealous as hell and want to punch the wall. Also, relieved you didn't sleep with anyone. But do I mind you're bisexual? Fuck no. What do you take me for? You're still you." He brushed his lips against hers. "The woman who orders extra rolls at restaurants because I eat every last one."

She savored his words, his scent, the solidness of

his body. He knew her too well and considered the mixed emotions she experienced.

He held her hands. "Have you used these toys with this woman?"

"No, not on anyone." She shuffled on her feet. "I was curious."

"Why didn't you tell me?"

"The fantasy is…strange."

"Not weird." His lips tugged into a shadow of a smile. "Since my discharge, my life fell apart, and I had no control. I'm up for some fun if you are."

"Really? You're still injured." Tension wound up tight in her body. Her skin flushed hotter than freshly brewed coffee.

"I'm fine." He kissed her briefly on the lips. "Tonight. Be ready."

****

Jenna had never tucked her kids to bed faster in her life. A weight had lifted off her shoulders after confiding in Marco. He was amazing and understanding and empathetic.

Marco supervised the girls brushing their teeth while she ironed and set their clothes out for tomorrow. She shivered even though the heater was on. Warmth suffused her body every time she considered the naughty toys. Her work worries dwindled to the back of her mind.

In her room, she prepared strawberries, truffles, and a whipped cream can on a platter and placed the tray on the bed. She picked up the tall gold perfume bottle and sprayed her wrists and neck. The violet scent always drove Marco wild. Tealight candles sparkled on the bedside tables. The toy bag sat in the corner of the room.

She deliberated the teddy in the wardrobe. Her lips tipped. A mischievous idea entered her mind. Removing her clothes, she lifted the whipped cream and sprayed it over her breasts and down *there*. The cold texture tingled her skin. She stuck half strawberries over her nipples. A giggle caught at her throat, wondering Marco's reaction.

Careful not to get food on the silver thousand thread count sheets, she rested on the bed. With cautious movements, she adjusted her position into the most seductive stance imaginable. One elbow on the mattress, she leaned on her side, relaxing her chin on her palm. The pose screamed 1960s porn star, and the whipped cream started to melt, running down her stomach.

She held the position, arms shaking. Knowing Marco, he was reading Eve's latest book obsession about the girls in a boarding school. Sighing, she leaned over to select a chocolate and popped the sweet into her mouth. The sticky caramel stuck her teeth together, and she struggled to chew.

Marco entered the room. The door thudded behind him.

She twisted her body to revert to the pose. Stumbling, she banged the tray. The platter jumped, and the contents fell back down in place. Lucky.

Marco chuckled and dropped his voice to a low and sexy whisper. "I wasn't expecting this type of welcome."

"I meant to be seductive."

His gaze flared over her breasts. "Believe me, you are."

He walked slowly to her like he savored the moment. But she wanted him here, right now. She suppressed a groan burning at the back of her throat.

"Lie on your back." He grabbed the rope from the bag. Fumbling, he raised her left hand and tied her wrist to the bedpost. He shifted to the other side and did the same with her right hand.

Jenna writhed against the restraints and gasped. He needed this, and so did she. For her, she submitted to someone while her job taunted her. For him, he longed to experience safety in the world. In some strange way, they both grabbed their power back.

His gaze held a gentle concern. "You okay?"

Too turned on to speak, she nodded, the space between her legs slick.

He smiled and shuffled lower, tying her feet apart. Her arms and legs stretched out to mimic a starfish. Heat curled her spine like a ribbon.

His gaze roamed from her head to her toes, and she squirmed under his scrutiny.

"I love you spread out nice and wide for me." Marco leaned over, licking the cream off her breasts, tongue gliding over her delicate skin. He sucked off the strawberries one by one.

Eager to touch him, her hands struggled against the restraints. The ropes held her tight, exciting her more. Too, too, too keyed up, any contact might tip her over the edge.

Cream still on his lips, he kissed her. He slipped his tongue into her mouth, reminding her of his cock also sliding easily into her. Their tongues tangled. He sucked and bit her bottom lip. She reached out. Every time she tried to wrap her arms around him, the rope held her down.

His mouth drifted back to her breasts, licking every last bit of cream. Arching her back, she thrust toward him. He sucked on her left nipple like she was the greatest treat on earth.

Jenna's pulse tripped in her throat. Brushing his lips over her stomach, he licked her belly button in small circles. Body wriggling against the ropes, she let out a strangled sound.

He grinned in a boyish way. "Hold still." His mouth drifted lower and lower, achingly slow, close to her sweet spot. He swerved to her ankles.

Her skin buzzed. "What are you doing? Get to the good part."

"I kinda like you laid out like this. No choice but to accept my every demand." His tongue wetted his lips as he spoke. Oh, she loved his voice—the rich velvet, and his seductive dips and growls.

He lifted her leg a little, stretching the rope between her foot and the bed, and licked his way up her calf. Lowering her leg, he grabbed her other one and continued the slow seduction.

Her leg almost buckled in his hand. His mouth finally clasped her burning core, and he licked the cream. If she knew the cream would've acted as a barrier to her sensitive spot, she would've never sprayed it on. She was like water held tight against a dam, bursting to escape.

Groaning against her, Marco took his time to lap up the cream. Vibrations quaked up her body. Her heart took off into a frantic sprint.

Then…he climbed off the bed.

She lifted her head as he chose the metal pleasure

balls from the bag. A pleading sound whimpered from her mouth.

Smirking, he strode to her. "Ready?"

Gasping, she nodded.

He slithered the two cool balls deep inside her heat. Hips up, she clenched the metal hard. The balls stretched her out.

His mouth glided over her folds, her pubic bone, across her hip. He licked her clit with a firm drag of his tongue.

Jenna hissed. The balls massaged her internal walls. Her head tilted back. She was close. Too, too, too close.

His tongue swirled round and round, and he nipped the tip of her clit. The walls of her pussy trembled. He licked her with his flattened tongue, forcing her inhibitions away. Her body jerked. She strained to grab his head, but those damn ropes tortured her again. Frustration added to her need. She clutched onto the strings, chafing her skin.

He sucked on her for several long seconds. Her mind grew woozy. She soared. Tremors overtook her. Too overcome with pleasure and pain, her legs shook. The balls tensed her stomach muscles, heightening every touch and sensation. Her body dissolved into jelly.

"I need to be inside you." He crawled up and kissed her mouth, tasting like whipped cream and her arousal.

"God, yes." The air left her lungs. She wanted to feel him. All of him.

"Let me remove these first." He shuffled lower and slid his finger inside her.

A few beats passed. Her orgasmic dizziness slowed. She lifted her head. "What's taking you so long?"

"Umm…" His voice croaked. "I can't find it."

"Ha ha ha. Very funny."

"No, I'm serious. The string or stick thingy that connected the balls fell off." He held up a silver thread.

"It can't be lost in there. Untie me."

"Where did you buy this from? It snapped off so easily." He removed the ropes from her hands and feet, rubbing the little red indents each time.

"The adult shop's bargain bin nearby my work." Jenna had never guessed an accident could happen skimping on a sex toy. Most normal people assumed the word "discounted" meant newer stock was arriving. She sat up straight, inserting a finger. Her fingertips grazed the metal. They could not grasp and pull it out. Sweat beads formed in her hairline, her skin flushed.

Marco kneeled at her entrance. "Let me help."

"We don't need multiple sets of fingers in here." Panting, she knocked his hand away. Her face radiated heat like a furnace. Slumping, she took deep breaths. "Pass a mirror."

He hurried to the ensuite bathroom. Seconds later, he held a small compact mirror.

She snatched it, angled the glass, and hunched her back. No sign of silver.

He lingered at the edge of the bed. "Are you okay?"

"A sex toy is stuck in my vagina. What do you think?" From her reflection, her face glowed bright red. She puffed, unable to steady her breaths. Her muscles hurt. The more she attempted to remove, the more the object shoved farther up.

He left the room.

She squatted and squeezed, but the balls didn't budge. They were supposed to be slick enough to slide out. Served her right for saving money on an item meant to be inside her.

Marco returned, holding his wallet and car keys.

"Where are you going?" She tried to retrieve the metal balls again. The room closed in.

This.

Wasn't.

Good.

He grabbed her clothes. "I'm taking you to the nearest hospital emergency room."

Chapter Nineteen

This was the most humiliating moment of Jenna's life. They arrived at the hospital reeking of lemon disinfectant. Her gaze darted around. Paranoid everyone knew why she was here, she lowered her head.

An older woman to her right coughed every few seconds. The child behind her blew his nose. People had normal illnesses. How she wished to swap places with any of them. At least her neighbor could mind the girls at such late notice.

"I'll wait for you over there." Marco pointed and walked to the back of the room.

The receptionist with blonde bouncy curls beamed behind the long desk. "Good evening. Can I help you?"

Jenna longed to wipe the grin off the woman's face. No one should be this happy. "I have an appointment with Dr. Atkinson under Jenna Kravitz."

"Yes, you're in our system. We've had a bus crash emergency since your husband called. Is your condition serious, or can your appointment wait?"

"Serious. Very serious."

The woman typed on a keyboard. "What is the nature of your illness?"

"Accident."

The greeter slid her thick purple glasses down her nose. "Sorry, can you please repeat that?"

"A checkup for my...parts," she half-whispered,

letting the hair cover her face. What a busybody. Anger boiled in her system at the receptionist, threatening to leak out like a bubbling pot on a stove.

Paramedics wheeled people with open wounds on stretchers through the entrance.

"I still didn't quite catch you. Please speak up." The receptionist tapped the desk with her long, fake fingernails.

Jenna slammed her fists onto the table. "I have a metal sex toy jammed up my vajayjay."

A sudden silence in the room hung like a cloud. The receptionist's hand froze mid-tap.

Jenna turned. Everyone stared. The coughing older woman had her mouth open wide enough for a ben wa ball to fit inside.

Jenna's collar tightened, face heating.

"Dr. Atkinson will be right with you." The receptionist lowered her voice.

"Now you decide to be discreet," she muttered as she strode to Marco.

He shrugged, biting his lip like his laughter might erupt at any moment. She glared. He straightened his face to serious.

Twenty minutes later, a five-foot-two woman in her early sixties with dark hair in a tight bun appeared. "Jenna Kravitz?" A hint of a British accent lit her voice.

"Yes." Jenna steadied her breathing to relax her muscles. It might help the doctor retract the balls if she were less tense.

Marco lingered behind. "Should I go in?"

"Yes, suffer the humiliation with me." She followed the doctor.

"I'm Dr. Atkinson. The receptionist informed me

of your…concern." Her eyes twinkled when they entered the room. She indicated to the blue cloth on the bed. "Pop the gown on and lie down. Sing out when you're ready."

Jenna closed the curtain, Marco by her side. She removed her pants and slipped on the gown.

"You'll be okay." Marco squeezed her shoulder. Easy for him to say not having a hard object shoved up his private parts.

With as much dignity as she could muster, she climbed onto the bed. "Ready, Dr. Atkinson."

The curtain scraped aside, and the doctor entered. Jenna wished she wore a smock to cover her head as well.

"Call me Fanny. No need for formalities given the…circumstances." Dr. Atkinson stifled a laugh as she placed on gloves.

Jenna's lips parted. "Wait. Is Fanny your first name?"

The doctor tapped Jenna's legs and gestured for her to spread them apart. "Yes. Ironic, right?"

****

The saying was, "the walk of shame." Even better, "the stride of pride." As Jenna tottered into the office the next afternoon—she'd asked Hayley if she could start late after her ordeal—she wished for either the walk or stride. Luckily, Dr. Atkinson had removed the less-than-desirable object swiftly.

Posters with cupcakes in the center lined the walls. They detailed a bake off for Friday. The proceeds contributed toward mental health research. She stopped at one sign, deciding to enter her family scone recipe to support Marco's turmoil. Around her, colleagues scribbled in notebooks. Some spoke loudly on the phone so the whole building heard. On the other side of the room, Angie slumped over, a hand over her forehead.

Jenna's brows pinched together. Maybe the mood was linked to Claudine. She charged toward Angie and sat on the spare chair. "Are you okay?"

Angie sat up straight and blinked. "Yeah, fine. My son's Parkinson's disease was playing up last night. I was awake until the early morning and have a splitting headache."

Tina strode by. Angie jumped in the chair, her whole body shaking.

Jenna took her hand. "Can I help you?"

"No. I'll be right as rain with a glass of water." Angie lifted the cup and drank. "I'll lock myself in the level twelve meeting room again to concentrate on work."

"Won't the broken lights worsen your headache? Are you sure you're okay? I care about you. Sebastian does too."

At the water cooler, Claudine waved to Nathan. A tick jumped in Angie's jaw. She sank lower into the seat.

"Is the problem Claudine? We're close, but if she's harassing you, I'm on your side." Jenna kept her voice low like Angie was a frightened child.

Angie choked out a laugh. "No one's bullying me. I pulled Claudine up yesterday on yet another mistake. Sebastian was quite irritated."

"But—"

Angie's face contorted. She banged the keyboard. "I have a lot of work to do."

"I'm worried."

Angie's face flashed in anger, eyes darkening. "I'm fine. Now, please excuse me." She picked up the laptop from the desk and headed to the elevator.

Jenna sighed, pondering Angie's beef with Claudine. She strolled to the desk and sat next to Vanessa.

Vanessa glanced sideways at Jenna. "You look tired."

"Are you politely implying I look like crap?" Jenna opened Sandeep's email from last night.

"Never." Vanessa winked, before continuing her work.

When the email popped up, the tightness in her shoulders released. The urgency was a stakeholder's upcoming report. As always, Sandeep stressed over the smallest issues.

Huffing, she hit the reply button and typed. "I already completed the analytics section two days ago. The report will be ready tomorrow. Please contact me for further questions."

She logged into AnaStone and checked the latest recommendations. Her body stiffened. Last night, one software suggestion should've bought SF Airline stock but completed the opposite. The same Romanian IP address had logged on.

Dammit, the technology team or Sandeep couldn't keep the hacker out.

Clicking into the spyware that kept track of everyone's work activities, she verified Claudine first. To her joy, Claudine hadn't signed in past five yesterday.

She examined Desiree's profile—wasn't online

either. To cover her bases, she scrolled through her colleague's emails. A message from the bank had arrived today.

"Thank you. We have received your transfer. Your payments are now up-to-date."

Her eyebrows inched up. Weeks ago, the bank threatened legal proceedings against Desiree. Now a payment occurred a day after the software error. Her head thumped as she confirmed if anyone else accessed AnaStone last night. Tina did, but her actions wouldn't corrupt the system. On Tina's emails, payroll had contacted her last week.

"We have processed your request for an advance on your bonus. Please allow two to three business days for the funds to appear in your account."

This message confirmed Tina's story. Another box ticked off.

Well, at least the culprit might not be Claudine. Relief washed over her like a warm shower. But the revelation didn't mean she could relax…not until she found the fraudster.

Claudine arrived at her seat, holding the baking contest flyer. "I think I'll enter. What to prepare…"

Jenna jumped and minimized the spyware program.

Vanessa swiveled in her chair. "I'll bake peanut butter cookies if I have time."

"Good idea. I'm doing my mom's scones." Jenna nodded.

"Can you both please come over after work to help me figure out a recipe?" Claudine sat and slid the flyer into her handbag. "No cake will be as good as Jenna's scones."

"I can't. Sebastian and I have a date night."

Vanessa twisted her mouth in apology. "Next time."

"I'll ask my parents to stay after they pick up the kids from school, but I don't see why not." Jenna plucked the cell from her handbag and knocked out a text. The atmosphere had been awkward with Claudine when Jenna went home after dinner. She welcomed the chance to smoothen the situation.

"Sounds good." Claudine gave a mischievous grin.

Ten feet away, Desiree pranced from cubicle to cubicle. Nathan followed. She waved her hand around, a giant ring reflecting in the light. The words "white gold," "expensive," and "twenty-four carats" were repeated often. God, Desiree was louder and more obvious than two robots having sex on a tin roof using bubble wrap as a condom.

They invaded Jenna's section.

Desiree held out her hand to show off the bling. "Nathan proposed. The ring is over twenty-five thousand dollars."

Claudine took Desiree's French manicured hand. "Wow, impressive."

Desiree flipped her long amber hair. "I know."

"Congrats. The jewelry will look beautiful with your new place." Jenna leaned forward, relishing the opportunity to grill her.

"Certainly does. I had an exclusive lobster and champagne dinner party last night to celebrate our engagement."

Vanessa whistled. "Must be nice rolling in money."

"I make smart investment choices."

Jenna tilted her head. "Which are?"

"I bought SF Airline shares predicting it'd go up." Desiree's lips puckered into a shriveled date.

Jenna's head pounded. "Oh? You must give me tips. Why did you decide SF Airline?"

Like Tina, Desiree had profited from AnaStone's mistakes. No sinister errors had occurred on Desiree's login activities minutes ago. Short of breaking into Desiree's house to set up the spyware on her personal computer, Jenna could do no more.

"They've been running at a loss for years. My flight attendant friend told me they're completing plane upgrades." Desiree lifted an eyebrow.

A colleague, sitting in a team of five, waved Desiree over. "Yay. Super happy for you, Desiree."

Desiree squealed and sauntered to the group, bragging more.

Well...a plausible explanation, but no matter the renovations, SF Airline was on its way to bankruptcy. Stone Corp threw a lifeline when accidentally buying more stock.

Jenna's gaze zeroed in on Nathan. The other week, he couldn't afford a ten-thousand-dollar ring. Now, Desiree wore a diamond as big as her head. "Congratulations. You must be thrilled."

Nathan shifted on his feet and yawned. Dark bags sat under his eyes. "Thanks."

"Well done picking the lovely ring," Claudine said, turning to her desk.

"Where did you end up looking for another job?" Jenna blurted before she remembered she had eavesdropped on Nathan searching for extra work. Hopefully, he didn't question her information sources.

"At the grocery shop down the road. I do night shifts after I'm done here. I didn't have time to look for another IT role."

Jenna's heart raced. After work, she'd visit the supermarket to check. But even if employed there, he still wouldn't be cashed up.

As she shook her head in disbelief, she wished the movement were a form of exercise. She sure as hell had been doing a lot of the action lately.

****

Claudine's aging yet elegant Victorian house in Mission District was beautiful. The last time she visited Claudine, she was too distracted to get her words right to appreciate her friend's exquisite taste. Every furniture piece and decoration suited her from the pewter ringed plates to the rectangular dining table featuring a unique parquetry inlay.

They shuffled back and forth in the long, narrow galley kitchen with geometric floorboards. A small wooden minimalistic Christmas tree stood at the end of the bench.

Concentrating, Jenna kneaded the dough like Claudine instructed. They had stopped by the supermarket Nathan worked at to buy supplies. Sure enough, he was stacking canned foods. His job equaled minimum wage. Yet he bought a massive ring.

Cupcakes and gingerbread men cooled on the rack. Each dessert gleamed pinks, blues, browns, and yellows.

"Your baking always rises to the occasion, Claudine."

"Oh, my God. The joke was terrible but thank you. Le Morning Sunshine is up for sale. My dream place. Unfortunately, my own café is a faraway goal."

"You will get there. If not Le Morning Sunshine, another café will pop up. I've tasted no dessert more delicious than yours."

Claudine dipped a teaspoon of sugar into a mixing bowl. "You're too kind."

Her vanilla perfume set Jenna into a heady daze. She resisted the urge to lean closer. "Can I use your bathroom?"

"Of course. Do you remember where it is?"

"Yup." She washed her hands and walked to the bathroom. Closing the door before she entered, she sidestepped to the study showcasing a computer with dual screens. Whipping out a USB spyware from her pants pocket, she slid the sneaky device into the slot.

Her stomach laddered toward her chest. After proving Claudine hadn't logged into Stone Corp last night, she wanted to put the matter to bed. But Claudine was smart. No chance she'd plot sketchy actions on a work computer. She must strike Claudine off her list. Claudine had helped her accept herself. She had become fond of her.

Waiting for the spyware, she snuck a glance at the door. She shuffled through the desk drawers—bills and random family photos. Picking up a notebook, she flipped through the pages. Inside had Claudine's handwritten recipes and café design drawings.

Convulsions riled her stomach at invading her colleague's private and personal items. Although she had questioned Claudine on multiple occasions about AnaStone, each time she suspected Claudine didn't offer the whole truth.

Footsteps echoed down the hall. "You okay?"

Jenna froze. "Fine. I'll be out in a sec." She kept her voice low to prevent Claudine hearing she stood in the study instead of the bathroom.

"Sure."

Footsteps tapped away. She yanked out the USB stick, shoved it into a pocket, and left the room. Plastering on a smile, she resumed her position at the kitchen bench and continued kneading the dough.

"Don't massage too much, or the dough will toughen." Claudine glided behind Jenna and wrapped her arms around her. "Only enough so the dough holds together without cracks."

Jenna shook, jittery from guilt. She silently promised to make up for the deception when she discovered the hacker's identity. "Our setup reminds me of the romance movie."

Claudine chuckled. "Pay attention."

"It's hard with the delicious smells around."

"I know." Claudine grazed her finger in the icing sugar and licked the grains off.

Lust rose from Jenna, surrounding her like a mist. Her body was no longer solid and had turned into melted chocolate. A purely physical reaction.

"I need to get the cake ready for the bake off." Claudine veered to the bench, sprinkled flour on the dough disk, and smeared some on Jenna's face.

Jenna's eyes widened. "You didn't just do that." She snatched a butter cube and rubbed it against Claudine's arm.

Claudine tossed her head back, laughing. She flung chopped apples.

Jenna raised her hands and blocked each one, pitching them back. Grabbing an egg, she cracked the shell over Claudine's head.

Claudine opened her mouth and lifted her gooey hair. She wiped her locks onto Jenna's and embraced her for a hug. The food mixed together.

Their laughter echoed through the room.

"This is why I love you." Claudine's eyes crinkled. "You're thorough in every task you do."

The giggles died in Jenna's throat. Love? She chewed her lip. They were meant to be friends. She had Marco complications and didn't entirely trust anyone at Stone Corp.

To stall time, she clutched a glass of water and sipped.

Claudine's smile faded, her face a little paler. "I didn't mean it like that. I mean...I love you as a friend."

"Oh, I see."

Claudine turned on the tap and washed out the egg in her hair. Jenna wiped her face with a napkin. After they cleaned themselves up, they continued working side by side. Strange they already knew each other's actions. When Jenna reached for the fridge, Claudine stepped aside. When Claudine stirred the mixture, Jenna handed cinnamon. Always in close contact but never bumping into one another.

One moment they were friends. Today, Claudine blurted the L word, no matter how innocent. Claudine's thoughts were a mystery.

****

"Tell me about Colin." Dr. Kim sat opposite Marco in a tranquil office. The abundance of natural light from the wide windows highlighted the freckles on her button nose and the silver streaks in her black hair.

Marco leaned back on the cushioned chair, distracted by the little water feature shaped as a wishing well on the white desk. The water trickling from the bricked bucket calmed him. "He was everyone's buddy."

"Sounds like a great guy. What was your favorite part about army life?"

"The friendships. We had each other's backs."

Dr. Kim wrote in her notebook. "Do you have a favorite memory?"

Marco pondered the question, and his lips tipped. "We worked hard, but we also talked shit. Mucked around. One time we put Stevo's hand in a bucket of warm water while he slept. He wet the bed."

The doctor chuckled. "No matter your age, bodily fluids never fail to amuse most men."

Marco laughed, relaxing into the reminiscence. He traced a hand over the leaves from the pot plant on the table beside him. A lot of greenery decorated the room. "Correct."

"Tell me a little about the incident that brought you here today."

"Why?"

Dr. Kim folded her hands on her lap. "For trauma to not hold power anymore, you need to be comfortable recalling the events."

He pictured smoke—his vision muddled, and his throat constricted. Bodies scattered around him, steamrolling any hope. Colin…his eyes opened wide, body still. Marco crawled to his side, shaking him to wake up, disbelieving someone with such a tall, powerful presence had now ceased to exist.

Glaring, he clutched the armrests on both sides. Someone couldn't plunge into his psyche, offer guidance, without experiencing his life. He didn't want to expose his deepest, darkest secrets. "Hard pass on the topic."

"Face your past. Be angry. Sad. Terrible accidents occur as an infantry soldier. You were doing your job."

His lungs squeezed tight. The wacko had no idea. The bomb was no accident. Fucking kid set out to harm and kill.

Taking shallow breaths, he curled his hands into fists. He stood. "I don't need this." His gaze darted to the door. Then he remembered why he should continue the session—for Jenna, his kids, to heal. Jenna had the courage to confide her bisexuality. He couldn't be a wuss now.

Dr. Kim's eyes shone with gentleness. "Fury is better than no emotion. We can work with this."

He glanced at the exit again, concentrating on his breathing like Jenna taught him. His mind spun faster than a CD in a player, but his wobbly legs dumped him back into the chair. "Fine."

****

"Babe," Claudine called out from the kitchen. "Do you want vanilla ice cream with your cake?"

"I'm not wasting calories on vanilla." Jenna joked as she examined the photos on Claudine's mantelpiece. One with her brother and sister outside a musical theatre show and another with her parents at a café.

The earlier awkwardness had dwindled. They relaxed into each other's company again with easy banter and friendly touches.

"It's my homemade vanilla bean ice cream. Fancier and healthier than store bought." Claudine left the kitchen, holding two sponge cake slices.

Jenna accepted the bowl. Ice cream was her weakness, and she'd never seriously say *no*. Licking her lips, she spooned a piece covered with ice cream. She slid the cold metal into her mouth. "Too good."

"Not as nice as your family's scone recipe. I will steal the ingredients out of you if it's the last thing I do."

"No chance." Jenna swallowed the light and fluffy texture and moaned.

"I love watching you eat. You look so happy." Claudine's gaze locked on hers, piercing and intense.

Jenna's chest dissolved into liquid, her heart leaving her body. Claudine's vanilla perfume hung in the air.

"Try this." Claudine picked up a shortbread from the plate and held it to Jenna's mouth.

Jenna took a bite, body on autopilot, brain not in control anymore.

A buzz vibrated in Jenna's pocket. She tore away from Claudine and slipped out the phone. Marco's face flashed on the display. "It's Marco. Might be about the kids."

Also, she hated to admit her true wishes, but she had gotten used to chatting to Marco most days. Her heart yearned even though they were together last night. He always cheered her up no matter her troubles.

She clicked the "accept" button. "Hi, Marco. What's up?"

Erratic breathing heaved from the other end.

"What's wrong? Did an accident happen with Keisha or Eve? Are they sick?" Her chest seized. Marco was usually calm, and she had only witnessed him distressed in a nightmare.

Claudine grasped Jenna's hand, her brows pulled together. "Everything okay?"

Jenna shook her head, clutching the cell closer to her ear. "Tell me, Marco."

"The girls are...good." A silence filled the line. "They're having fun with your parents."

The pinch in her shoulders loosened. "Then what's the matter?"

"I had my first therapy session today. More difficult than I expected." His voice wobbled.

She smacked her forehead, having completely forgotten his appointment. Her job anxiety was miniscule compared to his problems. She covered the receiver with one hand and peered at Claudine's worried face. "I'm taking the call in your room." She hurried away and yanked the door open. "What happened? You all right?"

The door closed behind her as she sat on the bed.

Marco took a shaky breath. "I told the doctor about the day Colin died. Confronting."

"Where are you?"

"In my car outside the therapist's office." His voice broke a little.

"How long have you sat there?" Jenna's heart clenched. Marco didn't discuss his experiences. Period. He'd be vulnerable right now.

"Not sure."

"Stay there. I'll come to you." Panic clawed her chest. He might do something stupid.

"I'm fine. No need." His voice strengthened in false pretense.

"Take deep breaths." She spoke in a volume barely above a whisper. "You're in your car and safe."

From his end, every single breath appeared forced. Confiding in her was a huge step.

"Keep going. Listen to my voice." She breathed in and out audibly, hoping he'd follow suit. "Take in your surroundings outside the window. What do you see?"

A pause before he spoke. "A couple is walking their dog. Looks a little like Scruffy."

"What else?"

"The dog stopped to pee on a pole."

Her stomach knotted, growing bigger and bigger, until worry burst out of her skin. "Good. Concentrate on the people and streets. I'll be right over. Don't move. Will you be okay until I'm there?"

"Yes. Thank you, Jenna."

"Be there soon. I lov…" Her mind hesitated mid-thought. "See you shortly." She hung up and rushed out of the room.

Claudine waited on the couch, chin leaning against her palms. "What's wrong? Are your kids well? Your parents? Brother?"

Jenna grabbed her handbag. "Yes, they're fine. I'm really sorry. I know we had plans today, but I have to go. Marco needs me."

Claudine's jaw tensed. "Marco needs you…" She repeated the words slowly. "Your ice cream melted."

Jenna fiddled inside her handbag, searching for keys. "Please don't be mad. I feel terrible I haven't taste tested all the cakes. Rain check? I was having fun."

"Didn't your ex hurt you?" Claudine strode to Jenna, reaching for the photo keychain Jenna held. Her fingers grazed across the image of Marco and their family. They sat on the dance studio's floor in front of the barre.

"Oh. Don't read too much into the photo. Eve gave me the keychain, and I promised I'd never take it off."

Jenna gripped the handbag over her shoulder.

A silence ballooned between them, inflating every passing second.

"You're still in love with him, aren't you?" Claudine's blue eyes pierced deep into hers, saying nothing, yet saying everything.

Jenna wobbled, barely remaining upright. "No...I mean...we have a lot of history."

Claudine let out a resigned breath and gave a soft smile. Grabbing Jenna's hands, she tugged her forward and wrapped her arms around her.

Jenna jerked before she clutched Claudine's back. Warmth clawed up Jenna's spine, jolting through her arms. They stayed connected for several long seconds. The embrace differed from others. Something meaningful. Something poignant. Something final.

Claudine tore away. "Go to him." She dropped Jenna's hands.

Jenna stumbled, getting her bearings. She shook her head multiple times. Opened her mouth to speak. Snapped her lips shut.

"Whatever attraction we've had..." Claudine set her hands to her sides. "Be with him. You deserve the world."

Jenna's eyes misted, every emotion in her head running an entire circuit. "I don't know what to say."

"Be happy."

Chapter Twenty

Ba boom boom, ba boom boom. Jenna's heart thumped like a drummer on speed as she sprinted out of the door and jumped into the car.

She lifted the keychain picture to eye level and ran a finger over Marco's face. Since their separation, she tried her hardest to forget him—too hurt and resentful.

But she had never stopped loving him. Claudine saw it as plain as day. Maybe why she never changed the keychain and still wore his perfume gift. He was a part of her. Her best friend in the entire world. Her family.

Fingers trembling, she stuck the key into the ignition and reversed fast out of the driveway. The looming possibility of unemployment hindered giving her entire self to someone. Family mattered more. Marco was her soulmate.

She clutched the steering wheel. Veering around a corner, she passed the strip of shops and restaurants. Every time she signaled, changed lanes, or entered another road, she strained her neck to check how far to go.

The psychiatrist's stone-gray clinic finally appeared. She parked next to Marco's white sedan at the front. Few other cars resided. She switched off the engine and raced to his car. Marco was resting his forehead against the steering wheel.

She opened the passenger door.

He twisted his neck in slow motion and blinked as if surprised she appeared.

She took his hand. "Are you okay?"

His face was ashen, eyes red-rimmed and puffy. "No, but I will be."

She hauled him into a fierce hug. "Yeah, you will."

He tugged her onto his lap, squishing her against the steering wheel. The gear shift jabbed her.

"I couldn't have survived therapy and this whole experience without you." He cupped her cheek. "I know you don't want to hear this, but I've loved you since I was seventeen. I exist for you. I'm complete when we're together and empty when we're apart."

"You never have to feel empty again." Tears brimmed Jenna's vision—now or never to confess. She sucked in a breath. "I love you, Marco. I always have."

Several beats passed. His gaze scanned her face. The corners of his lips lifted. And then he was kissing her. Soft at first, before his mouth pressed harder. Deeper. A feverish urgency. She'd never get enough of him. She blossomed like a flower and wanted to eat him. Drink him. Devour him. Clinging to him, she relished his familiarity, his musky scent, the way his mouth fit perfectly against hers.

When they finally came up for air, she took shaky, shallow breaths. "You're my life. I should've done more for you. I can attend your therapy sessions if you like?"

No matter what, she'd be there for him when things got too much and learn from a medical expert to help. He could count on her. She'd pick up the pieces over and over again.

His gaze flickered over her. "Yes. That'll be great."

They belonged together. He was her constant, her rock.

Squeezing him tight, she poured every ounce of love into his body. Tears blurred her vision. She wiped her eyes with the back of her hand. "Move back home?" She lifted her head.

His eyes shone. "There's no place I'd rather be."

****

Two hours later, Marco stood outside Jenna's house—no, *their* house—carrying the first cardboard box in his hands. The motion sensor switched on the porch light, illuminating the white archway, a light beacon leading him home. A green Christmas wreath with a red bow hung on the blue door.

Before he started the rest of his life with his family, he needed a second to savor the moment.

He picked up a ballet shoe from the box, first belonging to Keisha, then Eve before they grew too big. The slipper had a slight hole at the sole, the bottom blackened. Every time he looked at the broken footwear, he saw the times Jenna and he visited their kids' ballet class. When overseas, he often wished he could carry his daughters' hugs in a bottle. The inventor would've earned a fortune. Instead, he settled for packing the slipper every time he left to take a little piece of his family.

He clutched the slipper close to his heart and dropped it back into the box. With a sweaty hand, he inserted the key into the lock and nudged the door open. He stepped through the threshold. Happiness overtook him, elbowing out every other emotion.

Keisha and Eve raced to him. Scruffy jumped up

and down, her gray fluffy tail wagging.

"You're back." Keisha wrapped her arms around his waist.

"Glad you found the place okay." Jenna lingered at the living room, her wink turning his insides gooey.

Scooping up his daughters, he spun them.

Finger art displayed on the walls. School books scattered on the dining table. A huge smile spread across his face. He was finally home.

****

"Did your conversation go well with Marco?" Claudine squeezed her shoulder at the office the next morning.

Jenna secured a hand on hers. Her heart still buzzed. She swallowed a lump in her throat. Claudine ending any spark they had before it started touched her beyond words. "Yes, he's moving home."

Her cheeks hurt from constantly smiling. She had him back for good. Her personal life now felt at peace.

Claudine sat at her desk. "I'm thrilled for you. We can still be friends, right?"

"Of course. You're too important to me to give up."

Claudine's smile reached her eyes. She faced the computer.

Jenna relaxed into the chair, more at ease than she had been in a while. She had Marco, friends, family. The most important things in life.

She launched AnaStone. Python scripts in the LSTM model appeared. She gasped. Pressure built in her chest. The software was being manipulated into recommending Stone Corp to sell Giants department store stock. She'd read a news story on Giants' upcoming partnership with a major supermarket chain.

No, no, no. Why was the program still buggy? No matter the security, the hacker always broke through. She entered a code, manually stopping the trail.

A notification popped up. "Claudine De la Harp is now online."

Jenna spun. Claudine's desk was empty.

She twisted back to the screen. The Romanian IP address popped up but did nothing. Her blouse clung her arms and chest.

Claudine was reading and rewriting the data, feeding incorrect inputs to the model. Right in front of Jenna's eyes, Claudine hijacked the shell running AnaStone's scripts.

She was the culprit all along.

Fuck.

Chapter Twenty-One

After Jenna heated lunch in the microwave, she sat at the desk and stuffed a forkful of kale into her mouth. She was angry eating. *Angry* eating. She chomped on each tomato and ground the lettuce to a pulp. Why did the perpetrator have to be Claudine? The last time someone hacked the system, Claudine wasn't online. She must've found another way. Everyone's job was at stake because of the woman who took advantage of her.

To make matters worse, the police who arrested her bag snatcher didn't have extra information either. The thief remained adamant he acted alone. How she wished the cops would tell her there was a mistake with Claudine.

Finishing her salad, she picked up the laptop, not ready to meet Sebastian. Part of their catch–up was to brainstorm solving AnaStone's issue—too late now.

She knocked on Sebastian's door.

"Come in." A deep voice reverberated from the other side.

Sweat beads deposited on the cold metal handle when she twisted it. This was Sebastian—her friend's boyfriend who she'd dined with and shared multiple laughs. Yet her chest heaved like she entered her doom. Taking deep breaths, she closed the door, unsure how to start the conversation.

Sebastian's head was inches from the computer. He

lifted his chin, his square jaw tight. Small lines etched around his full lips. He belonged more in a fashion magazine rather than the head of a company. "Jenna. Thanks for coming. Take a seat."

Hands trembling, she sat opposite the CEO. Maybe she should confront Claudine before discussing her findings. Claudine might have had reasons.

Her nose twitched, and she closed her eyes and sneezed.

"Bless you." Sebastian slid a tissue box over.

"Thanks. I've had an allergic reaction to the universe, lately."

"Haven't we all? Another AnaStone error arose today." Sebastian walked to the table at the corner of the room. He lifted the jug and poured water into two glasses.

The liquid splashed against the cups, the rhythm in tune with the sloshing in Jenna's stomach.

He brought the two glasses to the desk and handed her one.

She grabbed the drink and gulped down half the contents. "I'm aware. The system works fine. I can't figure out who's hacking the program."

His emerald green eyes pinned on her. "Who do you believe the offender is? The police and our external consultants haven't discovered clues."

"I've worked on the mystery for the past weeks." Gaze averted, she thumbed the cold glass. "Someone with access to the software."

"Do you have suspicions?"

"Umm." She must speak to Claudine. Claudine had been kind when Jenna figured out her bisexuality and relationship with Marco.

"You must have an inkling. You know the software better than anyone. I followed up with the consultants yesterday. They couldn't track the hacking source."

She shook her head in furious motions. Claudine deserved courtesy. She placed the glass top and clutched her hands under the desk.

"I hoped you had an explanation because no one else does. I have to let people go next week." Sebastian rubbed his eyes. "There's more than a chance your role is also on the line. I'm sorry, Jenna. Stone Corp's at risk."

Her pulse pounded so loudly she didn't catch every word. No way she'd let staff lose their jobs. Too many people depended on their wages. Claudine would've understood her deception had a short lifespan.

With a heavy heart, the words propelled out of her mouth. "The issues started when Claudine joined."

"Proof?"

"Yes, she logged into AnaStone to change the codes and recommend the wrong outcome hours ago." Jenna slid her phone from her pocket and showed Sebastian the video recording she had quickly taken of Claudine completing the action. Guilt nibbled in her chest.

Sebastian's eyes widened. He shifted forward in his seat. "Let me look into this. Please send me a copy." He paused, stroking his chin. "Thank you, Jenna. Disclosing your friend couldn't have been easy."

She coughed, softening the lump in her throat. Her limbs weighed her down into the chair. "You're welcome."

She had formed a special bond with Claudine and helped her secure a job. In return, Claudine pulled the wool over her eyes. Despite the deception, her entire heart and soul still rotted from within.

****

The next three hours, Jenna didn't meet Claudine's gaze, who often smiled or initiated small talk. Jenna didn't trust her. Their entire relationship was a lie. She glared at the back of Claudine's head. Her stomach locked nausea up tight, fighting the urge to throw up.

Vanessa snapped her fingers. "Earth to Jenna."

She blinked. "Sorry, what?"

"I baked cookies last night after Sebastian and I got home from the movies. I feel so organized. Are your scones ready? You must've been busy with Marco moving back home. I'm so happy for you."

"Oh…how nice. Thank you." Last night on the phone, Jenna had filled Vanessa in on her tearful reunion. She noted to prepare scones tonight or tomorrow morning in time for the bake off. With the latest revelation, sweets were the last thing on her mind.

Vanessa wheeled her chair closer to Jenna. "Are you okay? You seem on edge."

Jenna's gaze drifted to Claudine, who was still clicking a presentation. She lowered her voice. "I told Sebastian who's infiltrating AnaStone."

"What the…oh, my…no wonder you're freaked out. Shall we go for a walk and talk?"

Jenna nodded.

A man and woman in security uniforms marched toward them. People peered up, curiosity on their faces.

Hayley stood from her desk and greeted the guards. The three walked to Claudine.

Blood drained from Jenna's head, gushing to her stomach. Sebastian must have filled Hayley in on their earlier conversation.

Claudine spun, her lips pale.

The two officers stood a little distance behind Hayley who leaned down to Claudine. "Please come with me."

Claudine's hands flew to her chest. She barked out a laugh. "What? Why?"

Hayley closed her eyes for a second. "We don't want a scene."

Colleagues whispered and nudged one another. Some strained their necks for a better view. Jenna shot lasers out of her eyes at each person, tempted to yell that someone's life wasn't a theatre show.

"Please come quietly." The female guard tugged Claudine's arm.

Claudine wriggled out of the guard's grip, her knees wobbling. "Why? I don't understand."

The male guard dragged Claudine to her feet and cuffed her hands behind her back. "We have to escort you out of the building for company misconduct."

A shrill siren rang at the back of Jenna's skull.

Tears welled in Claudine's eyes, her face frozen. "There must be a mistake. I did nothing wrong. Stone Corp has helped me a lot. Let me explain. Please."

Claudine stumbled back, gaze catching on Jenna. A small yelp escaped those lush lips. Jenna's stomach dropped into a sticky pit, her scalp crawling. Claudine was taken away so fast…and publicly.

Hayley's eyes hardened. "We found evidence you've hacked into AnaStone and caused a severe financial loss to the company."

"No. Not me. No. Just no." Claudine lifted her hands, but the cuffs didn't let her. She bowed her head.

Jenna's eyes misted, but she didn't dare move. This morning, they decided to be close friends. Claudine should be honest and tell the truth.

"Give your explanation to the police." Hayley nodded to the guards. "They're escorting you for questioning."

"Jenna, you know me. I didn't do this." Claudine kept glancing over her shoulder. Her eyes were earnest, imploring. The guards hauled her toward the elevator.

Jenna suppressed a shiver, chest cramping. Who was Claudine? Was the person she knew little more than a facade?

Chapter Twenty-Two

As soon as Jenna arrived home, Marco hurried to the front door. She burst into tears in his arms. His slow, steady heartbeats thudded against her cheek.

On her way back, she had called him to debrief. The expression on Claudine's face when security hauled her away...she'd never forget it. A part of her wished to message Claudine to check she was okay. The other part dismissed she had ever met her. She didn't know why she still cared. Claudine betrayed her.

"Shh, you're okay." Marco stroked her back. "Today's over now."

"Then why do I feel awful?" She glanced around the room, not intending her kids to see her upset.

"Because you're a good person." Marco's gaze followed Jenna's line of sight. "The girls and Scruffy are in Keisha's room playing a board game. Claudine was the one special to you, right?"

She nodded. She'd explained details to Marco last night when he moved some belongings over.

"Of course, you'll feel bad. You were close." He caressed her cheek with the backs of his fingers. "What can I do?"

"Help me forget today." She sniffed. Claudine would be on her mind for many more days, weeks, and months.

"You deserve a fun night."

"Maybe."

"It won't help anyone spending the rest of your existence miserable."

"Yes, I suppose tonight should be about us. We've been apart too long." She buried her face into his chest again. "I need to concentrate on the positives in my life."

"Let's go out if we haven't taken advantage of your parents' babysitting yet. I have an idea."

"They love looking after the girls." She traced a finger over his firm chest, tear streaks smudged on the material. "Don't tell Mom and Dad we're back together yet. They'll be pretty full-on and organize family trips. I plan to enjoy each other again."

"Of course. Your parents can be scary. Hopefully, the kids won't utter a word."

"We'll set up a scavenger hunt to occupy them. What do you have in mind for tonight?"

The left side of Marco's lips quirked up. "A night to reconnect in every way."

****

"Is tonight another yoga session?" Jenna admired the cozy room with a fireplace to the left. Couples in loose-fitting clothes already shared mats and sat in a circle on the floorboards. Delicate melodies with a drum soothed the air. The infuser's jasmine scent dosed her with sleepiness.

"Not quite." Marco winked in a boyish way. A contradiction to his bulging muscles and arm tattoos.

A woman in a white top and matching pants glided to the middle of the room. Rose petals lay scattered on the floor. "Welcome to your workshop, Sensory Tantra. My name is Sarita. Face your partners on the mat, please."

Jenna raised an eyebrow at Marco. "Tantra? Is this the type of class where we'll have sex at the beginning, and I'll give birth by the time we return home?"

He chuckled, leading her to a mat on the right. "We'll have fun. Especially if you still crave bondage experimentation."

A squeal of pleasure caught at her throat. No argument from her end.

The instructor circled the room, bringing a waft of lavender. "Tantra isn't only about sex. The practice involves connecting and being present and in tune with your partner. First, hold hands. Now, each of you say three positive statements and give the words with love. Watch which one your partner resonates with the most by their facial expressions and body language."

People broke off, talking in quiet whispers.

Jenna must admit, the activity was obscure enough to take her mind off Claudine. She tangled her fingers with Marco's. "I'll start. You're a great father."

Marco beamed. "You're the brainiest person."

It was always nice when someone complimented her mind. Relaxing into his comfortable presence, she stroked his skin with her thumbs. "You're kind."

Sarita patted Jenna's shoulder as she strolled by. "Keep going with your blessings, everyone. Doing great."

He brushed a lock of hair over her ear. "The girls adore you."

"Heyyy. I said the good parent praise first." Laughing, she smacked his hand.

"Doesn't mean my compliment is less true."

"Valid point." She kissed his cheek and forehead.

"You are safe with me."

Bright gold specks shone in his dark brown eyes. He squeezed her hands tighter. His breath hitched.

Ding, ding, ding. She had found a winning statement.

"Damn. I knew you'd find the right words first." His Adam's apple bobbed. "This is why you're the smart one."

"Too right."

"Okay, I thought of my third compliment." He rubbed the back of his shaved head. "You are enough. More than enough."

"Now, you've figured me out." Her eyes moistened. At work, she'd let her daughters down, and at home, her mind kept drifting to deadlines. Her thoughts never let her win.

Yes, over there was her kid cutting her own eyelashes with scissors. And didn't every parent sneak in front of the school drop-off line when desperate? Okay, she had been tempted once but chickened out. She wasn't perfect, but she was a good parent. Not to mention discovering Claudine as the fraudster, preventing further job losses.

Sarita stood in the center of the room and inclined her head. "Good job, everyone. Good. Yes. We'll begin the massages."

A giggle tickled Jenna's throat. "In front of everybody here?"

"The massages are with clothes on." Sarita cocked an eyebrow. "Tantra massages create new sensation pathways to the brain. The massage addresses issues whether physical, sexual, or mental to clear your mind and attain your full pleasure capacity."

Jenna pressed a hand over her lips, laughter vibrating in her chest.

Marco nudged her. "Pay attention."

Pretending to be a mature adult, she swallowed her amusement.

Sarita's gaze flittered to everyone. "Choose one person per couple to relax on their stomach to receive the massage first."

Out of everybody, Marco needed the mental release. The massage technique might teach her skills to help clear his mind. "You go."

"Sure." Marco adjusted his position to lie down.

Sarita tapped a foot in time to the soft and slow music beats. "Not everyone believes or understands this work. But I must say, each person who attends one of my sessions is very happy they came."

****

As soon as Marco and Jenna arrived home, they shooed her parents out of the door and double-checked the kids remained fast asleep.

Now alone, he drifted his hands to the small dip of her waist and up to her ribs. "I want you, badly."

He had worried about her when she finished work and was glad the workshop took her mind off her problems.

She cupped his jaw, following the shape with her fingertips. They kissed like they had learned in tantra—in tuned with each other and their surroundings. The cold bathroom floor chilled his feet, and the heated air tingled his skin.

Her lips were warm and full, tasting of minty toothpaste. He tugged on her lips with his teeth and scratched her back.

Her mouth opened, tongue dipping between his lips. The small, sweet vibrations of her moan melted him. He bent down, inhaling the fragrance of her neck. *Mmm* violets. Delicious.

He sensed how Jenna received the kiss like the teacher explained—her heart open and her love coursing into him. Undoing her buttons, he yanked her top off. She lifted his shirt over his head as they shoved the bathroom door open.

The thin bra straps were in the way of her plump, perfect breasts. He unhooked her bra and tossed the lacy fabric to the tiles. His cock twitched. Those beautiful breasts killed him. Leaning down, he tugged a hard, round nipple into his mouth, sucking hungrily. Her smooth mocha-colored skin glowed under his touch, and he wanted to lick, bite, and consume every part of her.

He stood and twisted the shower taps. The water cascaded onto the floor. She lowered her leggings and underwear. Her naked form drove him wild from her collarbone definition down to her wet folds.

From his pocket, he whipped out a blindfold and a golf ball sized black ring with two rabbit ears. He shoved his pants and briefs to his feet.

Jenna peered up underneath her long, thick eyelashes. "What are those?"

"I bought two play items earlier today. A vibrating cock ring." He slid the rubber ring onto his length. "And a mask."

She licked her lips and kneeled, kissing the tip of his cock. He inhaled a sharp breath. The sight of her gorgeous mouth wrapped around him and her hair covering her face almost made him come apart. She continued to kiss, lick, and suck, and oh, God…a storm already built inside his chest.

He swallowed, reluctantly nudging her to stand. "If you keep going like this, we won't test out the toys. I've been picturing you blindfolded all day while I do wicked things to you."

Jenna gave him a half-smile. "Sounds fun."

They stepped into the shower. Steam rose in the air and warm water washed over them. Her black curls clung to her neck. Droplets trickled down her nipples, chest red from his stubble scratches.

His dick swelled against the ring.

He held out the blindfold. "Want to try this on? It's waterproof."

Skin flushed, she nodded once. Guiding the blindfold over her head, he tightened the strings behind.

She reached out. "I can't see a thing."

****

Darkness stole Jenna's vision. Pleasure climbed her legs and raced along her spine. The entire day, she had been at a loss over Claudine. Now she desired to surrender to Marco more than anything in the world. He was in complete control, to do whatever he wished, while she remained blind.

Rummaging sounded from the shower rack, followed by a vibration below. Her body stirred in anticipation. Tiny pleas fled her lips.

A loofah scraped her chest, down to her stomach. The sponge traveled to her thighs and across to her ass. Her skin quivered. The cool shower gel foamed against her hot skin.

"I don't think I can wait long." She crooked two fingers for him to come closer. "Let's test whether the ring is any good."

"Turn around."

She obeyed, hands against the wall, wiggling her ass. Her breath trapped at her throat in anticipation.

Nothing happened. Jenna wished she could see him.

A sharp slap landed on her right butt cheek. Jumping, she choked out a small noise.

He soothed the soreness with his hand, the gel mollifying her skin.

"Did you like that?" He growled in her ear.

Too aroused and breathless to speak, she nodded. A fever tore through her. She leaned forward, ass angling up.

A smack landed on her left cheek. Wetness gushed out of her. It was liberating to relinquish control and lock her Claudine problems away. Another slap struck her stinging ass. A sponge rubbed her again. Kisses traced up and down her sides. The tip of his cock hovered at her entrance.

"Oh, God. Fuck me, Marco."

"Yes, ma'am." He glided deep into her. His hand slid in front of her and fumbled with the ring. Vibrations tingled against her swollen clit.

She panted, her eyes rolling back beneath the mask. Tension built between her thighs.

His groan rumbled deep in his throat. They fit nicely together—two halves of a jigsaw puzzle. Too good. Deliciously warm. Sex was better now they were back together. Soulmates fulfilling each other.

He thrust in and out of her, and she drew him back inside her each time, wet and greedy to devour him. The ring pulsated against her clit. She shoved her hips forward, meeting every plunge.

Warm water ran down her back, her face heating. With her vision taken away, every sensation heightened. She let out a jagged exhale, wanting to take, take, and take, and let go. A primal beast clawed out of her body, craving more.

The ring reverberated relentlessly on her firm nub. He gripped her waist, gasping and groaning. Oh, she loved the sounds—the sighs of pleasure, his cock slamming hard into her, their skin slapping against each other.

Pressure developed in her chest, her breathing faster than someone who had run a marathon. Losing her rhythm, she closed her eyes and gave in to the spiral.

Her legs spasmed. He held her shoulders steady. The orgasm hit her like an earthquake—bucking, thrashing, and shuddering her body. Her vision swam. Endorphins trickled from her brain down to her toes, unwinding every muscle.

Marco groaned against the back of her neck and slumped over her. She stilled, sweaty and heaving. He massaged her shoulders, spending the next few minutes washing her. She relaxed into his muscular arms—nice to be taken care of. The warm liquid rushed down her body.

They had journeyed a long way together. From using Marco as a stepping-stone for her confidence, to taking a full leap of faith. After embracing her attraction to women and renouncing control to Marco over and over again, she could now express her longings. She was free.

****

In the morning, Jenna had set her scones in the middle of the long table near her cubicle. Desserts of every kind scattered across the desk with gold tinsel lining the edges. The strawberry torte, pecan pie, and pineapple upside-down cake caught her eye. Her scones sat proudly in the center. After her shower escapade with Marco, she cooled her temperature enough to drag herself to the kitchen to bake.

Now time for the competition judging, Hayley and Vanessa stood beside her. Strange to be in this small team without Claudine although she had only worked at Stone Corp a few months. Her mind kept reverting to her former colleague, ruining today. Since Jenna read the bake off's flyer, she fantasized of a cheat day where she ate so much tastiness her stomach exploded, and she'd pass out in a food coma. Now the guilt denied her.

"Do we want to talk about Claudine?" Hayley nudged Vanessa and Jenna. "Stick pins in a voodoo doll of her? Chant a spell to protect our team? Her lies must've been a shock. I'm here to support or give hugs. Don't expect homemade muffins, though."

People circled the table, tasting the treats. They wrote their favorite down on paper and popped the verdict into a box. Sandeep hovered behind the voting counter, preparing to announce the winner.

"I can't believe she was so deceptive. She always appeared direct and honest. A lot of fun too." Vanessa shook her head. "Are we sure there hasn't been a mistake?"

"A clear trail linked her to hacking AnaStone." Jenna's hands clenched. She brought Claudine into Stone Corp, freeing a lioness among rabbits. Where was

Claudine now? Surely, she didn't sit in a jail cell.

"Ahhmm." Sandeep held up his long nose. A pile of paper was stacked next to the voting box.

The chatter stopped, and everyone faced him.

"I have tallied up the votes. Together, we have raised one thousand, four hundred, and twenty-six dollars to contribute toward Mental Health and Us." His hawked eyes glowered like he had achieved the amount single-handedly. Typical Sandeep, talking to produce sounds.

Whistles and cheers rang through the room.

Jenna's heart thumped against her ribcage. A huge donation. Fingers crossed she'd place in the competition.

Sandeep raised a hand to quiet everyone. "In third place, we have the pavlova by our very own Aussie, Henry Cunningham from the marketing team."

People applauded as a tall man collected his ribbon.

"Second place." Sandeep cleared his throat. "Jenna Kravitz from Business Analytics with her scones."

Her lips parted.

Hayley nudged her to the front. "Too good as always."

Vanessa jumped up and down, clapping her hands.

Jenna's gaze connected with Sandeep's. His brows furrowed. Every time they were in the same room, he pulled a face. Rolling her eyes, she accepted the ribbon. What a dickhead.

Hayley cheered the loudest. "I take full credit for my team member."

Jenna returned to stand beside her colleagues and high-fived them. She now contributed to PTSD treatment in her own way, even though she was no expert.

"And the winner is…" Sandeep's lips twisted. "Sebastian Stone's amazing Executive Assistant, Angie Petrova with *ptichye moloko*. I must say, her chocolate Russian cake was delicious."

Angie squeaked and sprang up from the chair, hurrying to Sandeep. They exchanged air kisses. Everyone was smiling and in a cheerful mood. A break beckoned around the corner.

Claudine's desk stayed empty. One person was missing among these celebrations—the woman who had given Jenna enough red flags to create an entire dress.

Angie popped up beside Jenna. The gold ribbon flashed on her chest. "Congrats."

"The sugar is calling me like I'm an ant." Hayley dragged Vanessa to sample more food.

"You too, Angie. The meringue and mousse in your cake were to die for," Jenna said.

"Thanks. How are you coping?"

Jenna sighed. "I'm relieved I've figured out the issues, but sad and conflicted at the same time. I can't believe I took ages to work out Claudine deceived me. She used another IP address mostly. I guess everyone slips up once, and she did by logging on as herself too."

"I'm here if you want to talk." Angie set a hand on her shoulder. "She's not worth agonizing over. It was surprising she knew how to change her location to Romania. Her work is poor quality."

"Ladies." Sandeep waved them over. "We need a picture of everyone who placed in the competition for the staff newsletter."

Angie tugged on Jenna's hand and led her toward Sandeep. "Chin up. You're worth a thousand Claudines."

An irritation niggled at the back of her mind. She stood between Angie and Henry and faced the camera. Her smile was weak. The case was done and dusted. Yet she couldn't let the issue go.

****

Cutout paper elves in red and green uniforms sat on top of Jenna's cubicle, different staff members' faces on the bodies. In Claudine's image, she winked. Jenna should remove the picture.

A signal popped up on the computer. Someone was using AnaStone with the same Romanian IP address. But Stone Corp revoked Claudine's access when she left. Jenna clicked through the program. The person was altering another recommendation. Claudine wouldn't be foolish enough to use the Eastern European location again.

A sudden gasp caught at her throat. She recollected the past few weeks' events. Jumping from the desk, she raced to the elevator and hit the "up" button five times. Every conversation and detail now clicked into place.

Tapping her foot, she whipped out her cell. Her body tightened like a rubber band close to snapping. She typed in a fury and sent a message to Vanessa, Hayley, Sandeep, and Sebastian.

—Get to the meeting room closest to the kitchen on level twelve, now!!!—

The doors finally pinged opened, and she rushed inside. She texted the police officer who arrived when she caught Damien selling her old phone, and Stone Corp's security department. The elevator halted at level twelve. She sprinted to the meeting room and barged through the door.

Angie was sitting at the far end on a laptop. Her head shot up, lips parted.

Jenna was the only person who knew the IP address was Romanian. When she had provided updates about the hacking, she informed the other teams to block everyone in general. Romania never came up. Angie mentioned the country in passing at the bake off.

Sebastian's sweet and reliable assistant was screwing over Stone Corp the whole time.

Chapter Twenty-Three

The light blinked above, enough to provoke an epileptic fit.

Jenna stood over Angie and crossed her arms. "What are you doing?"

"I'm working in peace." Angie typed on the laptop, fingers trembling.

Jenna bumped Angie aside and exited the Word document. Sure enough, AnaStone hid behind the file. The program was in the middle of a transaction to recommend Stone Corp selling blue-chip shares.

"You did this." Her mouth gaped. Angie had worked for the company for years and dedicated herself to Sebastian.

"How did you find me here?"

"No one else but you can stand the meeting room's flickering lights. I figured you weren't doing sketchy maneuvers in plain sight at your desk."

"This isn't what it looks like."

"You're not destroying Stone Corp?"

"Please don't tell anyone. I was desperate." Angie's voice wobbled.

Sebastian appeared in the doorway, broad shoulders sagging. "Why Angie?"

"Sebastian." Angie's shoulders slumped. "My loyalty is to you. I needed the cash."

Sebastian straightened to his full height. "What

was the urgency? I would've loaned you money or given you a pay advance."

"My son requires ongoing care. I had no choice." Angie stood on shaky legs. "Stone Corp's rival, TMC Investments, coerced me."

Jenna frowned. "Why?"

"Every altered recommendation benefited them and their partners. They did the hacking and required me present for questions. I had no choice." Angie quivered. "Today was the last time. I logged on to erase evidence, but TMC ordered one final trade."

Anger boiled in Jenna's system. TMC played dirty. First Damien snatching her bag, and now using Angie.

"What did they have on you?" Sebastian's words came out in cool, clipped tones.

"My son." A ghastly whiteness spread across Angie's face. "His Parkinson's is worse. Pain medication is over seven thousand dollars a month. TMC partners with Titans Pharmaceuticals and offered me cheaper treatment."

"We could've worked out an answer." Sebastian's expression remained stony. "You had other options."

"Simon tried to kill himself from his agony. I acted fast. Please don't call the police. He needs me." Angie threw her hands up, eyes wild.

Jenna wanted to reach out and comfort Angie, remembering Simon's complete anguish in the office. A parent moved mountains for their child. "I already alerted the police. I'm sorr…" Her voice trailed off. Sebastian was right. Angie had a small choice even though TMC took advantage of her vulnerability. "Why was Claudine caught, though? I heard you two arguing. Did you work together?"

Angie's face turned crimson red. "No. She hounded me from the start and was quite a nuisance. She had no proof but still warned me off and blocked my every cyber-attack. I told her about my son hoping she'd go away."

The words tangled in Jenna's mind. Her instincts were right about her friend. Claudine impeded Angie. Guilt bubbled inside her like a volcano, forcing up through her body. "Didn't she inform the police you were the real offender? Why did I catch her hijacking AnaStone?"

"She told the cops. The police questioned me but thought she was passing the blame." Angie exposed her teeth. "Claudine counter hacked me."

Jenna's mouth parted. Claudine protected her the entire time and never told her.

"You know what's appalling about you…besides everything?" Jenna's veins heated, hot as lava. "I understand your problems, but you still let an innocent person take the fall."

"Please, Sebastian. Tell the police the call was an accident. I'll make my mistakes up to you. To everyone. I've been part of your company since the beginning right alongside you." Angie softened her voice, pleading. "No one wishes to be on TMC's nasty side. They did the corrupting and needed me logged on. I wouldn't know how to do anything."

A knock resounded on the door. Two security officers marched inside.

The female guard trudged forward and grabbed Angie's arm. "We are here to take you to the police station."

Angie twisted her body, trying to wriggle out of

their grasp. "Please, Sebastian. You're like a son to me. What about Simon?"

Sebastian leaned a hand on the table. "He'll receive the help he needs."

"Sebastian, please." Angie's eyes reddened, deluded and feral. "You can still trust me. I can't leave my child." She kicked and punched, attempting to headbutt the guard holding her. The other guard secured Angie tight. Angie's nostrils flared. "I'll sue each and every one of you."

Other co-workers hovered closer to listen. Some with their jaws dropped. No one had suspected Angie, the mother hen who baked everyone treats.

"There must be a mistake," Tina squeaked ten feet away. "No chance Angie hurt anyone."

Sebastian did not sway, his face twisted in confusion. The elevator pinged, and the doors sprang open. Vanessa hurried to Sebastian's side and grabbed his hand.

Angie struggled every step of the way and tossed a last glare to Sebastian. "You'll regret this."

Jenna blinked rapidly, fingers cold. Poor Angie. TMC was ruthless and forced her to the breaking point. People didn't think straight when desperate.

Jenna had blamed Claudine for acts she didn't commit. Claudine's reputation was ruined while Jenna's life was wrapped up in a neat little bow.

Chapter Twenty-Four

The Christmas break was well and truly here, but Jenna didn't enjoy the holidays after taking off the rest of the year. A week had flown by since Angie's revelation, who was now out on bail. At first, Jenna wondered why Angie didn't complete the illegal activities at home to lessen the risk of getting caught. Then they learned Angie sometimes corrupted AnaStone during work hours to coincide a market announcement. TMC considered every scenario. With the latest turn of events, the police had enough evidence to start a full investigation on TMC. The rival investment firm deserved to pay after swarming Angie like vultures at her lowest point.

Jenna had called Claudine many times with more failure than a baby trying to walk. Her six texts stayed unanswered.

Head resting in the crook of Marco's shoulder and neck, she snuggled deeper into bed. Tears stung her eyes.

Marco tugged the blanket farther over her. "Talk to Claudine. The guilt is eating away at you."

"I can't when she's ignoring me." She wiped her eyes and smiled at his support.

He kissed her forehead. "Don't have regrets. My friend Bluebell messaged today. Her wife requested a divorce. Not everyone is as lucky as I am to be back with their one true love."

"Aww, I'm sorry about Bluebell." First time she heard Bluebell was married to a woman. Either way, the information didn't matter. She was secure in her relationship with Marco, but she shouldn't be so blessed. "I did terrible shit while figuring out AnaStone's problems."

"What exactly happened?"

She took a deep breath. "I eavesdropped on colleagues' conversations, sifted through their documents when they weren't at their desk, and snooped on them through USB spyware."

Marco sat up in bed and crossed his arms. "Wow, you did illegal things." His jaw tightened. "What about setting a good example to our kids?"

"I am awful. I'll confess to Hayley." She hung her head, gaze away. He was right. After the past weeks, she could barely look anyone in the eye.

"No, losing your job won't help the situation." Creases formed on Marco's forehead. "Try harder with Claudine."

"I want to reconnect. I really do."

"Didn't Hayley mention she bought a coffee shop? Bonjour Sunshine or a name similar? Visit in person."

"Brilliant idea." Her heart swelled with pride. Claudine achieved her goals to own her dream café, no thanks to her.

And now she had serious groveling to do, leaving her more uncomfortable than a long-tailed cat in a room full of rocking chairs.

****

Sitting in her car, Jenna rubbed her hands. A few feet away, a stunning brunette bustled from one table to another at Le Morning Sunshine. A cardboard image of Santa riding a sleigh with reindeers hung at the entrance.

Claudine beamed, writing a family's order in the outdoor seating area. A headband covered with mistletoe kept her long hair back.

Jenna opened the car door and walked to the café. Each step took her closer to the destination much sooner than she was ready.

Claudine peered up, bell earrings jingling.

"I'll be back with your food soon." Claudine smiled again at the family and dragged her feet toward Jenna. "What are you doing here?"

"Can we talk?" Jenna shifted on the balls of her feet.

Many beats passed before Claudine nodded. She ripped out the notepad's first page and handed the paper to a teenage waitress rushing past. Claudine sauntered to the far corner. No one occupied the tables on either side.

They sat. Jenna wrapped her puffer jacket tighter. Claudine's outdoor table choice set clear intentions of a brief conversation. Jenna racked her brain for the right words. Claudine remained silent.

"I'm here to say…" Jenna took a deep breath, forcing the words out. "Sorry your job ended terribly. You didn't deserve to take the fall." She exhaled. Waited for a reaction. A scream. Any response.

Claudine's lips stayed in a straight line. "You're right. I didn't."

"Why didn't you tell me you refuted Angie's online attempts?"

"No evidence. Angie was a favorite in the office

and close to Sebastian. She was in everyone's ear, spreading lies about my lack of ability. My word against hers."

Jenna's hand flew to her mouth. Angie did mention Claudine's work ethics whenever possible. Sebastian's former assistant was more calculating than she realized. "I would've believed you."

Down the road, carolers in identical red cloaks sang about sleigh bells and the snow. Their cheerfulness contradicted her mood.

"Really? Can you honestly say that? I was still on probation and needed my job. People treat whistleblowers worse than criminals." Claudine leaned back on the chair.

Jenna nodded. The repercussions for whistleblowers weren't ideal in any company.

Claudine continued. "Angie has a sick son. I've lived the turmoil of belonging in a broken family. A child shouldn't have to survive in those circumstances."

Jenna folded her hands on the table. "I understand. You had reasons not to confide in anyone. I feel terrible for Angie too, despite her actions. A child in pain would destroy a parent."

"Losing parents would destroy a child." Claudine averted her gaze. "When security dragged me out of the building, I almost died."

Heat climbed Jenna's neck. "I wish I could take my actions back."

"I spent hours at a police station and might've slept in a cell if my brother hadn't bailed me out." Claudine's eyes flashed.

"What can I do to make it up to you?"

Claudine's chest heaved. "You didn't check my

side of the story before throwing me under the bus. I expected more after our several open and honest conversations."

Silence set upon them as thick as today's fog.

A loud, carefree laugh erupted behind Jenna. Families dawdled by the café, waving their hands while chatting.

"I'm truly sorry." Jenna searched her handbag and removed a piece of paper. "I have a gift for you." She slid the note to Claudine.

Claudine frowned, picking up the peace offering. "What is this?" Her gaze flittered over the contents. "Is this…is this your family's secret scone recipe?"

Jenna nodded, breath hitched at her throat.

Claudine's eyebrows raised. "I thought your mom banned you telling anyone not family."

"You see…even though we're not deciding if we could develop something else anymore, you are one of my dearest friends." Jenna swallowed a lump in her throat. "There're countless qualities I admire about you. Your loyalty, passion, and fearlessness."

"I'm far from unafraid."

"You're always yourself. Seeing you free-spirited and confident…I became more assured to accept who I am. Having you around gave me courage to be myself. If that's not family, what is?"

Jenna's words hung between them. They'd come a long way since their first kiss and smirking teens sent her running for cover.

"You would've been okay on your own." Claudine's expression softened before she sighed. "To be fair, I can see why you thought I sold information to outsiders. I was new to the company and vague at times. I was trapped. Everyone adored Angie."

"Popularity contests don't interest me." Jenna took Claudine's hand. "Only you…because you're you. Thank you for protecting me. It means a lot you tried to stop Angie."

"I wanted to prove myself in the role and help even with no evidence. Show my uptight family I can be successful despite them turning their backs on me." Claudine didn't shift her hand away from Jenna's. "When I saw a way to block the hacking, I did it without thinking."

"Can we start again? I can't imagine not having you in my life."

"I've missed you." Claudine stood from the chair.

Jenna scrambled to her feet and flung her arms around Claudine. The embrace warmed her like whiskey on a snowy day. "I've missed you too." She held on to her tightly, cherishing Claudine's familiar vanilla scent. "Although we haven't known each other long, I'm lucky to have you."

Claudine unclutched her, eyes shimmering. "I'm glad you visited. How did you know I worked here?"

"Hayley." Jenna motioned a hand around the café. "This place is too cute. Very you."

Each wooden table had a daisy in a small vase. Outdoor heaters shaped like pyramids stood at every corner.

"Thanks, I belong here. When Sebastian called to apologize and offer my job back, I declined."

"I'm glad he did. His heart is in the right place," Jenna said.

The carolers arrived at the front, and patrons snapped photos and admired the singing.

Claudine rubbed her nose. "Too much had happened at Stone Corp. Sebastian provided compensation for unfair termination instead. I used the money plus my savings to buy this place." She tugged Jenna inside the café. The interior had slightly changed since the previous owner. Flowers carved the walls.

They stood in front of a stand of freshly baked croissants, cakes, muffins, and pastries.

Claudine pointed to the cabinet's middle shelf. "Your family scone recipe will be perfect here."

Jenna's heart ballooned. "I'm proud of you. I'll be honored to have a part of me here with you."

Claudine draped an arm over Jenna. "You always will be a part of me."

****

"You're back together? How marvelous." Mom squealed over Christmas lunch in Jenna and Marco's home.

Dad slapped Marco on the back.

In the living room's corner, the tree lights twinkled silver and gold. Holiday greeting cards lined the TV cabinet, including a gingerbread man one from Claudine. They remained in contact since they met at the café days ago and planned to catch up for dinner next week.

"The whole family together again." Mom twisted to Marco. "I always adored you. Not having you around felt like a son missing." Mom clasped Marco's hands while Dad nodded in approval.

"Hey, what about me? Your biological son." Josh scowled before he raised a hand to high-five Jenna. "I'm happy for you both. You were always meant to be."

Eve shoved a forkful of roast potato into her mouth. "I knew you'd be together by Christmas."

"How? We didn't even know." Jenna picked up the bowl with steamed broccoli and scraped vegetables onto Eve's plate and then Keisha's.

"When Dad asked me what I wanted for Christmas, I wished for this."

Jenna's heart melted like ice cream on hot pumpkin pie. She exchanged a soft glance with Marco.

"Well, if wishes coming true was that easy, maybe next Christmas I'll ask for a tower crammed with enough gold to swim in." Jenna ruffled her daughter's hair.

Josh finished his eggnog. "Did I tell everyone? I won the role for the major Hollywood movie. I'll say five lines, but the offer's a start."

A series of congratulations echoed from everyone at the table.

Jenna raised her fist for Josh to bump. "Way to go."

A happy moment. Even her parents appeared interested and asked about his future acting colleagues.

Once the excitement died down, Jenna gestured a hand to her daughters. "Can you both please grab more eggnog and cranberry sauce from the fridge?"

When they left, she faced her parents. "Not to dampen the mood, but there's more." She must be true to herself. The closest people in her life should genuinely know her, regardless of their potential reactions.

Marco patted her thigh under the table.

Jenna set her fork on the plate and fidgeted with the hem of her snowflake-patterned red sweater. "I

liked someone else while Marco and I were separated."
She held her breath, then let the air go. "An incredible
human being named Claudine."

Mom's chair scraped the floor, hands covering her
mouth.

"But Claudine's a girl's name." Dad furrowed his
brows. "Lordy, Lord."

"Yes, Claudine is a woman." Jenna's gaze scanned
her family, clenched fists on her lap.

Josh smiled, his eyes tender. "Good for you."

Her brother always came through. A small victory.
Wrapping her arms around her body, she guarded
herself like a curtain blocking out the sun's glare.

From the kitchen, Eve's laughter rang out. Keisha
was repeating her name over and over again in different
tones. "Keishaaa, Keiiisha, Kei-sha." Probably playing
with her talkback toy present.

Dad's eyes bulged. "You're married to Marco.
Does this mean you're a lesbian now? Or were you
going through a phase?"

"No. Just because Marco's my soulmate and my
relationship with Claudine never progressed, it doesn't
mean I'm not bisexual." She opened her mouth to
explain more but snapped her lips shut. The first time in
months, she was at peace with every aspect of her life.

"You're still with Marco forever, right?" Mom's
eyes widened.

Jenna sighed. "Yes. He's already moved back
home."

"Well...hallelujah." Mom dabbed her lips with a
napkin. "Anyone hungry? We cooked plenty of food."

Her mother chattered away about preparing each
dish and the activities they must plan as a family.

Jenna shook her head. She spilled her guts, and her parents moved on like they hadn't heard. A giddy mix of disappointment, relief, and love drifted through her. If only life resembled the movies where the main character's parents squished them in a hug and they talked, and talked, and talked the day away about their hopes and dreams.

Her mom and dad were one-track minded, acknowledging what they chose. But if she wanted them to accept her for who she was, she had to do the same. At least they didn't flat out reject her like Claudine's parents.

Jenna groaned at the food piles still on the table, letting the topic go. For now. "I can't eat every dish."

"Sure, you can. You need the energy to give us more grandchildren." Mom slid the ham over. "Know what I mean?"

Marco groaned, rubbing his stomach. "Who said a word about kids? Keisha and Eve keep us more than busy."

Mom's eyes twinkled as she nudged Jenna.

Despite Jenna's annoyance, she grinned at her mother's joke about her sex life. Maybe her parents could loosen up.

One bit at a time.

Eventually.

In the faraway future.

The kids returned to the table.

Dad raised a glass. "To family."

Everyone lifted theirs in return. "To family."

For a long time, her house hadn't been a home. She had found heaven back in Marco's arms. Eve was right in wishing for an unmaterialistic Christmas present. Her life overflowed with enough happiness and serenity already. The past months had been a rollercoaster from almost losing her job to acknowledging her confusing attraction toward women and reuniting with Marco. She wouldn't change a single moment.

Marco winked. Those smoldering dark eyes sparkled like jewels, like she was a treasure to be savored. A gift. He was her very own Christmas miracle. She leaned over and pecked his lips.

He hauled her into his warmth, deeper into a kiss filled with celebration, and joy, and new beginnings. And love. Yes, definitely love. River deep and mountain high levels of love.

Etched in Stone

Invested In You Book One

By Liv Arnold

Vanessa Lang lands her dream job at an investment firm, Stone Corp. When her kleptomaniac mother is caught shoplifting, Vanessa is forced to accept a deal with the detective—collect evidence of insider trading at her new job. Investigating Sebastian Stone comes with benefits. The drop-dead-gorgeous CEO introduces her to steamy encounters in public places, and in the midst of it all, she gathers information about his business. She soon has a difficult choice to make…save her mother or protect the man she loves.

About the Author

Liv Arnold has worked as a copywriter for several global companies and now runs her own freelance business. She grew up in Melbourne, Australia, and lives with her husband and their spoiled dog, who only eats freshly cooked meals. When she's not writing, Liv's avoiding the gym, devouring a cheese platter, or marathoning way too much TV. And, of course, she's a massive book addict and often reads until all hours of the night.

~*~

Visit Liv at:

www.livarnold.com
www.facebook.com/livarnoldauthor
www.instagram.com/liv_au
www.twitter.com/liv_au
www.goodreads.com/author/show/18845019.Liv_Arnold
www.bookbub.com/profile/liv-arnold

Thank you for purchasing
this publication of The Wild Rose Press, Inc.

For questions or more information
contact us at
info@thewildrosepress.com.

The Wild Rose Press, Inc.
www.thewildrosepress.com

Ingram Content Group UK Ltd.
Milton Keynes UK
UKHW022048190723
425454UK00009B/92